THE
PENDERWICKS
IN
SPRING

ALSO BY JEANNE BIRDSALL

The Penderwicks: A Summer Tale of Four Sisters,
Two Rabbits, and a Very Interesting Boy

The Penderwicks on Gardam Street

The Penderwicks at Point Mouette

THE PENDERWICKS IN SPRING

JEANNE BIRDSALL

Alfred A. Knopf
New York

THIS IS A BORZOI BOOK PUBLISHED BY ALFRED A. KNOPF

Visit us on the Web! randomhousekids.com

Educators and librarians, for a variety of teaching tools, visit us at RHTeachersLibrarians.com

Library of Congress Cataloging-in-Publication Data
Birdsall, Jeanne.
The Penderwicks in spring / Jeanne Birdsall. — First edition.
p. cm. — (The Penderwicks)
Sequel to: The Penderwicks at Point Mouette.
Summary: As spring arrives on Gardam Street, there are surprises in store for each Penderwick, from neighbor Nick Geiger's return from the war to Batty's new dog-walking business, but her plans to use her profits to surprise her family on her eleventh birthday go astray.
ISBN 978-0-375-87077-4 (trade) — ISBN 978-0-375-97077-1 (lib. bdg.) — ISBN 978-0-307-97459-4 (ebook)
[1. Family life—Massachusetts—Fiction. 2. Surprise—Fiction. 3. Moneymaking projects—Fiction. 4. Birthdays—Fiction. 5. Singing—Fiction. 6. Single-parent families—Fiction. 7. Massachusetts—Fiction.] I. Title.
PZ7.B51197Pei 2015
[Fic]—dc23
2014023537

The text of this book is set in 13-point Goudy.

Printed in the United States of America
March 2015
10 9 8 7 6 5 4 3 2 1

First Edition

For Elliot

CONTENTS

ONE   *Spring* 1

TWO   *Death of a Car* 14

THREE   *A Rock and Bach* 28

FOUR   *Chasing Rainbows* 44

FIVE   *Abandoned* 61

SIX   *PWTW* 76

SEVEN   *Duchess* 91

EIGHT   *Duets* 107

NINE   *Cilantro?* 119

TEN   *Spring Takes a Holiday* 138

ELEVEN   *Ninja Moves* 150

TWELVE   *Bribery* 165

THIRTEEN   *Dr. Who and Bunny Foo Foo* 177

FOURTEEN   *Still Life with Peacock Feather* 189

FIFTEEN   *Into the Woods* 201

SIXTEEN   *Dreaming* 219

SEVENTEEN   *Silence* 235

EIGHTEEN   *Beethoven* 249

NINETEEN   *Bus Stop* 261

TWENTY   *The MOOPSAB* 277

TWENTY-ONE   *The Secret Comes Out* 294

TWENTY-TWO   *Another Birthday* 307

TWENTY-THREE   *One More Gift* 325

CODA   *The Following Spring* 336

CHAPTER ONE
Spring

ONLY ONE LOW MOUND of snow still lurked in Batty Penderwick's yard, under the big oak tree out back, and soon that would be gone if Batty continued to stomp on it with such determination.

"Spring can't get here until the snow's all melted," she explained to her brother, Ben, who was celebrating the end of winter in his own way, by digging in the dirt for rocks. Rocks were his passion.

"Ms. Lambert said that spring came in March." Ben was in second grade and still believed everything his teacher told him. "It's April now."

"Officially spring came in March, but it can't really be here unless the snow is gone and the daffodils are in bloom. Dad said so." Having made it all the way to fifth grade, Batty had learned to be wary of teachers, but her father was much more trustworthy. "And since one of Mrs. Geiger's daffodils bloomed yesterday, if I can just get rid of—"

She was interrupted by a clunk—Ben's shovel had struck metal.

"Gold!" he cried.

Batty looked up from her stomping, but before she could explain the unlikelihood of finding gold in their yard, she caught a flash of red in an upper window of the house.

"Duck and cover!" she cried to Ben.

He didn't need to be told twice. He threw himself against the house and crouched, out of sight of that window. And just in time, too. The flash of red had resolved itself into a wild mop of curls atop a little girl, her nose pressed against the screen. This was two-year-old Lydia, the youngest of the Penderwick family, who was supposed to be napping. Recently she'd discovered that by standing on a pile of the toys in her crib, she could get a better view of the world. The family verdict was that it wouldn't be long before she figured out how to climb out of the crib altogether.

Lydia, so cherubic up there in her window, now roared like a furious foghorn. "BEN!"

Batty called up to her. "Go back to sleep, Lydia."

"Lydia is done," came the reply.

"No, you're not done, because nap time isn't over for another fifteen minutes."

Wobbling atop her precarious pile, Lydia pondered this, then went back to her original thought. "BEN!"

In his hiding place, Ben was whispering no, no, no at Batty. She sympathized. Lydia loved everyone she'd encountered in her short life—never had a Penderwick been so pleased with the human race—but she loved Ben most of all. This was a burden no boy should have to bear.

And, too, it was important that Lydia not get her own way all the time. Batty shook her head at the window and said, "Ben is busy, and you have to rest some more."

"But—" Mid-protest, Lydia fell off her pile of toys and disappeared from sight.

"Is she gone?" asked Ben.

"I think so. Stay where you are for a minute, just in case she pops up again."

Lydia was the most recent addition to the Penderwick family, bringing the total to eight. For the first half of Batty's life, there had been only five: Batty, her father, and her three older sisters, Rosalind, Skye, and Jane. Five had been a good number. Then Mr. Penderwick had married Ben's mother, Iantha, making seven, and seven had been an even better number, because everyone was so fond of Ben and Iantha. And now, eight—eight was a lot, especially when the eighth one was Lydia.

Batty glanced back up at the window. It was still empty, which meant that either Lydia had gone back to sleep or she was rebuilding her pile of toys from scratch. Batty had watched her do it once or twice, and it was no easy project.

"All clear for now," she told Ben.

"Then come see what I've found." He went back to where he'd been digging, scrabbled around with his shovel, and brought to light a flat piece of metal encrusted with rust and dirt. Although his previous non-rock finds had been worthless—a tiny and ancient glass bottle, various chunks of broken plastic, and a ring full of keys that opened nothing—Ben never gave up hope of discovering riches untold.

"It's only an old door hinge," said Batty. "Definitely not gold."

"Rats."

"Well, it's not like there were ever pirates burying treasure in western Massachusetts."

"I know that." He plunged his shovel back into the dirt. "Somebody else could have, though, like a banker, and maybe not just gold. Diamonds are possible, or mortgage bond fidelity securities."

Batty had a feeling he'd made up mortgage bond fidelity securities. It didn't matter. There wouldn't be any of them in their yard, either. Good thing Ben was so fond of the rocks he did find. And also mud, because he was covered with it now.

"How did you get mud on your head?" She went at him with the sleeve of her sweatshirt, rubbing off the muck obscuring his hair, the same bright red as Lydia's.

"Stop that," said Ben.

She gave him one last scrub, made sure Lydia

hadn't reappeared at the window, and went back to stomping on her pile of snow.

Batty knew why Ben had hoped to find buried wealth among the mud and rocks. While the Penderwicks weren't poor, money seemed to be tighter these days. The house, full-to-bursting even for seven people, had needed to expand when Lydia arrived, and that had been expensive, and then there'd been a new roof, and now there were years and years of college to pay for. The oldest sister, Rosalind, had already started, and Skye would go next year and Jane the year after. Not to mention the ongoing grocery bills, which Mr. Penderwick—when he thought no children were listening—had said were enormous. Actually, what he'd said was that they were *immoderatae*, which Batty looked up later in his Latin-English dictionary, knowing what all the Penderwick children learned at an early age: If their father said something incomprehensible, it usually turned out to be Latin. Rosalind had even been inspired to study Latin in school, but so far no one else had gone to that extreme.

The snow removal was working. Batty had gotten rid of the mushy upper layer and was now working on the colder, denser layer underneath. When this part of the mound proved less vulnerable to stomping, she used a stick to jab and pry at the icy snow until the stick jammed against something hard and snapped into pieces. A vision of buried gold—enough to pay for unlimited groceries—flashed into Batty's imagination. But it was gone in a second or two. Let second graders have their dreams. A fifth grader would, of course, know it was only a rock. She found a new stick to scrape away the snow. Beneath the snow were wet, rotting leaves. She poked and prodded at them, too, and found—

It wasn't a rock. It was a dog's rubber bone, left behind months ago to be buried first under autumn leaves, then winter snow. Just an old rubber bone, but Batty was already braced for what she knew would come—the rushing in her ears, the stab in her stomach, and the seeping away of the colors from her world. The soft blue spring sky, the yellow forsythia hedge, even Ben's bright red hair—all dulled, all gray and wretched.

Batty hid the bone in her pocket and kicked at the leaves and snow to cover up where she'd found it. Whether spring came that day or another hardly seemed to matter anymore. Much more important at this moment was to get upstairs to her room, where she could be alone.

"Ben," she said. "I'm going inside."

"But I've found another good rock." He was digging with renewed determination.

"Show it to me later." She slipped past him, turning away to hide her crumpled face, her fight to keep the tears from coming too soon.

The only other person at home that afternoon was seventeen-year-old Skye, whose turn it was to make sure none of the younger siblings injured themselves or each other, especially Lydia. Skye, among all the Penderwicks, was the least likely to want to discuss grief or any other emotion, particularly, it seemed, if the emotions were Batty's, though Batty didn't know why—it had always been this way.

But still, she paused in the kitchen, listening, hoping to figure out where Skye was. It didn't take long.

"No, no, the random variable x is discrete!"

Batty peered into the dining room, and yes, there was Skye at the big table, tapping on her computer with one hand and tugging at her blond hair with the other. Skye was the only blond Penderwick, gleaming alone among the redheads—Iantha, Ben, and Lydia—and the brunettes, that is, everyone else. Some of them thought that Skye should treat her golden locks with more respect, but Skye had other ideas, keeping her hair cropped short and, whenever she was thinking hard, pulling and yanking at it until it looked like she'd been through a tornado. This could be a useful barometer for those around her. The messier the hair, the more oblivious its owner, and right now Skye's hair was going in thirteen different directions. Batty, still holding back her tears, was able to get through the dining room unnoticed and make a break for the stairs.

The baby gates at both the top and bottom, necessary to protect Lydia from too much adventure, slowed Batty down, but in moments she was upstairs, with only one hurdle left, Lydia, who had the keen hearing of a panther. Cautiously, Batty tiptoed past Lydia's room, without incident, and now was safe in her own bedroom and scrambling into her closet, her sanctuary. She dug her way toward the back, past stuffed animals, piles of board games and jigsaw puzzles, several plastic buckets full of shells, and an old favorite unicorn blanket, until she reached what she needed, a zippered canvas bag with VALLEY VETERINARY HOSPITAL printed on the front.

Batty kept a flashlight back there for emergencies, but didn't need it to see what was inside that bag: a well-worn dog collar and tags, a half-chewed tennis ball, a tuft of rough black hair curled carefully into a tiny pillbox. Now to add the rubber bone Batty had found under the snow and leaves. She wiped it clean with a stray sock, then reverently slid it into the canvas bag. There, done. All that was left of big, black, clumsy, loving Hound Penderwick, the best dog the world had ever known.

Hugging the bag, Batty curled up and let the tears come. Her father had promised that the hurt, the terrible loneliness, would fade someday, but Hound had been dead for six months and Batty was still struggling to understand a world without him. Her earliest memories were of Hound. She'd heard all the stories about how he'd adopted her when she was a tiny infant newly home from the hospital. Her mother had just died of cancer, her father and older sisters were ripped open with grief—and Hound, who until then had been a goofy young dog with no apparent skills or intelligence, decided to become Batty's best friend and loyal protector, and he stayed that way as they grew up together, year after happy year. And then last autumn his heart had stopped working properly. The veterinarian said that they just had to care for him and love him, and Batty had loved him, and loved him, and loved him, but it hadn't been enough. No one in her family had ever said that Hound's dying was her fault, but she knew the truth. She hadn't been able to keep him with her, to stop him from leaving her behind.

Her face now a wet mess, Batty groped around on the floor, hoping to find another sock to use as a handkerchief. Instead, she got hold of a twitching tail attached to a large orange cat.

"I'm sorry, Asimov," said Batty. "I didn't know you were in here."

Asimov didn't immediately accept her apology. As the Penderwicks' only cat, he considered himself far too fabulous to be overlooked, but at last he honored Batty by snuggling next to her, and while she knew he'd abandon her in a flash at the far-off sound of a can opener, she allowed herself a little comfort, a little lifting of the awful gray.

"I'm sorry I couldn't keep Hound alive. I know you miss him, too."

Here Batty was being generous. Asimov lived

like a Buddhist, in the moment, not bothering with the dead and gone. But it was true that while Hound lived, Asimov had loved him as much as a cat can love.

"And I know you're not ready for another dog, either."

Asimov narrowed his eyes at her, wishing she would talk less and scratch his head more. Batty sighed, and scratched his head, and missed anew how Hound had understood every word she said. Her dad and Iantha had promised there wouldn't be a new dog in the family until Batty was ready. But how could she ever be ready? How could she ever trust herself with a dog again? She barely trusted herself anymore with Asimov, who had never even been her particular cat, letting others in the family feed him and make sure he was doing well.

Too soon her closet was invaded by distant cries from Lydia. "BEN, BEN, BEN!" Batty shut her ears against the noise for as long as she could, in the forlorn hope that Skye would be roused out of her concentration. But the wailing only got louder until Batty couldn't stand it anymore.

She crawled out of the closet and set off toward Lydia's room. By the time she got there, the noise was over, but instead of peaceful silence, Batty heard strange little grunts. Suspicious, she pushed open the door to find her little sister in the middle of an escape attempt. Like an ungainly ballerina at her barre, Lydia was balanced with one foot propped up on the crib's railing and the other on a teetering pile of toys.

"I can see you," said Batty.

Lydia slowly lowered her foot from the railing, then carefully stepped down off the toys, all the while trying to look like doing so was her own idea. When she was once again standing solid, she tossed her head back and forth, making her red cloud of hair sway invitingly.

"Rapunzel, Rapunzel," she said.

"No Rapunzels," Batty replied sternly. They'd had this conversation dozens of times.

Lydia threw herself down in the crib and closed her eyes. "Snow White is dead. Kiss Snow White, Prince."

"No royalty at all. If you want to get out of that crib, stand up and be an American."

"Sad Snow White."

"I'm ignoring you."

While Lydia stuck with being Snow White, Batty looked around the room. It had been hers until the house had expanded. Batty loved her new room, but it still pained her to see the depths to which the old room had been lowered. Frills, ruffles, and princess paraphernalia were everywhere. Even when Batty was Lydia's age, there had been none of that nonsense. Only stuffed animals and, of course, Hound. At least Batty's Hound ceiling was still there. It had been one of Iantha's first projects after marrying Mr.

Penderwick, pasting glow-in-the-dark stars up there for Batty in the shape of a real constellation—Canis Major, the Great Dog—and painting an outline of a Hound-shaped dog all around the stars. So that he could watch over her always, Iantha had said. Well, now he was watching over Lydia, thought Batty. He wouldn't have approved of the frilly stuff, either.

"No Snow White?" asked Lydia.

"Nope. Now hang on so I can get you out of there. Legs, too, Lydia."

When you're not yet eleven years old and not very large yourself, a toddler being hauled from a crib feels like a ton of lead. But with Lydia's arms and legs wrapped around her, Batty could just manage it. That was only the first struggle, though, because as soon as Lydia was set down, she dashed into the corner to grab a golden crown from her toy shelf. Batty dove after her and there was a brief and undignified tug-of-war, which Lydia won by refusing to let go.

"If you have to wear the crown, okay," said Batty, defeated, "but just stop *talking* about princesses."

On went the crown. It had been a gift from Aunt Claire, the family's favorite relative, and someone who should have known better, and *had* known better throughout the childhoods of the original set of sisters. But since then, she and her husband, Turron, had produced twin boys, Marty and Enam, whose energy and enthusiasm for life seemed to have rattled Aunt Claire's common sense. The crown wasn't the only thing. Tutus also arrived at irregular intervals. Mr. Penderwick had been heard threatening to retaliate with drum sets for Marty and Enam, but Iantha always calmed him down.

Still, a crown and tutus do not a princess mania make, so Aunt Claire couldn't be assigned all the blame. While Batty was certain that princesses couldn't ruin a life, as the senior member of the younger Penderwick siblings, she felt responsible for the honor and dignity of all three. Ben had many talents and not just with rocks, and Batty planned to become a professional pianist, but who could tell with Lydia? So far she was dragging down the team.

"La-la-la-la-la-la kiss, kiss," sang Lydia.

"Also no kissing," said Batty. "Where are your shoes?"

Lydia found her shoes in the corner, buried under one of the tutus, and brought them to Batty.

"Outside?" she asked, lifting one foot at a time to receive its shoe.

"Yes, outside. Let's go look for signs of spring."

CHAPTER TWO
Death of a Car

HOLDING HANDS, Batty and Lydia went out into the spring sunshine. Across their street—Gardam Street—Mrs. Geiger's first daffodil glowed proudly among a smattering of purple hyacinths and white crocuses. But what Lydia noticed first was the family car parked in the driveway and, in the driver's seat, the third-oldest Penderwick sister. This was sixteen-year-old Jane, and she was reading a book propped up on the steering wheel.

Lydia broke into a run, clutching at her crown to keep it from tumbling off.

"Snow White is dead!" she shouted to Jane.

"The prince will kiss her awake!" Jane threw open the car door and swung Lydia up onto her lap, covering her with kisses.

"You know we agreed not to encourage her," said Batty when she caught up.

"Sorry," answered Jane, but she snuck in a few more princely kisses anyway.

On the passenger's seat of the car was a stack of books—the one that Jane had been reading, plus a dozen others. This was typical for Jane, who wanted to be a published author someday and believed that the only way to learn how to write was to read, read, read. So she was always in the middle of at least one book and felt safe only if she had several more on standby. Tucked into her stack was also a blue notebook, the kind Jane used for writing down ideas that came to her, bits and pieces of conversations she'd heard, anything she thought she might write about one day. Batty figured that by now Jane had filled dozens of these blue notebooks—most of them kept in boxes under her bed.

Lydia pointed at the book on top of the pile. "Lydia wants story."

"That one's in French," said Jane. "You wouldn't understand. Even I can't understand it without looking up most of the words."

"*Oui.*" Lydia had picked up a few words from Jane, and was proud of herself for it.

"All right, but just a little bit. This is by a man named Dumas, who wrote about hopeless passion and bitter revenge—" Jane paused. "You're probably too young for the details. Just listen. '*Une belle jeune fille aux cheveux noirs comme le jais, aux yeux veloutés comme ceux de la gazelle—' "*

Batty let the words wash over her, understanding nothing. Life would have been easier, she thought, if Skye and Jane had followed Rosalind and their dad into Latin. Skye had started on that path, taking Latin in seventh grade, but she soon tired of being compared unfavorably to Rosalind—Mr. Smith's favorite Latin student ever—and switched to Spanish. After that, Jane didn't even attempt Latin, instead studying French, because it was "romantic." Lydia was able to pick up words from all three languages, but the polyglot confusion had the opposite effect on Batty. She hoped to avoid studying any languages, except maybe Italian, because so many of the notations on her piano scores were in that language.

But now Lydia, bored with Dumas, kicked over Jane's stack of books, and when Jane stopped reading so that she could stack them up again, Batty asked her why she was sitting in the car. It wasn't, after all, the most comfortable place to read a book.

"I'm letting it rest. I thought I heard a strange noise, and then I thought that the noise might stop after the car rested a little. Here, you take Lydia and I'll drive—you tell me if you hear anything. It could be my imagination." Jane said this part about her imagination with eager optimism. The car was old and already beset by many minor injuries. Another could send it to its grave.

As soon as Jane backed the car down the driveway, Batty heard the noise, actually three noises—a simultaneous squeal and moan, followed by a thunk.

"I heard it!" she called to Jane.

"Are you sure? I'll drive it forward again."

The noise was the same with the car going forward, and even Lydia said so, but Jane drove it back and forth several more times, hoping that if her sisters wouldn't agree about the noise being her imagination, maybe it would get bored with itself and disappear.

"Now it's getting louder," said Batty.

Loud enough even to summon Ben out of the backyard, his curiosity stronger than his desire to find buried riches. He'd picked up even more mud since Batty saw him last, which she'd thought impossible.

"Ben, Ben, Ben!" Lydia tried to dive out of Batty's arms, but Batty held on tightly, keeping her away from Ben and his dirt. One filthy Penderwick was plenty.

"What's Jane doing?" he asked.

"Hoping that noise will go away."

THUNK! It was the loudest one yet, but the cry from Jane was louder still.

"Now it's stuck!" She was fiddling with levers and pedals, but the car wouldn't move at all, either forward or backward.

"At least the noise stopped," said Ben.

"That's not necessarily a good thing." Jane frowned. "Better go get Skye."

Ben went inside to yank Skye out of her world of

mathematics. When she arrived, blinking in the sunshine, she switched places with Jane and did more fiddling. But the car wouldn't move for her, either.

"I've killed it, haven't I," said Jane. *"Le morte d'auto."*

"It's at least gravely wounded." Skye got out again and looked under the hood. Everyone looked with her, but nothing in there was obviously broken.

"I think the sound came from beneath the car," said Batty.

"Maybe a big stick got caught underneath," said Ben. That had happened once to his best friend Rafael's car, and Ben secretly hoped to observe it sometime for himself.

"I don't think so." But now Skye scooted under the car and everyone followed her, even Lydia, who thought they were playing a game made up just for her.

"Snow White is dead," she said, wriggling happily. "Lydia loves Skye."

"You can't suck me into your princess stuff," said Skye. "I'll tell you instead about telescopes that find stars so old they existed almost at the beginning of the universe. Isn't that more exciting than princesses?"

"Crown!" said Lydia. It had slid off her wild red curls.

"It'll stay on if you don't wriggle so much." Batty grabbed the crown and crammed it back on.

"Skye, what should we do about the car?" Jane asked.

"Because there's no big stick under here." Ben had looked carefully.

Skye sighed. "I guess it's time to call Dad with the bad news."

So Skye called Mr. Penderwick, who called Ernie's Service Station, who agreed to send a tow truck for the car.

The excitement created by the arrival of the large red tow truck, with its brute strength, broad straps, boom, and clanking chains, kept the younger Penderwicks from thinking about consequences. But once the car had been dragged away, thoughts turned to what its brokenness meant for the family. They owned one more vehicle, an old and ungainly clunker nicknamed Van Allen, but that wouldn't be enough to handle so many people who needed to go in so many different directions at all different times. If the car was truly dead, another one would have to be bought.

"Are cars expensive?" Ben asked Batty.

"I think so."

He eyed Lydia speculatively. "Maybe we could make money by renting her out to lonely families."

"But since it would be Lydia being rented out, the money would be hers and she'd want to use it for more crowns and tutus."

"Lydia, you'd give me any money you made, right?" asked Ben.

"*Sí*," she agreed.

"And I'd give it to Dad and Mom," he said. "Do you think they'd let us do it?"

Since the Penderwicks weren't the kind of family to rent out children, Ben didn't bother to wait for an answer, but returned to the backyard in search of buried valuables. When Lydia tried to follow him, Batty took her to the front steps, a good place to sit when looking for spring and, because the afternoon was almost gone, to wait for their parents to come home.

"Lydia, do you see Mrs. Geiger's first daffodil?" She pointed across the street.

"Purple flower," said Lydia.

"No, that's a hyacinth. I mean the yellow one."

"Lydia likes purple. So does Tzina."

Tzina was one of Lydia's friends from day care, and was often brought into discussions as an authority. So, Batty thought, purple it was.

From overhead came a familiar chorus. Batty leaned back to look—yes, it was a V-shaped flock of Canada geese. They could be coming up from the south, or maybe it was one of the flocks that lived in Massachusetts all year long, making their way from one feeding ground to another. Batty had always thrilled to their honking, haunting cries. As had Hound. They would race together across the yard, trying to keep up with the big birds traveling on the wind, and afterward, when the birds were gone, Batty would imitate their call, *ahaawln haawln*, and Hound would lick her face—

"Goldie put Frank in a box," said Lydia.

Batty came back into the present. "Hmm?"

"*Goldie* put *Frank* in a box."

The part about Goldie made sense—she ran Lydia's day care. But who Frank was and why Goldie would put him into a box was beyond understanding. Batty had learned long ago that asking Lydia direct questions rarely got results. It was best to go roundabout and hope they ended up at the truth.

"What kind of box?" she asked.

Lydia thought hard. "Blue."

"Did he like being in there?"

This was the wrong question. Lydia's lower lip started to quiver, and Batty—not for the first time—wished that Lydia had put off talking until she could make sense, like when she was five or six. And now she was crying.

"I'm sorry," said Batty helplessly. "I don't know who Frank is."

"He *died* and Goldie put him in a *box* and Lydia couldn't kiss him."

With this, Batty could be reasonably certain that Frank wasn't one of the children at the day care. She went over the names of the animals living there: Leon the Madagascar hissing cockroach, Baloney the hamster, and—oh, dear—Francis the guinea pig, aka Frank. And now she remembered that Lydia had talked about loving Frank a lot, especially when compared to Leon.

"I know that's sad, but you really shouldn't kiss

guinea pigs, even when they're alive." Batty pulled Lydia onto her lap. "Come on, I'll sing a song for you."

Except for Batty, the Penderwick family wasn't much for singing. Not because they wouldn't have liked to, but because they couldn't carry tunes, and so sounded—as Mr. Penderwick had once said after they'd all sung "Happy Birthday" to someone or other—like a flock of depressed sheep.

However, Batty could not only carry a tune, she sounded nothing like a sheep, even one in a good mood, so she sang often to Lydia. Today she started with "Swinging on a Star," one of Lydia's favorites— full of moonbeams and a funny-looking mule—and soon Lydia's crying slowed down. But Batty had forgotten that in a later verse the mule was replaced by a pig, and since the pig reminded Lydia of guinea pigs, the crying got worse again. Batty quickly changed to another favorite, "A Ram Sam Sam," which had a little hand dance to go along with it. But Lydia's crying had already taken on a life of its own, and even the joy of wiggling her fingers to "guli guli guli guli guli" couldn't stop it now.

Thus it was a very good thing when Van Allen pulled into the driveway a few minutes later.

"Lydia, look!" said Batty. "Mom's home. Isn't that wonderful?"

For Lydia, the arrival of her mother meant another person to help with her mourning. As Iantha climbed down out of Van Allen, Lydia reached out imploring arms.

"Crisis?" Iantha called to Batty.

"Sort of, yes, please!"

Iantha was a calm mother who didn't believe in adding to the chaos of woe. Smiling, she came to the girls, managing somehow to hug Batty and scoop up Lydia simultaneously. As Lydia sobbed about boxes and kisses, Batty tried to present a logical version of the Frank-the-dead-guinea-pig story. It was one of Iantha's many skills that she could listen to lots of people speaking at the same time and still get hold of the important parts. She'd explained once that it was because she was a scientist—an astrophysicist— and therefore had to take in opposing views, but Batty didn't think that was it. Skye was planning to become an astrophysicist, too, and she wasn't particularly good at listening to even a single person at a time. Maybe she would learn that when she went away to college next year.

"Thank goodness she didn't kiss Frank," Iantha said when Batty finished. "I would've had to write Goldie a note about germs, and I'm really not that kind of parent. And how was your day, Batty?"

"Good." Except for finding Hound's bone, and Batty didn't want to talk about that.

Now came a redoubling of Lydia's sobs—she'd heard *germs* as *worms*, which reminded her that her friend Jordy had said that dead guinea pigs were eaten by worms—and Iantha thought it best to take her inside and give her a snack.

The sun had shifted, and shadows crawled across

23

the front steps. Batty shivered in the sudden chill but stayed where she was, waiting for her father to arrive. He would be home soon and here was a rare chance to have him to herself, even for just a few minutes. She drove away the shivers by humming the Bach prelude she'd been practicing for that evening's piano lesson, her fingers energetically playing along on an imaginary piano.

She hadn't long to wait. Her father arrived before she ran out of Bach, dropped off by a colleague—a botany professor, like Mr. Penderwick—whose car wasn't broken. Batty ran over to help with the large cooler being lifted out of the car. She knew that this contained plant samples collected from the field. Her dad was always happiest when he'd been out collecting real plants instead of just talking about them in a lecture hall.

"Ah, one of my many daughters. But which one?"

"The best one," she answered. It was one of their jokes. "Daddy, your glasses."

"Whoops." They were dangling precariously from the cooler handle. He rescued them before they smashed onto the ground, and put them in his pocket.

"Wouldn't it be simpler if you just wore them?"

"That's the theory," he said cheerfully.

They carried the cooler to the front steps and opened it, so that she could see the bits of plants he'd carefully trimmed from their hosts and stored in plastic bags. Each was marked with the exact location of the host plant, including latitude and longitude readings. He'd let Batty and Ben play with the portable GPS he used to get those readings, and they both knew the exact location of their home: latitude 42.320529, longitude -72.632236. Ben liked to give that as his address instead of Gardam Street, Cameron, Massachusetts, but Batty considered that showing off.

"What plant is this?" she asked, pointing to a slender twig with small, dangling, white bell-shaped flowers.

"*Chamaedaphne calyculata*," he said. "Or leatherleaf, which doesn't sound as glamorous, does it? The leaves contain poison, though according to some, rabbits eat it."

"I wouldn't like for a rabbit to be poisoned."

"Nor would I, but they know how to take care of themselves out there." Mr. Penderwick closed the cooler. "And what's your news today?"

"Well, the car. Is it badly hurt?"

"Afraid so. Ernie already took a look and declared it dead on arrival."

"Oh, Daddy."

"Don't 'Oh, Daddy' me. Cars aren't your worry. What other news?"

"Ben found a hinge that wasn't gold and Lydia is upset because she wasn't allowed to try mouth-to-mouth resuscitation on a dead guinea pig."

"That's everyone else. What about Batty? Today is Thursday, so piano lesson tonight. Are you prepared?"

"Of course." He knew she was always ready for

anything to do with music. She'd been practicing the Prelude and Fugue no. 9 in E Major until she could play it in her sleep.

"How about homework?"

Homework was a different story. At first she couldn't remember if she had any.

"We're supposed to learn the different kinds of clouds," she answered finally.

"I can help with that. In Latin, *cumulus* means 'heap' or 'pile,' so those are the big fluffy clouds, and *cirrus* means 'ringlet of hair,' so those are the wispy ones. Logical."

"That's just more for me to remember."

He went on, pleased to have an excuse to speak Latin. "And *nimbus* means 'rainstorm,' so those are the rainclouds. And then there are the *stratus*—"

"Stop, you're making it worse!" She covered her ears.

"You win," he said, laughing. "All Penderwicks home and accounted for?"

"Except for Rosalind, of course."

"And how long until Rosalind comes home from college?"

Batty had been keeping a running total since Rosalind's last visit in February. Her college wasn't that far away, in Rhode Island, and she came home for holidays and breaks. But that wasn't often enough for anyone, especially Batty.

"She'll be home in three weeks and two days.

Twenty-three days." It was easy to remember—Rosalind would get home on the day just before Batty's eleventh birthday.

"Getting closer, thank goodness." He picked up his cooler. "I'm ready to mingle with the hordes. How about you?"

"Ready," she said, and they went into the house.

CHAPTER THREE
A Rock and Bach

BEN PROUDLY MANAGED HIS OWN BATH TIME, from running the water all the way through the final rinse. It was a new-won responsibility, and one that he treasured. His friend Rafael, not yet trusted with filling bathtubs (there had once been a flood), envied Ben greatly and repeatedly begged his mother to follow the Penderwick parents' example.

Now that Ben was old enough to bathe alone, he considered himself old enough to expect privacy while he did so. Most particularly from Lydia, who wasn't supposed to roam free through the house but could give almost anyone the slip. Their father made a joke of it, calling Lydia the Great Getaway Artist and saying that she should go into bank robbery when she grew up. Ben didn't think it was funny, especially when he was in a bathroom with no lock on the door.

He compensated by setting up an early-warning system, a hanger leaning against the door. This was most important for those bath times when he had something to hide not just from Lydia but from anyone who thought he shouldn't take rocks into the bathtub with him, which was just about everybody in the family.

This evening, with his early-warning system in place and his filthy clothes off and stuffed into the hamper, he stepped into the tub, carefully clutching the one rock he'd found that had extra-exciting possibilities. Whitish gray with darker gray speckles, it was shaped like a big egg. Ben cleaned it with the special toothbrush he kept just for rocks, then rinsed it off under the spigot, turning it round and round. Maybe, he thought, just maybe it had once been an actual egg. Rafael talked about fossilized dinosaur eggs that had been discovered in Mongolia, but that didn't mean some couldn't be found in Massachusetts, too. Because Massachusetts had been roamed by dinosaurs, too, right?

Ben wrapped the rock in a washcloth and set it gently on the bathtub ledge. He'd be the luckiest boy ever if it turned out to be a dinosaur egg. He'd be on television, and scientists from around the world would visit and ask if he would let them touch it. Or he could sell it to a museum for a whole lot of money, like a billion dollars. With a billion dollars, he could buy his parents a car to replace the dead one.

A small noise caught his attention—someone was

slowly and stealthily turning the doorknob. Lydia! With a great splash, Ben leapt out of the tub just as his warning hanger tipped over. He shoved the door shut again and leaned on it with all his might.

"You can't come in!"

"Yes, inside!"

"No, never, go away."

This time Lydia didn't reply, but Ben stayed by the door, suspecting she wouldn't give up so easily. He was right. A moment later, the sound of huffing and puffing came rising up from the vicinity of his feet. He crouched down and looked under the door. One bright and hopeful eye gazed back at him.

"Lydia *loves* Ben."

He grabbed his towel and stuffed it against the crack under the door, blocking out that eye.

"Ben, Ben," cried Lydia in heartbreaking tones.

He took the rest of the towels from the racks and piled them on top of the first towel and was about to shove the hamper on top of all that when he heard extra footsteps and scuffling.

"She's bothering me again!" he shouted to whichever Penderwick was out there.

"It's okay. I've got her," Jane answered from the other side of the door. Then came the sounds of Lydia being unwillingly borne away.

Relieved, and cold from all that standing around, Ben went back to his bath, and to spending the money he'd get from his dinosaur egg. *Two* cars for his parents would be even better, and after that, there should be enough money left to buy a movie studio, because he and Rafael wanted to make science-fiction movies. And when Batty was finally ready for a new dog—which Ben hoped would be soon—Ben would get a dog, no, a hundred dogs, because only a hundred could start to make up for Hound, the greatest dog who had ever lived. And he and Rafael would train the hundred dogs to work on movie sets, in case they needed alien dogs in their science-fiction movies.

When Ben was as clean as he was likely to get, he slipped out of the bathroom with the egg rock wrapped in a towel, successfully navigating the route to his bedroom without getting caught by any sisters. Unfortunately, his bedroom door didn't have a lock, either. His parents had promised he could get one when he turned twelve, but that was four years away and he was hoping that Lydia would have glommed on to someone else long before then. In the meantime, he was reduced to using an early-warning system here, too. After clearing a space for his egg rock on the bottom bunk, which was so full of interesting things that Ben always slept on the top bunk, he was about to put the hanger in place.

Someone was already turning the doorknob.

"Go away!" he shouted, throwing the hanger and himself against the door. "You're driving me insane!"

"It's Mom."

"Sorry." Ben let his mother into the room. "I

thought you were Lydia. She tried to bust in on my bath again."

"I heard about that, but you're okay for the rest of the evening. She's just gone to sleep."

"She could wake up and try to escape. Maybe you should tie her to the crib." He'd suggested this many times, but no one would take him up on the idea.

"That would be dangerous, as well as impolite. I never tied you to anything, did I?"

"I don't remember."

"Take my word for it. I didn't."

Ben knew why his mother was there. She'd come to say good night because she was going back to her office at the university and wouldn't be home again until after he was asleep. Ben was proud of his mother for being an astrophysicist—Rafael's mother was a psychologist, and neither boy thought brains any-where near as fascinating as stars—but he didn't like it when she went out to work at night. And he didn't like it when his father did, either. So he'd developed a strategy to keep people at home—keep them talking as long as he could. Though it hadn't yet worked, Ben never stopped trying.

"Mom, I found this today." He showed her the rock. "Do you think it's a dinosaur egg turned into a fossil?"

"I'm afraid not."

"Are you sure? Because it would be worth a lot of money."

"I'm sure, honey."

This was a setback. But Ben was too attached to this rock to give up right away. "Maybe it's an outer-space rock, worn into this funny shape by its passage through the earth's atmosphere. That would be worth lots of money, too."

"Not that, either. Although it's a very nice rock, it's just a rock."

"You're absolutely positive, right? Because Rafael says there are lots of space rocks around that nobody knows about. We're going to make a movie about it someday called *Secret Rock Invasion*. He's going to be the scientist and I'm going to be the alien in charge of sneaking the rocks to Earth."

One of the extra-good things about his mother was that she liked science fiction. Ben knew this and milked it as long as he could, all the way to the Delta Quadrant and rocks that formed whenever an extra-terrestrial burped. But since she was still a grown-up, she kissed him good night and left for work long before he was ready to let her go.

"Plus, no dinosaur egg," he said, plopping himself down on the edge of the bottom bunk. "And no billion dollars."

Batty's piano lessons were always good, but that evening's was a great one. Her teacher, Mr. Trice, demonstrated how the Bach would sound if played by Scott Joplin, which led to Batty playing a Scott Joplin piece as if she were Bach. Which led to much hilarity—Mr. Trice was like that. He insisted that music had to be fun, or why bother?

Batty had never before tried to *think* like Bach—or like Scott Joplin—and was eager to do more of it when she got back home. But when she arrived, she found the way to her piano blocked by teenagers. This was happening more and more often, and she sometimes wished the piano could be moved out of the living room and up to her own room, where no teenagers ever went. Tonight the teenagers were: Jane, Artie, whom Jane had known since elementary school, and a boy named Donovan, a more recent addition. Jane actually had two friends named Donovan, both stocky soccer players with dark hair and glasses. At first Batty had thought they were brothers, with Donovan as their last name. But they were each Donovan Something Else—Batty never could remember what—and it didn't matter anyway. Whichever Donovan was there, Batty was too shy to play Bach or Joplin in front of him. Or Artie, either, though she was more used to him.

She went upstairs and knocked on Ben's door, using their private signal—three quick knocks and a slap—and waited while he removed his hanger warning system and opened the door.

"Did you bring me anything from Keiko?" he asked.

She held up a paper bag full of cookies. Keiko,

who was Mr. Trice's daughter and also Batty's best friend, liked baking with her own made-up recipes. Since sometimes disaster ensued, she used Ben to test her odder concoctions before they were let out into the wider world.

"I'm not supposed to say what's in them until you try one."

"But no sweet potatoes?" He'd gotten sick just once from Keiko's cooking, when he'd eaten three slices of her sweet potato meringue pie.

"No sweet potatoes."

Ben took a cookie. It turned out to be almost normal, chocolate with small chunks of lemon rind.

"It's good," Ben mumbled through a mouthful.

Now that he hadn't frothed at the mouth or fallen over dead, Batty took one for herself.

"The living room is full of teenagers again," she said, "and I want to play the piano. Will you watch with me to see if they leave?"

Ben didn't care about the teenagers in the living room, but he'd follow that bag of cookies anywhere. They settled at the top of the steps, where they could spy down on the front hall from behind the baby gate. Batty didn't blame Jane for having boys visit. It must be nice when you're sixteen, especially for Jane, who was always doing research for the books she planned to write. And Keiko thought Batty should be grateful to have all those boys available for observation— any information she could gather would prepare them both for the fraught teen years, which were coming whether they liked it or not. Maybe so, thought Batty, but it would be easier to be grateful if the boys didn't so often keep her from the piano.

"I thought one of my rocks was a dinosaur egg." Ben spoke quietly. Lydia's room was right there, and the last thing he wanted was to wake her up. "But Mom said no. I would have sold it and we would have been rich."

"We don't need to be rich."

"I know, but still."

Batty knew what he meant. At dinner, Skye had said she'd take on more math tutoring—she already had three students—and Jane had offered to start sewing the family's clothes to save money. Although Mr. Penderwick and Iantha had told them to stop, stop, stop, none of that was necessary and everyone should leave the money issues to the adults, Batty knew her sisters wouldn't stop. And Rosalind had a job at college, working in the library. Someday, when Batty was a teenager, she'd want to make money, too. She had come up with a name for a future neighborhood odd-jobs business, Penderwick Willing to Work, or PWTW. But the "Work" part of it was still a mystery, and it would have to be something a shy person could do. Keiko thought that Batty would outgrow her shyness by her teen years, but Batty wasn't so sure.

"Ben, go down and see what those boys are doing," she said.

"Can I have the last cookie?"

"When you come back."

She watched him labor through the baby gates, down and up again. When he returned, he said, "The Donovans are lying on the floor, and Artie's doing handstands. I wish I could do a handstand. Also, they're eating pretzels again. We never have any pretzels left anymore."

So now *both* Donovans were in the living room. When had the other one gotten into the house? Instead of going away, the boys were multiplying. Batty couldn't help thinking they didn't spread themselves around very well. Surely there were teenage girls right this minute without any boys at all in their houses.

Then the doorbell rang, and Jane let in yet another teenager. At least this one was a girl, Jane's friend Eliza, improving the girl-to-boy ratio. But Batty was no closer to her piano. Good thing she did her serious practicing in the mornings before school, before these invasions.

"I suppose I should give up and just do my homework," she said.

"I already did mine," said Ben. "Subtraction and spelling."

Ah, subtraction and spelling. Those were the good old days, thought Batty, dragging herself back to her room to learn clouds. Plus, there was her book report problem. She needed to write ten before the end of the year, and while she'd had all year to get started, so far she hadn't written any. It wasn't that Batty didn't like to read. She loved reading (not as much as Jane did, but neither did anyone else in the world). For Batty, though, reading was like having a private conversation with the book's characters. Writing a report—making it all public—wrecked that. She'd tried reading books she didn't like just so they wouldn't be ruined when she had to write about them, but she never could get past the first few, awful pages.

And this was Thursday night, and every Friday, her teacher Ms. Rho, obsessive book report enthusiast, made a big fuss over the chart that recorded how many reports each student had handed in so far. Maybe Batty could force herself to write one tonight for Ms. Rho—just one—and thus avoid what she'd had to endure every Friday for months now, her teacher's look of disappointment, tinged with the tiniest bit of scorn.

Batty drifted toward her little bookcase, meaning to look at the books, but first she had to stop by the bed to say hello to two stuffed animals lounging on the pillow. One was Funty, a blue elephant who had been with Batty forever. The other was a tiger named Gibson, one of a revolving set of friends who got to hang out with Funty. A few months ago it had been Ursula the bear. Next up would be Fred, the other bear.

"Hi, guys," she said.

"Hi, Batty," she replied, then sighed, and made it all the way to the bookcase.

And greeted the pictures she kept there of Hound. None of them were much good, mostly fuzzy and out-of-focus snapshots, as if he'd always been dashing away from or toward the camera. It was her fault, Batty knew, that she'd never thought to get a better one while he was still alive. Occasionally she was haunted by a vague memory of one framed picture that had captured his essential Hound-ness, his empathy and intelligence, but she'd searched for it through the entire house and had found nothing. Probably she'd made it up.

"Hi, sweet dog," she said, this time with no reply.

Okay, book reports. She bent down to look at the bottom shelf, where her least favorite books ended up. She pulled out one that she'd managed to get through, about an interesting kind of magic but with a lot of extra-silly stuff about groundhogs thrown in. If she could stand thinking about it again, she could possibly squeeze a book report out of it.

But the bookcase was near the window, and the window was open, and in through the window wafted the heady scent of damp earth and fresh green growing things, drawing Batty like a siren song. And soon the groundhog book had dropped to the floor and Batty was leaning out the window, breathing in spring.

Now, what was this? Teenagers in the yard? Couldn't they be content taking over the inside? Must they be outside, too? These were Skye's friends, kicking around a soccer ball, calling softly to each other. Batty recognized most of them—Pearson, Katy,

Molly, Asante—and there was Skye, her blond hair shimmering in the deepening dusk. Batty couldn't remember a time when Skye wasn't constantly doing soccer drills, and Jane, too, though Jane never worked as hard as Skye.

Molly was the first to notice Batty up there in the window. "Hey, Batty. Come down and play?"

"No, thanks." Batty had known Molly for years and wasn't shy with her. It wasn't just shyness, though, that kept Batty from wanting to join them at soccer but also her complete lack of talent for kicking, throwing, or catching balls of any size or shape. Although she didn't mind, not really, it was impossible not to have some envy for Skye's strength and grace, her relentless pursuit of perfection.

Now Molly was down there trying to convince Skye that they should once again try to teach Batty some rudimentary skills.

"There's no point," Batty heard Skye say. "She's hopeless at sports."

"I am hopeless, Molly!" Batty called down. "It's true!"

Skye looked up at her sister. "That reminds me— Jeffrey's visiting this weekend. He said I should let you know he'll be here on Saturday."

Batty almost fell out the window with excitement. "When? When on Saturday?"

But Skye had already turned away, dribbling the ball back into the game.

Well, Saturday was good enough, no matter what

time he arrived. Jeffrey! Jeffrey, Jeffrey, Jeffrey! A teenager, yes, but one of the few outside Batty's family that she was always delighted to see. Indeed, he wasn't truly outside the family, having been brought in as an honorary member one summer years ago when the four original Penderwick sisters first met him. They would have gone further if they could, adopting him even, to get him away from his selfish and awful mother, but because such matters are more easily dreamt of than done, the second choice—making him an honorary Penderwick—had been settled upon. And so Jeffrey had remained all these years, even after he'd found his missing—and quite wonderfully unselfish—father, making life much nicer for both of them.

But for Batty, Jeffrey was even more than an honorary brother. That first summer—she'd been little, only four years old—he'd rescued her twice, first from being stomped on by an angry bull, and again when she was about to run in front of a speeding car. Some of the family (Skye, for example) had thought that Batty shouldn't have put herself into situations from which she needed rescuing, but others felt that Jeffrey's selfless courage had bound him more closely to the family, which made the rescues a good thing. Mr. Penderwick even said that because Jeffrey saved Batty's life, he would forever own a piece of her soul. Batty hadn't understood what that meant when she was four, and she still didn't, but she liked it nonetheless.

Jeffrey and Batty had another special bond not

shared by the rest of the Penderwicks—music. A brilliant and dedicated musician, he'd been the first to recognize that Batty, too, had musical talent, the first to teach her the piano, the first to believe she might someday be as brilliant and dedicated as he was. It was Batty's dream to make this come true.

And now he was visiting! It had been too long since he'd come—weeks and weeks. He would drive his little black car out from Boston, where he was in boarding school, and they would play the piano together and talk about music—or at least they would do as much of that as Batty could manage, since he would also want to spend time with everyone else in the family, especially Skye. They all loved him, and he was Skye's best friend.

His upcoming visit called for celebration! For music!

On Batty's desk was an old-fashioned record player that Iantha had found for her several years ago at a garage sale. It was one of Batty's most prized possessions, along with the ever-growing collection of secondhand albums she played on it. Many were of classical music, and also musicals—Batty adored musicals—plus a trove of Frank Sinatra, Lena Horne, and Judy Garland albums that Jeffrey had found in his mother's attic and passed on to Batty. And sometimes he would send her records, discovered in vintage shops, by all sorts of artists, like Johnny Cash, Joni Mitchell, and the Beatles, and lots of Motown. He'd promised that when she turned twelve, they'd start on a serious history of rock and roll, and when she was fourteen, he'd move her on to jazz, but for now, he wanted her listening to anything and everything and soaking it in.

What was just right for tonight? Batty flipped through her pile of favorites. Here was what she wanted: Marvin Gaye and her very extra-special favorite Marvin Gaye song, "I Heard It Through the Grapevine." She slipped the album out of its sleeve, set it on the turntable, and carefully set the needle down on the song's first groove. The opening notes came, the rhythm, the shake of the tambourine, and Batty snatched up Funty and Gibson and spun them around the room, the groundhog book and its unwritten book report completely forgotten.

CHAPTER FOUR
Chasing Rainbows

FIRST THING EVERY FRIDAY MORNING, before Ms. Rho had time to go over the awful book report chart, Batty and the rest of the Wildwood Elementary fifth graders gathered to sing. This would have been an enjoyable break from normal classroom labors if the music teacher hadn't been dull and pompous. Batty had long suspected that Mr. Rudkin knew nothing about music. Keiko went further, saying he would be better off teaching raccoons than children.

So there was a lot of interest this morning in the rumors flying around that Mr. Rudkin was gone. As Batty and Keiko joined the line of students snaking into the auditorium, they heard several possible explanations. That Mr. Rudkin had bored himself to death was the cruelest, that he had run away to marry a rock star the least likely.

"And Henry said that Mr. Rudkin's gone into hiding because the FBI is after him," Keiko told Batty as they made their way up to the stage.

"Henry's nuts." He was one of their classmates, and prone to exaggeration. Still, Batty couldn't help hoping it was true about the FBI. A public elementary school is not a good place to hide from the government. Maybe Mr. Rudkin would disappear forever.

The fifth graders crowded onto the risers higgledy-piggledy. Mr. Rudkin had never bothered to sort them into any order, so each week was a free-for-all of trying to be close to your friends and far from your enemies. Keiko and Batty always stood next to each other and, if they could manage it, behind someone tall enough to block them from Mr. Rudkin. Today they chose a spot on the fourth riser behind the basketball-playing Wise twins, then wished they hadn't when the school principal arrived—definitely without Mr. Rudkin, but instead with a short woman with lots of wavy gray hair and impressively large eyeglasses. To get better views, Batty leaned one way and Keiko the other.

"Who do you think she is?" asked Keiko.

The school principal raised his hand in the air, the Wildwood signal for silence, and all the students had to raise their hands in the air, too. The gray-haired woman did not, which gave Batty a twinge of optimism. Mr. Rudkin had usually spent half of class with his hand in the air, making it difficult to get much singing done.

"Good morning and hands down, fifth grade,"

said the principal. "I'm sorry to have to tell you that a medical condition will keep Mr. Rudkin from us for the rest of the year."

An arm shot up again from the midst of a cluster of boys that included Henry the FBI insider. This was not a request for silence but a request to interrupt.

"It's Vasudev," Keiko whispered to Batty, who already knew that, since he was in their class. Keiko was keeping close tabs on several boys—Henry, Vasudev, a sixth grader named Eric, and a movie star named Ryan. She hadn't yet committed to the idea of having a crush, but thought she should know who was worthy, just in case she suddenly felt the need to give away her heart.

The principal pointed to Vasudev. "Yes?"

"What kind of a medical condition?"

"Nothing life-threatening—and more important, none of your business." The principal rubbed his forehead, which he often did in the presence of the fifth grade. "We have, however, found a substitute for you. Let's give a round of applause to Mrs. Grunfeld for stepping in on such short notice."

As it sank in that Mr. Rudkin was really and truly gone, the applause grew increasingly enthusiastic, until the principal again raised his hand for silence. He issued a few dire warnings about what would happen if they didn't behave, then made his escape, and the students were left alone with Mrs. Grunfeld.

"According to Mr. Rudkin's lesson plans, you've

46

been singing 'Shenandoah.' Now you will sing it for me," she said, taking a pitch pipe from her pocket and blowing into it. "That is your starting note. One and two and three and four—"

The fifth grade had never done a good job with "Shenandoah" for Mr. Rudkin. Neither he nor they had cared enough to find the charm in the old folk song. But today it sounded absolutely ghastly. Batty knew what was going on, because it had happened before. Several of the boys were singing off-key on purpose. Mr. Rudkin had never been able to figure out who was making the awful noise—those were the classes during which everyone spent lots of time with their hands in the air for silence.

They'd barely gotten through the second line about longing to see Shenandoah when Mrs. Grunfeld made a slashing gesture across her throat.

"Cut," she said quietly but with such authority that everyone stopped singing, even the off-key singers, whom Mrs. Grunfeld now pointed to, one at a time. "You, you, you, and you, move to the first row, where you will stand quietly while the others sing. You'll be allowed to rejoin the singing only when you request it. Please note that I didn't say *if* you request it, but *when*. And I believe *you* will be the first to request it, Mr. . . ."

"Lowenthal," said Henry. He couldn't believe they'd been caught.

"Good. Now the rest of you must move, too. Those

who can sing without sending dogs into fits, stand on the left, and those who think you are a little better than that, move to the right. And if the tallest stand at the back and the shortest at the front, I will be able to see all your faces."

The next few minutes were a confusion of giggling and pushing as everyone sorted themselves out according to their perceived abilities and relative heights. Batty and Keiko moved together to the far right and down to the second row, because Batty wasn't tall and Keiko was a little shorter. To Keiko's regret, many of the boys ended up on the left, probably hoping that they might later be tested against a dog.

"Now let us try again," said Mrs. Grunfeld. "And please, everyone, stand up straight. Your lungs can't work when you're slouching like teenage reprobates."

The fifth graders straightened up until they were more telephone poles than reprobates.

Oh Shenandoah,
I long to see you,
Away, you rolling river.
Oh Shenandoah,
I long to hear you,
Away, I'm bound away,
'Cross the wide Missouri.

"Cut," said Mrs. Grunfeld.

This time there had been no misbehaving boys, and Batty thought that Hound, at least, would not have been sent into fits. She was curious to see what this interesting teacher would do next.

"Second row, just the four girls at the end, please. Start again."

The four at the end were Keiko and Batty, and two girls from a different class, Melle and Abby. They all exchanged nervous looks—none liked being the center of attention. Batty liked it least of all. She bent her knees to look shorter and shook her hair in front of her face.

"Now, please." Mrs. Grunfeld blew into her pitch pipe again.

The girls got through two entire verses before they were cut off. In silence they waited for a verdict, but to their collective relief, none came. Mrs. Grunfeld simply smiled and went on.

"Thank you, girls. I think I've had enough of rivers for now. What other songs have you been working on?" She read from a list on a music stand. "'All Quiet Along the Potomac Tonight,' 'The Song of the Volga Boatmen,' 'Swanee River.' They *all* seem to be about rivers."

A helpful boy in the front row explained. "Mr. Rudkin thought we could learn geography while we were singing."

"How much geography have you learned so far? That's what I thought. Forget rivers. We will begin with a song that teaches you nothing."

The remainder of the class sped by. Mrs. Grunfeld started them off with a deliciously silly song called

"That's Amore." After that they sang "Twist and Shout"—for which Mrs. Grunfeld demonstrated how to do the dance called the twist, explaining that some music was inextricable from dance, and here was a good example. By this time, the boys who had been forbidden to sing were showing signs of regret, tapping their feet along with the music, and when at the end of the class Mrs. Grunfeld was leading the group in a rousing rendition of "I Go to Rio," all four were singing along. Henry had in fact been the first to politely ask if they could do so.

The mood of the students filing out of the auditorium was very different from when they'd come in. Everyone was crazy about the new teacher. One girl did protest that the twist was a dance for grandparents, but when Vasudev asked if she wanted Mr. Rudkin back, that was the end of complaints.

Batty was preoccupied with why she, Keiko, Melle, and Abby had been asked to sing together.

"What do you think Mrs. Grunfeld was listening for?" she asked Keiko.

"Our dulcet tones." Keiko was working on her twist moves. "Why don't you ask her? She's coming over here."

Mrs. Grunfeld was indeed making her way toward them. Batty froze, suddenly more wild deer than fifth-grade girl. Mrs. Grunfeld said hello and asked for Batty's name. Since Batty was still frozen, Keiko answered.

"She's Batty Penderwick."

"Thank you. But she's not mute, is she?"

Keiko nudged her friend. "Say something, Batty."

"I'm not mute."

"That's good," said Mrs. Grunfeld, smiling. "I wonder if you would mind stopping by the music room at the end of classes today."

"Yes, all right. I mean, no, I wouldn't mind."

Mrs. Grunfeld moved away, and Batty grabbed Keiko for support.

"Am I in trouble?"

"I don't think so," answered Keiko. "She smiled at you."

"She could have been smiling to soften the blow."

"Teachers only do that while they're delivering the blow, not five hours before the blow. Speaking of which, you didn't happen to write a book report last night, did you?"

"Rats, no." Batty hummed a little Marvin Gaye. "I guess I forgot again."

Ms. Rho's book report chart hung directly in Batty's line of sight, a constant reminder of her ongoing failure. By shifting a little sideways she could avoid seeing it, but then she was pointed right at Henry, who made faces at her, and she couldn't help laughing. Then Ms. Rho would tell her for the hundredth time to face forward, and there, again, was that awful blank line next to B. PENDERWICK. Only one other student had a blank line, Vasudev, and he didn't provide any

51

comfort, since he'd already written the required ten but kept forgetting to turn them in. Most of the rest of the class had around five stars on the chart, one star for each book report. Keiko had eight. And then there was Ginevra Santoleri, who already had fourteen and this morning popped up with another two. Ms. Rho made a great display of taping an extra piece of paper to the side of the chart to accommodate the overflow of stars.

Today, though, the chart had, for Batty, lost its usual sting. She was too busy thinking over the wondrous surprise of Mrs. Grunfeld and, mostly, why she wanted to meet Batty after school. This thinking lasted through lessons on clouds, exponents, and the effects of global warming on the Greenland tundra. It wasn't until they were in the midst of ancient Egypt that Batty thought she'd found her answer. She must have been playing her imaginary piano while singing in chorus, and Mrs. Grunfeld had noticed and now wanted to ask her to accompany the chorus on the piano. If this was so, Batty knew she was much too shy to play in front of the entire fifth grade. She would tell Mrs. Grunfeld no. But also thank her for "I Go to Rio," because that had been great.

After the last bell, Batty had to collect Ben before heading over to the music room. He was too young to walk home by himself, especially since the first rock he came across would distract him, and the next thing would be that no one knew where he was and the Penderwick family would go into a panic. When she reached the second-grade hallway, she found what seemed to be a huge exploded map of the United States. Large white cutouts of states were scuttling here and there, the biggest ones so big that they overwhelmed the second graders carrying them. Oregon was spinning in circles, unable to get its bearings. Alaska had bumped into the wall, New York had crashed into Nevada, and Mississippi was tripping Texas, who dropped her lunchbox.

Batty picked up the lunchbox and handed it back to Texas.

"Thank you, Batty." This was Remy, who had been friends with Ben way back when they were both at Goldie's day care.

"You've got a big state there, Remy," she said.

"All the little states were taken first. I would have liked Delaware. My aunt Courtney works at a museum there." Remy shifted Texas to a more secure position and wandered off, narrowly missing Iowa.

Now Batty was accosted by Minnesota and Florida, also known as Ben and Rafael. Ben was excited to have Minnesota. He peered at Batty—just barely—over the northern edge and explained, "We get to decorate these with stuff from the state, and Ms. Lambert says that Minnesota has lots of rocks."

"Every state has lots of rocks," said Batty. "Rocks are everywhere."

"But Minnesota is special. Ms. Lambert said so."

"I took Florida because of the alligators," said Rafael. "And also because the rocks there grow right out of the ground. It's the only state where this happens. Something in the soil."

Batty had learned long ago not to try to straighten out Rafael's wild imaginings. Any attempt just sent him further from reality.

"Ben, we have to go," she said.

He turned solemnly to Rafael. They had special ways of parting, including using codes and salutes, but Batty was too eager to get to Mrs. Grunfeld to wait for all that to happen. She took hold of Ben and pulled him and Minnesota toward the music room.

"Where are we going?" he asked when they veered past the hall that led to the school entrance.

"I have to stop by the music room."

"You're going to see Mr. Rudkin?" Even the second graders disliked him.

"No, he's gone. There's a new teacher, and she wants to talk to me."

"Why? Are you in *trouble*?" This was even stranger than choosing to see Mr. Rudkin. Batty never got into trouble in school. "Is it about your book reports?"

Ben knew about Batty's unwritten book reports and expected her to be thrown in school jail any minute.

"It can't be that. Music teachers don't care about book reports," answered Batty.

When Batty knocked on the door with MUSIC on it, Mrs. Grunfeld opened it right away, smiling.

"Hello again, Batty. Thank you for coming. You and whoever is behind Minnesota."

"That's my brother, Ben, and he can wait out here."

"Is Batty in trouble?" asked Ben.

"Of course not," answered Mrs. Grunfeld. "You may come in with her if you'd like."

But Ben preferred to stay in the hall and ponder the glories of a state with lots of rocks, and Batty went in alone. She was glad to see a piano in the corner. It bore out her theory about being an accompanist.

"I've asked you here so that you could sing for me," said Mrs. Grunfeld.

"Sing!" Batty almost turned to leave. She couldn't sing alone, here, in front of this person who knew so much about music. "Why?"

"This morning in chorus I thought I heard—" She paused. "I'll know better after you sing."

"But I never sing for anyone except my sister Lydia, who's two years old and doesn't count."

"Would it help if I closed my eyes? Or we could both close our eyes, and then you will sing." Mrs. Grunfeld closed her eyes. "You see. I am no longer here."

"Mrs. Grunfeld, please don't make me."

She opened her eyes. "My dear, I wouldn't dream of making you sing. I'm just hoping you will do so, as a favor to me."

A favor? What kind of teacher was this? "I guess I can try. What should I sing?"

55

"Anything except 'Shenandoah.'" Mrs. Grunfeld closed her eyes again, waiting.

Batty searched her memory, but her entire repertoire was gone, fled, vanished. Maybe it was the stress of standing here on display, out in the middle of the room. Batty looked longingly at the piano bench.

"Maybe I could manage if I sat at the piano," she said.

"Do you play? Excellent. Go ahead, dear, and open yourself to the music."

Batty sat and let her fingers rest on the white keys. The feel of the piano gave her courage, and now a song came creeping back into her mind. It was on one of the albums Jeffrey had given her, with lyrics set to music by Chopin. Tentatively, Batty picked out the melody—having her back to Mrs. Grunfeld helped, no matter whose eyes were closed—then dropped her hands into her lap and started to sing.

"I'm always chasing rainbows, watching clouds drifting by. My schemes are just like all my dreams . . ."

She had chosen well. Chopin's exquisite melody pulled her in, letting her forget herself, until all at once she came to the end and was jolted back into the Wildwood Elementary School music room with a teacher she'd just met that morning. She swiveled around on the bench, with no idea of what to expect. Mrs. Grunfeld still had her eyes closed.

"That was the key of G, Batty? Try it in C."

Surely it was time for explanations. "But—"

"And a little more slowly this time. Larghetto."

So Batty sang "I'm Always Chasing Rainbows" again, more slowly and in the key of C. Halfway through, she realized that this was a much better key for her and that larghetto gave her the time she needed to appreciate Chopin's melodic intervals. Huh, she thought. She'd never bothered to consider such things in terms of singing.

This time when Batty finished and turned around, Mrs. Grunfeld's eyes were open and she looked pleased with herself.

"Thank you, Batty," she said. "I was correct this morning. You have a beautiful voice. Rare and beautiful."

"Excuse me?"

"You don't agree?"

Batty didn't agree or disagree. Music for her was the piano. "I just never thought about it."

"And your family. They don't sing?"

"No." Batty didn't want to mention that they sounded like depressed sheep. "Mrs. Grunfeld, are you sure? That I can sing, I mean?"

"Yes, quite sure."

Batty slid back and forth on the piano bench, trying to let this all sink in. It was true that lately her voice had felt richer, like molasses instead of maple syrup, but she'd paid no attention, thinking it was just part of growing older.

Mrs. Grunfeld said, "Since this is news for you, I can assume you've had no voice training."

"You mean lessons?"

"Yes, lessons. When and if you do decide you want training, you must choose a teacher who won't make you do that awful belting everyone is being taught these days. People see it on television and think it's the correct way to sing." Mrs. Grunfeld stretched out her arms and sang, loudly, with an extra tremor in her voice that could have been dramatic, but just sounded silly.

"I *have* seen people sing like that on television." Batty was increasingly impressed with Mrs. Grunfeld's breadth of knowledge.

"Very bad for children's voices, too."

"I won't belt, I swear," said Batty, surprised to find herself promising not to do something she'd never considered doing. "Not for years and years, if ever."

"Excellent." Mrs. Grunfeld nodded, pleased. "If you ever have questions about singing, come to me. Yes? I will be here every Tuesday and Friday."

"Thank you, Mrs. Grunfeld."

"You're welcome. And thank you for singing for me. It was an unlooked-for treat, like finding an orchid blooming in a daisy field."

Batty left in a daze. An orchid in a daisy field! Her father would love that description.

"What happened?" asked Ben. "I heard someone screeching."

"That was Mrs. Grunfeld belting."

"Why?"

"It's a long story." A story Batty wasn't yet ready to tell Ben. It was only right that she tell her father and Iantha first. "So never mind, and promise you won't mention it at home or to Rafael or anybody."

"Okay." He didn't think some lady screeching was interesting enough to repeat.

"Penderwick Family Honor!"

"Okay! Penderwick Family Honor. Will you carry Minnesota home for me?"

Hidden behind Minnesota, Batty imagined her father's face—*all* their faces—when she sang for the family, the surprise and pride. "I'm Always Chasing Rainbows" would be a good song to begin with, and then maybe a Beatles song. Her father loved the Beatles.

But then she thought of Rosalind. She really should wait until Rosy got home. Could she keep such an excellent secret for so long, twenty-two days now? And—oh!—if she could wait that long, she should wait just one extra day and sing for the whole family on her birthday. As an extra-special birthday present for herself.

She and Minnesota abruptly stopped dead on the sidewalk. "Jeffrey's coming tomorrow!"

"I know that," said Ben. "Skye said he'd bring me a Celtics T-shirt. They just beat the Knicks. Rafael says there's also a Celtics team in Scotland, but they play soccer. And that someday the two Celtics teams will play each other, but in a game neither play, like ice hockey or cricket."

Batty had stopped listening when Ben began quoting Rafael, diving deep into plans of her own. Jeffrey's coming this weekend was perfect timing. He could help her put together a singing concert for her birthday. They'd done little concerts before, including one when she was five and just learning the piano. This, though, this would be the best ever. The Grand Eleventh Birthday Concert! And Keiko could help her figure out what to wear—something serious and dignified, yet creative and glamorous.

"It will be wonderful!" she said.

Ben was surprised but pleased by her enthusiasm for the Celtics teams. "Especially if they play ice hockey."

CHAPTER FIVE
Abandoned

A LONG ROW OF HYDRANGEA BUSHES ran along one side of the Penderwick home. Now, in the spring, they were mere clumps of sticks, drab and bare, with an occasional withered blossom from last year that had hung on through the winter storms. To Ben, the drabness made as little impression as would the delirious beauty that always arrived midsummer, when the bushes drooped with masses of multi-flowered pompoms, large as grapefruits, in shades of pinks, blues, and purples. No, what he cared about was the space between the bushes and the house, a narrow corridor of privacy he'd claimed as his own the previous summer. There, he'd stored the rocks not exciting enough to be taken inside, and he and Rafael had constructed things from them—roads, bridges, and building-like structures that could double as military installations and alien-invasion forces.

After breakfast on Saturday morning, Ben shoved through the hydrangeas, set down a large cardboard box, then brushed away the dead leaves and sticks that had accumulated since the previous fall. The winter hadn't done damage to his work. Good. Sometimes he thought he'd like to build real roads and bridges when he grew up. And maybe he could convince Rafael to be an architect, like after they'd made several movies and wanted to move on to new careers. Together they could build whole cities.

Ben crouched down and opened the cardboard box. First out, one of his most prized possessions, a model UH-60 Black Hawk helicopter, with real doors and seats. This had been a gift from Nick, oldest son of the Geiger family across the street, handed over before he'd gone overseas to fly around in helicopters just like this one, helping to fight a war. Lieutenant Nick Geiger of the United States Army, that's who he was now. Ben's mom had shown him on a map where Nick was fighting: a place with mountains, desert, and lots of small villages, all very far away.

Nick—and his younger brother, Tommy—had grown up mixed together with the Penderwicks, sometimes babysitting for them, and always making good jokes, plus teaching sports to everyone from Rosalind on down, though not as far as Lydia, and also failing with Batty, hopeless as she was at sports. Nick had taught Ben football and had promised to start on basketball the next time he came home on leave. He was due home sometime this spring. It couldn't be soon enough for Ben, who missed him terribly.

With the Black Hawk safely out, he dumped the rest of the box onto the ground. Here was a hodgepodge of action toys, many of them inherited from Nick and Tommy, plus a battered Millennium Falcon from Ben's mom. There were several from Ben's father, too, his birth father, that is, not his dad. These were all *Star Trek* figures, especially from *The Next Generation*, Worf, Troi, Picard, and a few evil-looking Romulans. All that Ben knew about this father, who had died in a car crash before Ben was even born, came from stories his mom told him. Sometimes he and Batty talked about their dead parents, but not often and usually not with sadness. It's hard to be sad about people you've never met, especially when the parents you ended up with are so good at being parents.

Ben's box had also yielded up a Chinook with only one set of rotor blades, a transporter room with a big crack down the middle, and lots more figures. Other than the *Next Generation* ones, Ben could identify only about half, including Luke Skywalker, Chewbacca, Spock, and Ginny Weasley, whose red hair was almost the same shade as his. The rest of the figures he used for his own purposes. An authoritative man in a blue uniform was Nick. And there was one mean-looking guy all in black that Ben called Dexter

Dupree, after a man famous among the Penderwicks for his loathsome personality. Dexter had once been married to Jeffrey's mother, but they'd divorced several years ago, after which she'd managed to marry and divorce another man, and was rumored to be engaged yet again. Ben set Dexter on a rock and spoke to him in his deepest voice, using the military code he'd learned from Nick.

"Ready for defeat, Delta-Echo-Xray-Tango-Echo-Romeo?"

"Never, never," squeaked Dexter, who wasn't smart enough for code.

"Ha, ha, ha. You're doomed."

Ben balanced Nick on the Black Hawk—he was too big to fit inside—just out of reach of the rotor blades. "This is your leader, November-India-Charlie-Kilo. Prepare for departure. Start engines. *Schwoof, schwoof, schwoof, schwoof*—"

"There you are."

His position had been discovered by a person or persons unknown! Ben tipped Nick into the underbrush for safety, then parked the Black Hawk behind the Millennium Falcon.

"You're entering a war zone," he said in the deep voice. "Prepare to defend yourself."

"Okay." The intruder turned out to be Skye, now shoving through the bushes. "In the mood for some goalkeeping?"

Skye was always trying to put him into an old

catcher's mask and chest protector—more hand-me-downs from the Geiger brothers—so she could shoot soccer balls at him. This was not Ben's idea of fun.

"No," he answered.

"What's Captain Apollo doing?" She pointed down at the man in the blue uniform, half hidden by a dried-up hydrangea bloom.

"That's Nick."

"Nick as a Colonial Warrior? I guess that works."

"He's coming home soon, right, Skye?"

"We hope so, buddy. The Geigers will let us know as soon as they hear anything." She kicked aside more dead leaves. "Okay if I sit down?"

He scooted over to make room, and down she came, squashing Dexter with her knee.

"Sorry, Spike," she said.

"That's Dexter," said Ben.

"Actually, this is Spike from *Buffy the Vampire Slayer*. He's a bad guy. So Dexter works, I guess."

"Good." Ben had gotten the bad part right.

She picked out a female Romulan. "This can be Jeffrey's mom, Mrs. T-D-M—"

"I thought she was Mrs. Tifton now." After Jeffrey's mother had divorced the husband after Dexter, Mr. Menduzio, the Penderwicks had decided it was simpler to stick with calling her Mrs. Tifton, no matter how many more times she got married and divorced.

"You're right. Horrid woman. Okay, so the Romulan is Mrs. Tifton, and you've got Dexter, so this

Dalek can be Menduzio." She smashed the Dalek into the Romulan. "Exterminate! Exterminate!"

"Mercy, mercy!" shrieked Ben, tossing Dexter into the fray.

"No mercy for you, horrible parent and step-parents," said Skye. *"Blam, blast, boom, blom!"*

"I'm melting! Melting!"

Skye put down her now quite defeated figures.

"So, Ben," she said. "You're a boy."

"Yes," he answered warily. It didn't seem like a good way for the conversation to go.

"And you have friends who are girls, right? Like Remy?"

"That was a hundred years ago."

"Well, if she were still your friend, would you make the mistake of wanting to move past friendship and into romance?"

Ben was confused. Skye usually made more sense than this. "Are you wanting to be romantic about Nick?" he asked tentatively.

"Nick! Good grief, no!"

"Then what are you talking about?"

"Let me put it another way," said Skye. "Jeffrey's getting all weird and talking about wanting me to be his girlfriend."

"Oh. That is weird."

"So I told him not to come this weekend."

"Not come *here?*" Ben couldn't believe what he was hearing. Jeffrey was an honorary Penderwick,

66

always welcome at their house. Plus, there was that Celtics T-shirt he'd promised to bring Ben.

"Only for this weekend, so that he has time to get sensible again. I said he could visit for my birthday. That's only two weeks from now—not too long, right?"

"I guess not." He turned the rotors on his Black Hawk. "So you're not going to make him disappear like Rosalind did with Tommy?"

"Rosalind didn't—"

"Yes, she did, Skye." Tommy Geiger had been Rosalind's boyfriend for years and years and then suddenly wasn't anymore when they went to college. Batty had tried to explain it to Ben—something about new beginnings and exploring options—but none of it had made sense to him. "Tommy didn't even come over to see us when he was home at Christmas. And I wanted to show him my presents. I *always* show him my presents."

"Okay, she sort of did, but it wasn't all her fault. They decided together that they needed a break. Anyway, I figure they'll get back together one of these days. And I'm not breaking up with Jeffrey—I'm wisely keeping us from getting together in the first place. It's completely different from Rosalind and Tommy." Skye picked up the Dalek and squeezed it mercilessly. "I just don't want a boyfriend right now. I want to get out of high school and go to college and learn, learn, learn, and soak up the universe. I wish you understood."

"Well, I don't want a girlfriend, but not just now. Never."

Which meant he did understand that part, but not about soaking up the universe.

"Thank you, that's a help, anyway. If you won't do soccer with me, I'm going to take a long bike ride to think. Will you tell everyone about Jeffrey not coming? I can't tell Jane because she's still asleep, and I can't tell Dad or Iantha because they'll get all concerned and make me feel awful."

"But I'm busy!" protested Ben. It was times like this when he most wished he had brothers. Or if he couldn't have actual brothers, that Nick, Tommy, and Jeffrey would stay where they could do the most good—on Gardam Street with Ben.

"Please."

"Oh, all right." It was hard for him to refuse Skye when she lowered her dignity enough to say please. "But you have to tell Batty."

"Why can't you tell her, too?"

"Because she's looking forward to him coming the most." Which meant she might cry, and Ben didn't think he should have to deal with crying when this was clearly Skye's problem.

But after Skye said please three more times, he gave in.

Ben found both his parents in the kitchen, drinking coffee. Lydia was there, too, sitting on the floor, making mysterious patterns with spoons. Ben and Rafael sometimes wondered if she picked up signals from aliens trying to connect with earthlings. If so, the aliens had picked the wrong human, that's for sure.

"Lydia loves Ben," she said, looking up from her spoons.

"I know that." He turned to his parents. "Skye said to tell you Jeffrey isn't coming this weekend."

"Why not?" his mom asked. "Is he all right?"

"He wants to be Skye's boyfriend." Ben wasn't sure if that fell into the category of being all right. "And she doesn't want a boyfriend because of soaking up the universe. But she said Jeffrey could come for her birthday."

Ben's parents were exchanging the kind of looks that meant they'd be discussing this after Ben left the room. That was fine with him. He was already weary of talking about it, and there was still Batty to tell.

"Is Batty upstairs?" he asked. "'Cause I need to see her."

"Yes, she is, but wait a minute," said his dad. "We're shopping for a car today. Want to come along?"

"Is Lydia going?"

"She is, because we're also going to look for a big-girl bed, which Lydia is very excited about, isn't she?"

"*Non.*" Lydia had no interest in a big-girl bed.

Iantha said to Ben, "Tell your sister how much fun it is to sleep in a real bed."

Ben wasn't sure he wanted Lydia to get a new bed. Her attempts to get out of the crib were becoming

69

ever more determined. What would life be when she could simply roll out of bed and go wherever she liked? "She'll really be able to escape now."

"Yes, but without the danger of falling on her head when she climbs out of the crib."

"Oh, yeah, that," he said, trying to sound enthusiastic. "Lydia, sleeping in a real bed is fun."

Lydia gave him a suspicious look, then moved one of her spoons a quarter inch further left.

"I think I'll stay home," said Ben, and trudged upstairs.

Batty was in her room, listening to Beethoven's Fifth Symphony, a piece of music thrilling enough to keep her from going crazy waiting for Jeffrey. It was the only Beethoven symphony she owned, and was marred by a scratch in the beginning of the fourth movement. Someday when she had lots of money, she was going to buy all of Beethoven's symphonies, with no scratches on any of them.

The Beethoven served another purpose. It was loud enough to drown out any singing that might suddenly pop out of Batty. Her family was used to her humming—anybody can hum—but this was different, more like she'd become inhabited by a sprite fond of bursting into song at any old time. It had started the evening before, but while Batty had managed to keep it quiet when anyone else was around, she definitely needed to learn more control.

Here came the fourth-movement scratch—*iehn-iehn, iehn-iehn, iehn-iehn*. Batty rushed to turn off the record player. In the sudden silence, she heard Ben's private signal.

"Come in," she said.

He did, looking grumpy.

"That music was so loud you couldn't hear me knock."

"Sorry," she said.

And then it happened—her sprite tried to sing. Batty clapped her hand over her mouth and hoped Ben hadn't noticed.

He'd noticed. "What was that sound?"

"What sound?" is what Batty said, except that it sounded like *whu sohn* because her hand was still over her mouth.

"That sound you just made."

"Maybe your stomach was growling."

He stared at her suspiciously. His stomach hadn't growled. "There it goes again!"

"Maybe it's *my* stomach!"

She started to push him toward the door, but he resisted. "If it's your stomach, why is your hand over your mouth?"

She took away her hand but kept her teeth clenched, just in case, and tried again to get him out of the room.

"Stop pushing me. I have to give you a message from Skye."

Batty's sprite disappeared, and Batty stopped shoving her brother.

"What message?"

"I'll tell you, but you can't cry."

"Just tell me."

"Jeffrey's not coming this weekend."

She sat down on her bed with a *thwump*. "Why?"

"Skye said he couldn't because he wants to be her boyfriend and she doesn't want to be his girlfriend."

Batty was horrified. They'd already been through all this. A few years earlier Jeffrey had decided that Skye should be his girlfriend, and she told him he was an idiot. Then he fell for a girl named Margot at his school in Boston who turned out to actually be an idiot, obsessed with clothes and money, which Jeffrey finally realized, then came to his senses and swore he was done with romance and would now turn his life completely over to music. He'd even asked Mr. Penderwick for a Latin motto that would express just that. *Musica anima mea est.* "Music is my life." So why was he starting up with love again? Was he turning into a boringly normal teenager?

"This is a disaster," she said.

"Don't cry."

"Stop telling me not to cry. I'm not, anyway." Or just a tiny little bit, because of the shock.

"But Skye said Jeffrey could come for her birthday, so he won't disappear forever like Tommy did," said Ben. "Okay, that's all, so I'll go now. And don't push me out!"

Wiping her eyes, Batty realized that she shouldn't have pushed him, singing sprite or no singing sprite. She didn't like it when her older sisters tried to get rid of her.

"I'm sorry I did that," she said.

But Ben had already left the room, head held high.

At one end of Gardam Street, halfway round a cul-de-sac, was the path into a forty-acre slice of paradise called Quigley Woods, a wild realm of trees, rocks, and water, and a favorite refuge for all the Penderwicks. Batty hadn't yet gone there this spring—so not since Hound's death—but she went now, needing to be alone and think.

Winter had more of a hold here than on the lawns of Gardam Street. Patches of snow stubbornly lingered in the shadows, far too many for Batty to stomp away. She broke into a run to warm herself up, racing under the still-barren trees. After a dip in the path and just before a low, crumbling stone wall, she turned off onto a path that led down to her favorite spot in the woods, chosen long ago with Hound. She had picked it for the ancient willow tree, both huge and graceful, and Hound, for the creek that ran under the willow's vast canopy, where he could splash in the shallows while still keeping a watchful eye on Batty. But when she reached the willow, she found it already occupied by a male cardinal, furious with this human galumphing into his home.

"Please stay," she said. "I've come to visit, that's all."

But the bird flew off, a red and unforgiving blur. Abandoned, Batty looked up through the bare willow branches to the soft blue sky. Maybe she shouldn't have come here yet. Not until she'd stopped missing Hound so terribly.

She sat down and leaned against the willow, glad for its familiar support, and tossed a stick into the creek. Her dad had once told her that Hound wouldn't want Batty to mourn for long, that he'd loved her too much to want her miserable. She asked her dad how he could be certain, and he said that years ago someone had told him that very thing, before she died. "*My mother, you mean,*" Batty said, and he answered yes.

It hadn't helped.

She wondered what Hound would have made of this singing business. He hadn't been a particularly musical dog, showing no preference for Mozart or Motown, Beyoncé or Beethoven, if he'd ever even noticed the difference. Jeffrey had called him the perfect audience, since he would wag his tail for anything Batty played on the piano, even deliberate discord. She tried to picture him there in front of her, already wet from his first dip in the creek, his tongue hanging out with excitement, his brown eyes warm with love.

"I wish I hadn't let you die." She said it to the creek and the trees and the sky and the bird that had flown away, so there came no answer. Never an answer.

She had so been looking forward to seeing Jeffrey, to singing for him. Oh, now she was about to cry again. Except—except that Hound had never wasted time feeling sorry for himself, and Batty shouldn't, either.

She watched the creek, the sun glancing off the water, and listened to its gentle plashing.

Maybe this wasn't a disaster with Skye and Jeffrey. If Skye had said he could come in two weeks for her birthday, she must be counting on the boyfriend-girlfriend stuff to blow over pretty quickly. And since Skye's birthday was eight days before Batty's, there would still be time for Jeffrey to help plan the Grand Eleventh Birthday Concert.

"I'll just have to wait a little longer," she said. "I can do that."

And while she waited, she could start learning about this voice Mrs. Grunfeld had discovered. After all, *Musica anima mea est* was Batty's motto, too.

She stood up, planting her feet firmly on the ground, sheltered under her willow tree. What was it that Mrs. Grunfeld had said? *"Open yourself to the music."* All right. Two deep breaths.

Batty started to sing.

CHAPTER SIX
PWTW

SEVEN, NINE, MAYBE TEN SONGS LATER—Batty had lost count—she was wandering back through Quigley Woods, stunned with joy. It had come to her, this happiness, during the third song, "Here Comes the Sun," when for just one instant she'd heard her voice as if it belonged to someone else. A voice that soared out across the creek and up through the willow branches, so rich and glorious it lured back the red cardinal, astonished by this phenomenon, a human who sang as beautifully as a bird.

It wasn't that Batty hadn't believed Mrs. Grunfeld about her voice. While the orchid in the daisy field had seemed like an exaggeration, Batty had understood that she could sing well. But this was different. Mrs. Grunfeld hadn't exaggerated. This voice—the one Batty had heard there in the woods—was indeed an orchid, and a great gift, one that she would need to take care of. No belting, for example.

What a lucky girl she was!

Close to the edge of the woods now, she stepped off the path to sit on a fallen log. There were practical considerations to explore before she broke back into the real world of Gardam Street. Like the training Mrs. Grunfeld had mentioned. Yes, Batty wanted singing lessons—she was certain of that now. And she wanted them from the person who had brought on this magic—Mrs. Grunfeld.

But lessons cost money. Batty knew that she could go to her parents for the money—tell them about Mrs. Grunfeld, then sing for them—and that they would figure out a way to pay for the lessons. But that would mean giving up the surprise of the Grand Eleventh Birthday Concert, and Batty didn't want to do that, now less than ever. Besides, she was too proud to ask for more money, not with the new car and her sisters' college fees, not to mention the *immoderatae* grocery bills. For a moment, Batty considered giving up her piano lessons, exchanging one kind of lesson for another, but no, she couldn't do that. The piano was too important to her, voice or no voice.

She would have to earn the money for voice lessons on her own. Which meant launching her Penderwick Willing to Work business not when she became a teenager, not when she'd grown out of her shyness, but now, immediately.

She got up and leapt back onto the path and

headed home. First, she had to apologize properly to Ben for being so rude to him—she was too happy to have anyone angry with her. Then she'd get started on PWTW. Maybe she'd ask Ben to help with the details. He loved coming up with ideas, and as long as Rafael wasn't there to encourage the wackier parts of his imagination, sometimes the ideas were decent.

When she burst into the house, Iantha called out from the living room. "Is that you, Battikins?"

Batty smoothed down her hair in an attempt to look less exuberant, and went in. Iantha was sitting cross-legged on the floor, using pins to mark the hem of the dress Jane was wearing, one that Jane had made herself. It was cotton, sprigged with tiny yellow and orange flowers, not particularly stylish but individual, a dress that an author might wear.

"Yes, it's me," Batty answered. "You look nice in that dress, Jane."

"Thank you. I even designed it, believe it or not," said Jane. "Wow, you look really happy. What's happened?"

"Nothing." Batty tried looking less happy. This voice secret was going to be difficult to keep.

"Turn, Jane," said Iantha, and stuck a few more pins into Jane's hem. "Batty, you do know that Jeffrey's not coming, right?"

"Ben told me. I'm very upset." She tried to look like it.

"But you look happy." Jane was looking at her with what their father called her "writer's gimlet eye."

Batty pinched her own leg to make her face look unhappy. If Jane decided that Batty's emotions would make for good research, she'd be relentless in trying to figure out what they were.

"Jane, turn," said Iantha. "And stop trying to make Batty look not happy. Happy is good. And Jeffrey and Skye will work it out somehow."

"They have to, don't they?" said Jane. "Skye can't banish someone who belongs to all of us."

"Right, and turn again. Batty, do you want to come car-shopping? We're leaving soon."

"No, thanks. I have—things to do." She started out of the room. "Do you know where Ben is?"

"Outside digging up rocks."

Batty went through the house, picking up a pad of paper and a pen as she went, and out the back door, where she found Ben attacking a new spot. He'd already dug up three interesting rocks, making himself filthy once again.

"I'm sorry about before," she told him.

"I know it was you making that noise," he said. "And it wasn't your stomach."

"You're right. I'm sorry."

"It wasn't regular humming, like you usually do. It was like a fire engine siren. And then you pushed me."

"I was very rude, and I'm *sorry*. Good grief, Ben, please stop being mad."

He picked up one of his rocks and inspected it carefully. "I guess I could."

"You could? Because I have something to tell you."

Batty waited—he seemed to be listening. "I have to figure out how to make money."

Ben wasn't sure how he felt about this. If Batty started making money, he and Lydia would be the only non-earners in the family. This was not a way he wanted to be linked with Lydia.

"Why? Are you going to help pay for the new car?"

"No, I need money for music stuff." She hoped he wouldn't ask what kind of music stuff, but he was still thinking about the car.

"Maybe you could pay for a tire." Ben thought it would be fun to own one of the tires on the new car. He could paint his name on the side. BEN BEN BEN BEN, rolling around and around.

"Not even for a tire."

"Oh. Well, *how* are you going to make money?"

"I'll have a business called Penderwick Willing to Work."

"But what kind of work?"

This was the problem, she told him, figuring out what work an almost eleven-year-old could do. Batty wished she was learning work skills at school, instead of clouds and exponents. Fixing shoes, for example, might not be a bad job. And she wouldn't have to talk to strangers, except when they brought her the shoes. Even then, she wouldn't have to look at their faces— just their feet.

But Ben, as she'd hoped, wanted to help, and Batty put the pen and paper to use. Across the top she wrote *PWTW (Penderwick Willing to Work)* and then two ideas that had come to her as she ran home. She was proud of them—*Light Cleaning (Dusting, etc.)* and *Light Lawn Work (Weeding)*—but knew they were only a weak beginning.

"It's going to be a neighborhood odd-jobs business," she said, "and this is all I've got so far. I can't do carpentry or plumbing. I'm not sure I even know how to weed. But I can't have an entire business based on dusting."

"Nick and Tommy used to cut lawns," said Ben. "When Nick comes home, he could teach you how."

"There's no point, since I'm too young to use the lawn mower." The family rule was that you had to be twelve. Less chance of losing toes that way.

"Well, then, maybe when Tommy's home for the summer, you could follow along behind him and pick up the grass he's cut." Ben pictured bonding with Tommy over hard labor, having long discussions about basketball and Nick. He could do it if Batty didn't want to.

"Tommy doesn't even talk to us anymore, Ben. Not since he and Rosalind split up."

"Skye figures they'll get back together."

"I hope so." The whole family hoped so, except perhaps Rosalind. No one knew what she hoped. "But still, I need jobs that don't involve Geigers."

"You could dig up rocks," he said, then graciously added, "I could show you how."

"No one pays to have their rocks dug up."

"Batty, you said you wanted my ideas, so write down 'Digging Up Rocks.' And if anyone wants it done, I'll do it."

"But this is *my* business!"

"Write it down. Please."

Without enthusiasm, Batty wrote *Digging Up Rocks*.

Encouraged by his success, Ben had another idea. "How about home security? I can watch Gardam Street out my window with those binoculars Skye gave me. They have night vision and everything."

"You're asleep at night. And what about when you're at school? Robbers can come during the day."

"Write it down anyway."

"No." Digging up rocks was silly enough.

Ben scowled at his rocks, thinking. "You could teach piano."

"I already rejected that. Anyone who would pay a fifth grader to teach them would be awful, and awful music hurts my brain. I thought of babysitting, but what if the Yees asked?"

Batty and Ben both shivered at the idea of babysitting for the rambunctious Yee children, who lived on the cul-de-sac.

"How about pet-sitting?" Ben suggested. "The DiGintas have fish."

Batty was pretty sure fish were even harder to keep alive than dogs. Keiko had kept fish for a while, including one she'd named Ryan, after that movie star she liked, but one of the other fish ate Ryan, then died itself, and Keiko had cried for a whole day.

"No pet-sitting," said Batty.

"Washing windows?" Once last summer Ben had helped his mother wash the windows with the hose, and he hadn't forgotten how much fun it had been to get wet and soapy.

"I guess so." Batty wrote down *Washing Windows*. "As long as they're on the first floor, because we're probably not allowed to climb high ladders."

They struggled on, but after another half hour had added only *Companionship* and *Taking Out Trash*. It was a decent first step, though, and Batty hoped that neighbors would come up with their own ideas for chores she could manage. But now she had to figure out how to tell her parents about PWTW. Since she'd run back from Quigley Woods, she'd focused only on how to make money. She hadn't taken even a moment to wonder whether her parents would approve.

"How do I get Dad and Mom to let me do this?" she asked Ben.

"I don't know." His requests to their parents were usually less complicated, like asking if Rafael could spend the night.

"I should ask them one at a time. Divide and conquer, like Dad says, except he says it in Latin. Who do I ask first?"

Another long discussion ensued, during which they analyzed each parent's soft spots, but in the end they could agree only to toss a coin. Batty went back into the kitchen to borrow a nickel from the spare-change jar by the phone.

"Heads for asking Mom first, tails for Dad," she said, tossing the coin high into the air.

It was heads.

Their parents arrived home in the late afternoon, bearing photographs of the car they'd bought after a long and arduous search. It was a blindingly bright turquoise minivan with a peculiar orange racing stripe across the hood, plus at least a dozen bumper stickers that no Penderwick agreed with.

"It's awful," said Skye, looking at the pictures.

"We know," said Iantha. "But we got them to knock five hundred off for the racing stripe."

"And another hundred off for the bumper stickers," said Mr. Penderwick. "And we can bring it home this week."

"It's flashy," said Ben admiringly. He liked the orange racing stripe.

"*Flashy* is just the right word," said Jane. "I hereby dub it Flashvan, and we can scrape off the bumper stickers."

"And Lydia's big-girl bed will be delivered on Thursday," said Iantha. "She helped pick it out, didn't you, sweetheart?"

Lydia put on her I-can't-hear-you face and showed Asimov the balloon she'd been given by the car sales-woman. Under the impression that every floating thing was a bird, he gave it an irate swipe. The balloon popped, and Lydia crumpled into loud misery.

"She needs a nap," said Iantha, gathering her up and heading toward the steps.

Ben poked Batty. "Follow them," he whispered.

She shook her head. No one could be receptive to daughter-run businesses with Lydia wailing in their ear. But when Iantha came back downstairs, she was never alone long enough for Batty to tackle her with PWTW. It wasn't until dinner was over, when her mom went into the basement to do laundry, that Batty got her chance. She followed Iantha down the creaky wooden steps, nervously clutching her list of odd jobs, now a neatly typed and official-looking flyer.

Batty had always been fascinated by the basement, with its hulking, humming furnace, the maze of overhead pipes, dim corners full of shadows, plus the hoarded treasures of years past—dusty vases, broken chairs, battered Frisbees, ancient clocks with their hands all set to different times, discarded doors and windows from earlier versions of the house, and one mysterious and solitary wooden shutter that seemed never to have belonged anywhere.

Tonight wasn't the time to linger and look about, though. The washer and dryer were along the back wall, and that's where Batty found Iantha. She was leaning over the washer, pulling out wet laundry one piece at a time, each sparkling where it had never sparkled before. "Glitter. Glitter. More glitter."

"Where did it all come from?" asked Batty.

"Aha!" Iantha pulled a small plastic tube from the pocket of a tiny pair of flowered jeans. The tube was labeled GLITTER, it had no cap, and it was empty. "Lydia must be bringing home art supplies from Goldie's again."

This wasn't the first Lydia-versus-laundry mishap. The last time it had been a purple crayon that melted all over Ben's shirts. He was going to hate glitter even more.

"Maybe she shouldn't be allowed to have pockets."

"Too late." Iantha pulled out Skye's favorite soccer jersey, all asparkle. "I'll have to wash this load again."

"Mom." Batty readied her PWTW flyer. "I want to start a business."

"Glitter removal, I hope."

"Mom!"

Iantha let drop a twinkling sock and turned to Batty. "You're serious?"

"I want to make some money."

"Honey, what could you want that you think we can't buy for you? Do you need new clothes?"

"No, I thought I'd use it for music stuff." She held her breath, hoping that *stuff* would work for her mom as well as it had for Ben.

It didn't. "What kind of stuff?" Iantha asked.

"Like records and sheet music and maybe I'll want more music lessons someday," she burbled, hoping that the definition of *someday* really actually meant this coming week. Then she had an inspiration. "You know, like how Jeffrey plays both the piano and the clarinet."

"You want to take clarinet lessons? That's exciting. Let's talk to your dad about it."

"No, thank you, not now, anyway." Batty had no interest in playing the clarinet. "Here, look."

She handed over the flyer and watched anxiously as Iantha read it.

"Digging up rocks?"

"Don't pay attention to that one. Ben made me write it down, but it's my business, not his. I know he's much too young to have a job."

"And you're not?"

"No! I don't want to buy a tire for the new car or anything. Promise."

"Good, because Flashvan already has four tires." Iantha smiled. "PWTW. That's clever. Did you think that up?"

"Yes." Being called clever was a good sign.

"I'm awfully proud of you for taking responsibility, but, Batty, between school and piano, you already work so hard. I want you to have fun while you're a child."

"I don't work that hard at school," said Batty, thinking of those unwritten book reports.

"Still, how could"—Iantha scanned the flyer again—"*dusting* be fun for you?"

Batty couldn't lie and pretend that dusting would be fun. "Please, Mom."

"Have you asked your father yet? No? Go tell him about PWTW, and then we'll talk."

Much encouraged that she hadn't gotten a definite refusal, Batty took the PWTW flyer back upstairs to where her father was emptying the dishwasher. Before she could begin her spiel, there was a knock at the front door. Mr. Penderwick left to answer it, and came back grumbling.

"Boys for Jane. I asked them their names and they both said Donovan, thinking they could fool me. So I didn't offer them any pretzels."

"There *are* two Donovans," said Batty.

"Really? Well, I still won't offer them any pretzels. *Locustae*, swarming the house and devouring all the snacks."

"Daddy—" Then Batty said all over again what she'd said to Iantha. At the end, her father was shaking his head.

"Isn't it enough that Skye's tutoring half the high school and Jane plans to turn herself into a clothing factory? Now my ten-year-old wants to go into business for herself?"

"Almost eleven. Please, Daddy. I know what I'm doing."

Jane flew into the kitchen, looking for the pretzels. "Know what you're doing about what, Batty?"

"She wants to start a neighborhood odd-jobs business," said their father. "And I think she's too young."

"Didn't you and Aunt Claire have some vaguely shady business when you were Batty's age?" asked Jane.

"There was nothing shady about it," he said with dignity. "We helped neighbors clean out their garages, then sold what they gave us at tag sales."

"To the other neighbors." Jane took not only the pretzels from the cabinet, but also a giant bag of tortilla chips.

"And I was twelve, which is older than almost eleven," he added.

"So Aunt Claire was only nine!" said Batty eagerly.

Her father frowned, and tried to change the subject. "Jane, leave some food for the family!"

"I'll pay you back for all of it when I publish my first book, I promise. Do we have any cookies?"

"It's not the money, it's the innumerable trips to the grocery store," he said.

"Yes, Daddy." Jane kissed him on the cheek, found a bag of cookies to add to her loot, grabbed several bottles of drinks from the refrigerator, and left.

"No one listens to me," he said.

"I do," said Batty.

He went back to the PWTW flyer, studying it carefully. "I must say this is impressive. My daughter, an entrepreneur. But if we let you do this, there must be rules."

"Yes! Rules!" She could handle any rules, as long as she was getting closer to singing lessons.

"We will wait, however, until Iantha comes back upstairs. No more of this *divide et impera.*"

There it was—the Latin for "divide and conquer." "Okay, Daddy."

When Iantha came back upstairs, the three of them retreated to the cozy book-filled study the

Penderwick parents shared, though unequally. With the exception of Iantha's neat desk, from which she could research her way into the heavens, the room overflowed with Mr. Penderwick's botanical samples, all in different stages of preservation, some still drying between sheets of newspaper, some pressed flat in glass frames, and on his desk, a few in the last stage, carefully pasted onto sheets of white paper, turning them into pieces of art with delicate smears of dried color. Batty snuggled into an open space on the couch between two of these—one with a touch of rusty orange and the other a smoky blue—hoping their beauty would bestow luck.

Batty and her parents worked on the rules until they were all satisfied, finally agreeing on three. She couldn't accept a job without first checking back with them. Her schoolwork couldn't suffer. And to begin, she would limit her business to Gardam Street, where her parents already knew and trusted the neighbors.

"And for heaven's sake," added her father when they were finished, "make sure you mention your age on this flyer. People might think Iantha and I are offering to do their light dusting!"

CHAPTER SEVEN
Duchess

On Sunday morning Batty headed downstairs. She had with her the PWTW flyers, neatly typed and printed out from Iantha's computer (with the added note *I am almost eleven years old and reliable for my age*). After breakfast she would distribute them to the houses on Gardam Street. Despite her unwavering determination to make money, she was feeling shy and hoped that Ben would go with her.

In the kitchen, her father was pouring batter into the waffle iron, Lydia was in her high chair, wearing her favorite bib, the one with lambs on it, and Ben was in a chair far away from Lydia.

"Good morning." Batty kissed her dad's cheek while sniffing greedily at the sizzling waffle.

"Don't go near Lydia," said Ben. "She's grotesquely sticky."

"Lydia is beautiful," Lydia said, offended.

"That's true, Lydia," said her father, "although in this family we concentrate on brains, not beauty. But you are also very sticky. Have you been eating your waffle or bonding with it?"

Batty took a wet towel to Lydia, who fought her manfully. The process wasn't made easier by Asimov, who decided it was a good time to try to steal Lydia's waffle.

"No, no, *gato!*" cried Lydia, but Asimov ignored her, not knowing that *gato* is Spanish for "cat."

"More Spanish!" Mr. Penderwick shook his spatula. "Skye's getting ahead of me again. Lydia, what is the Latin for 'five'? *Unus, duo, tres, quattuor,* then what?"

"*Armaweerum.*"

"No, but that does sound like the start of the *Aeneid*. How clever of you to remember that."

"*Oui,*" said Lydia.

"Rafael and I are going to study Klingon when we're in high school," said Ben.

"Fine goal," said Mr. Penderwick, sliding a hot waffle onto a plate. "Ready to eat, Batty?"

"Yes, please. Yum." She sat down, and dug in. There is nothing so delicious on a Sunday morning as a waffle fresh out of the waffle iron, smeared with butter and real maple syrup. "Ben, will you come with me to distribute the PWTW flyers?"

"Can't. Rafael is coming over, and we're going to build and battle."

"What about taking Lydia along?" Mr. Penderwick asked.

Batty looked doubtfully at Lydia, now with a chunk of waffle stuck in her red curls. Not exactly the businesslike appearance Batty hoped to project. But a talkative baby sister was always good cover for a shy person. "Lydia, will you come with me to distribute my flyers?"

"Lydia wants to build and battle." Lydia waved her fork for emphasis.

"Oh, no, you don't," said Ben. "Go with Batty. It will be much more fun."

"And you can ride in your stroller," added Batty.

This caught Lydia's attention. She was always willing to go somewhere if she could ride there in regal splendor. Today was no exception, so after breakfast, she allowed herself to be cleaned and readied for an outing. She wanted her crown and several tutus, one atop the other, and also an attendant. For this she chose her pink-and-green-striped doll, which Skye had named Baby Zingo as a joke. Except that Lydia thought it an excellent name, and now they were stuck with it. When Lydia and Baby Zingo had at last been loaded into the stroller, Batty slid the PWTW flyers into its pocket and resolutely set out to meet her future.

Gardam Street had ten houses, five on each side. Because knocking on nine doors was beyond her, even with Lydia's company, Batty had come up with a compromise. She would distribute flyers to every house, quietly slipping them into mailboxes, but she must also—to prove her resolve—knock on at least one door. It was tempting to choose the Geigers'. Batty had been in and out of their home all her life and had little shyness left for any of them, certainly not for Nick and Tommy, but not even for their parents.

Choosing the Geigers was too cowardly, though, and they got only a flyer, just like the other families up and down the street. Batty decided to knock on the door of the second-least-scary family, the Ayvazians, down on the corner, who were old, tiny, and kind, and always had excellent treats on Halloween.

Mrs. Ayvazian opened the door at Batty's knock and beamed. "It's some Penderwicks! How nice! Come in, come in."

Before Batty could explain about the flyer, Mrs. Ayvazian had helped Lydia out of her stroller and was bustling them both into the house. Mr. Ayvazian was in the living room, sitting at a table piled high with books, papers, and photographs.

"Look who's come to visit, Harvey." Mrs. Ayvazian turned back to the girls. "He's writing his memoirs."

"I've made it past Vietnam," said Mr. Ayvazian. "Hope to reach Reagan by Christmas."

"And how is Miss Lydia?" said Mrs. Ayvazian.

"Goldie put Frank in a box," she answered.

"Not now, Lydia," said Batty.

Her storytelling thwarted, Lydia decided to show off her tutus. She executed a giddy triple twirl, then

94

set off on a series of hops that put Mr. Ayvazian's table at risk. Batty lunged, getting hold of a tutu or three just in time. One good bump to that table and all the papers, books, and photographs would be on the floor, and that would be the end of earning money for a while, since it wouldn't be fair to charge the Ayvazians to clean up a mess Lydia had made.

"How about some cider donuts for our guests?" Mr. Ayvazian asked.

"Of course," said Mrs. Ayvazian. "Who would like some donuts?"

"Lydia," said Lydia.

"No, you wouldn't," said Batty, determined to keep this strictly business. She handed a flyer to Mrs. Ayvazian. "No thanks for either of us, Mrs. Ayvazian. I've come looking for work."

"Work? Goodness."

"I'm the Penderwick Willing to Work and I can do most anything—well, some things, like dusting."

"I do my own dusting," said Mrs. Ayvazian, "and Harvey handles the outside, except for the gutters, of course."

"I don't know much about gutters." Except for the time Tommy had lodged a baseball in one, causing a small flood.

"That dog could use a walk," said Mr. Ayvazian.

"Why didn't I think of that? Batty, would you consider walking a dog?" Mrs. Ayvazian asked.

The last thing in the world Batty wanted was to

walk a dog. She hadn't even been able to protect her own dog. How ever could she be trusted with someone else's? But she couldn't say any of this to Mrs. Ayvazian. Besides, there didn't seem to be a dog in the house. There never had been a dog at the Ayvazians'.

"I didn't think you had a dog, Mrs. Ayvazian," she said, hoping this was all a misunderstanding.

"Duchess, dear, say hello to Batty and Lydia." Mrs. Ayvazian lowered her voice, as if the invisible dog could hear her. "She arrived only last week. My brother moved to Florida and thought she would be better off here with us. I think she misses him something awful."

"Well, she should miss him. He spoiled her rotten." Mr. Ayvazian didn't lower *his* voice. Since there was still no dog in sight, Batty didn't know whether this was a good or bad sign.

Could it be that the Ayvazians were losing their minds? This happened sometimes to old people, Batty had heard, although usually it made them do things like misplace keys, not hallucinate dogs. She was trying to figure out a polite way of getting Lydia safely out of the house when she heard a grunt coming from behind a blue armchair.

Then, slowly, while Batty and Lydia stared in amazement, an oddly shaped brown animal—like an overstuffed hot dog with teeny legs—dragged itself out into the open.

"*Gato*," said Lydia uncertainly.

96

Batty hoped that the dog—for it was not a cat but a terribly overweight dachshund—didn't understand Spanish. Never had she seen a look of such shame on an animal's face. It was clear that Duchess already knew she was tubby—being called a cat could have pushed her over the edge.

"Have you ever met a dog that needed exercise more than this one?" asked Mr. Ayvazian. "Laziest dog I ever met."

"She's not lazy, Harvey, just a little out of shape." Mrs. Ayvazian gave Duchess an encouraging pat on the head. "Would you like to take a walk with Batty and Lydia?"

"I really hadn't considered walking dogs," said Batty. Especially not this dog, who looked like she would die of a heart attack at any moment. "I don't think I'd be any good at it."

"Anyone can walk a dog," said Mr. Ayvazian.

"And you were so good with dear old Hound," added Mrs. Ayvazian.

Should Batty explain how she hadn't been good enough with Hound to keep him alive? No, she couldn't say that to these nice people. She'd simply take Lydia and leave, and hope to find work at another house.

But Lydia had decided to like this strange-looking dog.

"*Gato,*" she said again, this time with pleasure.

Sensing approval, Duchess toddled over and

snuffled at Lydia's ankles. Lydia giggled, and Batty felt that she was losing control over the situation. The feeling grew stronger when Duchess gazed into her eyes, pleading for sympathy.

Batty turned to the Ayvazians. "Are you certain Duchess would survive a walk?"

"Of course she will, dear," said Mrs. Ayvazian.

Mr. Ayvazian made a stronger point. "What she won't survive is staying behind that chair for too much longer."

"Then I guess we could try."

"Wonderful! Now, where did I put that harness?" Mrs. Ayvazian whisked out of the room, and Duchess cautiously lowered herself to the floor, staying there when her mistress returned with the harness and, with great effort, maneuvered it around the dog's massive chest.

Next Mrs. Ayvazian clipped on the leash, and the expedition was ready for departure. Astonishingly, Duchess managed to hoist herself up and stagger toward the door.

Mr. Ayvazian abandoned his memoirs and, belying his great age, picked up Duchess and carried her outside. "There, you miserable excuse for a dog. Go for a walk with these nice girls and count yourself lucky if I let you back into the house."

But Batty noticed how gently he set Duchess down, and how he gave her an extra scratch under the chin.

"How far should we take her?" she asked, knowing it was an optimistic question, since it was doubtful they would manage to take Duchess anywhere at all.

Mr. Ayvazian thought. "How about around the cul-de-sac and back?"

"Yes, we don't want to wear her out on the first day," said Mrs. Ayvazian, helping Lydia into her stroller. "Enjoy yourself, Duchess. Good-bye."

So they set out, two girls and a dog, bravely, and very, very slowly.

As soon as Rafael arrived, Ben took him behind the hydrangea bushes to show off the roads, hills, and bridges built from stone. They added another hill or two and an airstrip, then put together two entire teams: Team Golf-Oscar-Oscar-Delta (GOOD), under the command of Lieutenant Geiger, and Team Bravo-Alpha-Delta (BAD), under the command of Dexter. Team BAD used the Chinook to attack Team GOOD's base camp. Team GOOD fought them off with guts and the Black Hawk, then went on the attack themselves, chasing Team BAD out of the hydrangeas and into the front yard with much yelling and running around, until the Chinook crashed into the maple tree and Dexter plunged to his doom. It was then that Ben noticed the odd procession making its way up Gardam Street. Batty slowly pushing Lydia in her stroller—this he understood—but what kind of creature was that, struggling to keep up with them?

"Batty's got a huge guinea pig on a leash," said Rafael, squinting to bring the scene into better focus. "Like the hugest one in the whole world."

"Its nose is too pointy for a guinea pig. More like the hugest rat in the whole world."

Neither of the boys wanted to meet a huge rat, but they refused to run away from something Lydia didn't seem to be afraid of. So they stood their ground and, as the procession came closer, were relieved to see that the giant rat was only a fat dog with short legs.

"Don't laugh," said Batty when she reached them. "Her name is Duchess, and she lives with the Ayvazians."

No one laughed—the situation was too dire for that. Duchess had collapsed, panting. She was doing her best for these children, but she hadn't walked this far in a long time. Ben and Rafael ran inside and brought back water, which she would drink only right from their hands. Even after that, she seemed incapable of going any further, let alone all the way around the cul-de-sac.

"I should take her back home," said Batty, "but I don't think she can make it that far. She's going to die. I shouldn't have taken this job."

"We could carry her," said Rafael.

"No, we can't," said Ben. "Look at her."

"Out," said Lydia, who had been trying unsuccessfully to escape her stroller and get closer to Ben.

"Not yet, Lydia."

Ben gave Duchess more water, then stroked her ears and head. "Poor dog."

"*Out!*" said Lydia.

"Would the dog fit in the stroller?" asked Rafael.

It was worth a try. Lydia was let out of the stroller and warned that she'd have to wear Duchess's harness and leash if she didn't behave, then the effort to install Duchess began. They found that her bulk wasn't as big a problem as her floppiness. It was as though the signals from her brain couldn't reach all the way to her back end. Batty, Ben, and Rafael had to work together, lifting the front half of Duchess in first, then, with a great heave, the rest of her. But once they'd accomplished it, Duchess seemed grateful, even attempting a doggy smile—though she didn't like it when Lydia tried to put the crown on her head.

The walk could now resume. Batty pushed the stroller, Rafael held Lydia's hand, and Ben walked in front to keep watch over Duchess, all the way around the cul-de-sac and back down the street to the Ayvazians' house. Relieved that the ordeal was over, Batty knocked on their door. The Ayvazians were bound to be dismayed that she'd brought Duchess back in a stroller and would give up on this nonsense, then Batty would be free of the responsibility.

That's not what happened. Mrs. Ayvazian took one look at Duchess and said that she'd never seen such an improvement, and Mr. Ayvazian tried to put

Batty on his permanent payroll, with a twenty-dollar advance for the coming week.

Twenty dollars! That would go a long way toward paying for singing lessons. Still, Batty hesitated.

"I promised my parents I wouldn't accept a job without checking with them first." This was a stalling technique, since Batty was sure her parents would agree to the arrangement. They'd known the Ayvazians forever.

"You go ahead and ask your parents, and if it's okay with them, I'll pay you tomorrow after you take Duchess for another walk."

"But, Mr. Ayvazian." Batty tried one more time to get out of this. "I'm not sure Duchess liked it."

He leaned down to whisper in her ear. "Mrs. Ayvazian likes it, and that's what I care about the most."

Indeed, not only was Mrs. Ayvazian pleased with Duchess, she was delighted to have even more children return than had set out. Before Batty knew what was happening, everyone was inside the house, eating cider donuts and watching while Duchess maneuvered her way back into her hiding place behind the blue armchair, where she could recover from her perilous voyage around the cul-de-sac.

As soon as she got back home, Batty sought refuge at the back of her closet, asking Hound's forgiveness for letting a new dog into her life. Asimov followed her there and provided some comfort, at least, and didn't seem to mind when Batty took out Hound's old rubber bone and cried over it. Crying helped a little—enough, anyway, to let her rejoin the family. And when her parents were proud and enthusiastic about her first job, Batty tried to look enthusiastic, too. After all, more jobs might come from other neighbors. Having something to do besides walking a dog would lessen the sting.

Then at dinnertime came a phone call from the Geigers, with news so very wonderful it swept away all cares and worries. Nick had just landed in the United States, he was safe at his base in Kentucky, and he would be heading north—and home—soon.

Cheering and applause broke out around the Penderwick table. Nick! Nick! Jane lifted Lydia from her high chair and danced around the kitchen with her, Skye pumped her fists in the air, Mr. Penderwick and Iantha smiled happily at each other—and Batty saw that Ben was weeping, tears dripping down his face.

"He's been worried about Nick," she said.

"Oh, sweetheart." His mother went over to hug him. "Everyone's been worried."

"Maybe we need to make Welcome Home posters," said Jane. "Would you like that, Ben?"

Ben nodded, smeared his tears around with his napkin, managed a smile—and the poster team took over the kitchen. Space was cleared on the kitchen floor, large sheets of cardboard scrounged up, and markers and crayons distributed. Skye and Jane wrote messages for Nick in giant block letters and gave them to the younger siblings. Over by the refrigerator, Ben enthusiastically filled in *W, E, L, C, O, M, E, H, O, M,* and *E* on one poster. In front of the sink, Batty worked on another, coloring in *M, I, S, S, E, D, Y, O,* and *U* while trying to keep Lydia from completely wrecking the letters *W* and *E.*

After a while, a few of Jane's boys showed up and were pulled into the poster-making business. One was Artie, and the other one was someone new, a French boy named Jérôme who'd only just come to the United States as an exchange student. It took him a while to understand what they were doing, partly because Jane insisted on explaining in French.

"*Nick est* . . . sort of a . . . *un grand frère, qui* . . . *rentrer* . . . Artie, what's third-person future?"

"I don't know. I take German," said Artie.

"Nick is a brother?" asked Jérôme, who'd understood that much.

"*Oui!*" Jane was thrilled with her ability to communicate.

"He's *like* an older brother," said Skye. "Jane, Jérôme's English is probably better than your French."

"But it's good practice for me, if he doesn't mind."

"*Mais, non.*" Jérôme nodded politely. "Jane speaks beautifully."

As Jane beamed happily and went on butchering the French language, the rest of them bent to the

104

task. Artie quickly became the star of the group, with his seemingly effortless drawing of a Black Hawk, declared by Ben to be museum-quality art.

"If I had paint, I could make it even better," said Artie. "Even just some black and white would help."

Ben took off to ask his mother if they had any paint in the house and came back with the answer—there was plenty in the basement, lots of cans of different colors.

"I'll go," said Batty. If regular American teenagers made her shy, one from a foreign country made her want to hide under the kitchen table. This was a good excuse to take a break, and gather her courage.

Humming "High Hopes," a great song for courage-gathering, she ran down to the basement and over toward the corner where the paint cans were stored. She seldom went this way—it meant going past the big black oil tank that years ago Skye had said was a child-eating monster. Skye had even given it a name: Hanfligurtson. Though now that Batty thought about it, Hanfligurtson sounded more like something Jane would make up. So maybe they'd both been in on it.

"But of course I'm too old now to believe in—" Batty stopped, pulling up beside a heap of old bicycles, sleds, and a kiddie pool or two. The bikes and sleds hadn't grabbed her attention, no. It was what was peeking out from under one of the pools: a small red wagon that Batty hadn't thought about in years. Aunt Claire had given it to her when she was four, and she and Hound had played with it for months after, sharing many adventures.

Another Hound haunting. Would they never come to an end?

Her humming had fled, replaced by a fierce desire to drag the wagon upstairs and hide it in her closet with the rest of her secret treasures.

"Batty! Did you find the paint?" Ben was calling from the top of the stairs.

"Not yet," she answered, catching her breath.

"You sound funny."

"No, I don't. I'll be up in a minute." She shoved the wagon back under the kiddie pool and went to get the paint.

CHAPTER EIGHT
Duets

USUALLY ON SCHOOL DAYS Batty woke up to her alarm clock playing "Chain Gang." This Monday, she woke when something touched the tip of her nose. At first she sleepily brushed whatever it was away, half remembering when Hound used to snuffle her awake. But the nose-touching kept happening until Batty had to open her eyes and deal with it. Her room was still dark—the sun wasn't yet up—but there was just enough light to see a small finger coming at her again and, behind the finger, brown eyes, lots of red hair, and a princess crown.

"Lydia is hungry," said the nose toucher.

Batty turned on her bedside lamp, trying to grasp the situation. The clock said it was only a quarter of six, fifteen minutes before the alarm would go off. "Did you climb out of your crib?"

"*Oui.*" Lydia did an interpretive dance of her breakout, which ended with her standing on her feet, thank goodness, rather than on her head. Then she repeated her message: "Lydia is hungry."

So the expected had happened—Lydia had figured out how to escape the crib. Good thing the big-girl bed was arriving soon. And now Batty was stuck with Lydia. Yawning, she got them both downstairs, provided Lydia with a banana and a sippy cup of milk, and parked her in the living room near the piano.

"I'm going to practice now, and you're going to stay in here and not get into trouble. You can dance if you want. Okay?"

Lydia nodded happily, her mouth full of banana, and Batty went to her piano and began with the Hanon exercises Mr. Trice insisted upon for warming up. Batty didn't find them boring, though. Indeed, she lost herself in the pleasure of feeling her fingers fly, gaining always in strength, flexibility, and accuracy.

Lost, that is, until she heard Lydia crying "Ben, Ben!" and then the slam of the front door. Panicked, Batty leapt off the piano bench. Had Lydia made it out the front door? No, there she was at the window, still calling for Ben. Because *he* had escaped and was racing through the dawn—in his pajamas—to the Geigers' house.

Now what? Couldn't a girl have a peaceful morning for practicing the piano? Batty picked up Lydia and flew out of the house in pursuit of her little brother, in her bare feet, across the chilly dew-drenched grass. By the time she caught up with Ben, cursing her fate as the eldest of the youngest Penderwicks, he was around back of the Geigers' house, peeking into their kitchen window.

"What are you *doing?*" she whispered.

"I want to know if Nick is home yet."

"He couldn't possibly be. It's much too soon."

"You don't know that."

"His truck isn't here, is it?"

"Oh." No, Nick's blue pickup truck with the Red Sox decal wasn't in the driveway. Pressing her advantage, Batty used Lydia as a battering ram to push Ben away from the window. It was too late.

Mr. Geiger's voice drifted out to them. "Connie, I believe we're being staked out for a robbery. We really should have bought that alarm system."

Ben whispered to Batty. "I told you to put home security on the PWTW list."

"He means *us*, you numbskull." She called in through the window, "It's not robbers, Mr. Geiger. Just Batty, Ben, and Lydia."

"Never mind, Connie," they heard him say. "Just those annoying kids from across the street."

But Mrs. Geiger was already opening the back door and inviting them in. She even understood without being told what they were doing there.

"Nick's not here yet, but isn't it wonderful about him coming home?" She was almost hopping up and down with excitement. "He's leaving Kentucky this morning to drive to Delaware for a quick visit with

Tommy at college, and after that he'll drive up here and arrive tomorrow night, sometime after eleven."

"Tomorrow," said Ben. And he actually did hop. "Tomorrow, tomorrow, tomorrow."

"Tomorrow *night*," warned Batty. "You might be asleep and not see him until after school on Wednesday."

"Tomorrow *night*, tomorrow *night*, tomorrow *night*." Ben hopped into Mr. Geiger, almost making him spill his coffee.

"Connie, get these kids out of here," he said, handing a blueberry muffin to Ben.

"Lydia is hungry," said Lydia, so Mr. Geiger gave her some muffin, too.

Mrs. Geiger went on. "And he's going to stay for almost three weeks. Three weeks before he has to go back to that awful war. A good, long visit!"

"Three *weeks*, three *weeks*, three *weeks*!" said Ben.

Batty tried to grab Ben as he hopped by, but now Mr. Geiger was hopping, too, so she gave up, and put down Lydia, who also started hopping. The phone rang. Mrs. Geiger answered it.

"Yes, Iantha, they're here. I'll send them right home." She laughed. "No, Bill and I like it. You know we do."

"We'll go back now," said Batty as soon as Mrs. Geiger hung up. "Ben, stop bouncing around!"

"But we are dancing with joy," said Mr. Geiger, putting on a glum face.

"Batty, dear, before you go, I spoke with the Ayvazians last night," said Mrs. Geiger. "They told me how sweet and kind you were to Duchess, and how good it will be for the little dog. They were so pleased."

"I wasn't that sweet and kind." Batty had been careful, but not the rest of it. She remembered a few unkind words while getting Duchess into the stroller.

"They thought so. And, if you still have time, I'd like to hire you, too."

"Wow! Really?" This was wonderful news. Batty was 100 percent certain there were no dogs secretly living behind any of the Geigers' armchairs. "What do you need doing? Dusting?"

"Dusting!" said Mr. Geiger. "I do the dusting, thank you very much."

"Shh, Bill," said Mrs. Geiger. "No, I'm opening up a new flower bed in the backyard, and I could use help with digging up rocks."

"That's me!" cried Ben. "I am the digger of rocks!"

With Ben accelerating from a dance of joy into an extravaganza of ecstasy, it took Batty another few minutes to get her siblings back outside and across the street. The sun was up by now, another gorgeous spring day beginning. She passed Ben and Lydia off to Iantha, who fussed over their bare and bedewed feet, then sat them down for breakfast. She wanted Batty to eat, too, but Batty excused herself for a few moments, slipping down to the basement instead.

It hadn't occurred to her that the Ayvazians might

111

have thought her sweet and kind. But now that they did, well. She went back to the pile of bikes and sleds, and this time tugged the little red wagon all the way out from under the pool. Yes, it was as she'd thought— just the right size for Duchess, and much lower to the ground than Lydia's stroller. And it wasn't in bad shape, just dusty and with several scrapes in the paint.

Batty picked up the handle and pulled the wagon a few feet—the clatter of the wheels bringing back such memories. If only she could be sure that Hound wouldn't mind.

She had all day to think about it.

That afternoon, Batty carried the red wagon up from the basement, scrubbed it until it shined, found an old blanket to make it a more comfortable ride, filled a bottle of water for Duchess, and dragged it down Gardam Street. Mrs. Ayvazian opened their front door with a big smile. Alongside her was Duchess, her tail wagging with pleasure.

"She's ready for you," said Mrs. Ayvazian. "We told her you were coming, and she's been sitting by the door waiting."

Mr. Ayvazian came up behind his wife. "And we told her it was time to make it outside on her own."

"*You* told her that, Harvey," said Mrs. Ayvazian. "Humph."

Batty softly whistled and held out her hand. With a great heave and greater determination, Duchess rose up, made her way through the doorway and down the step—with only a minor amount of stomach-scraping—and over to Batty.

"Well, here we go," said Batty, picking up the leash.

"Good-bye, good-bye," said the Ayvazians.

Like on the day before, they moved slowly, maybe even more slowly, since Batty wanted to conserve the dog's energy, getting her as far up Gardam Street as possible before resorting to the wagon. She should also try getting to know Duchess a little better, since they were going to be spending time together. But how to begin? Conversation with Hound had always flowed so naturally.

"I guess I could tell you about school today," she said. "Ginevra turned in three more book reports and Ms. Rho just about fainted with happiness. Also, Vasudev finally remembered to turn in all of his, so now I'm the only one with no stars. I guess I really do need to write a book report one of these days."

Duchess had no reply, being too consumed with forward motion to think about book reports.

"I passed the test on clouds, so that was good. Then, at recess, Melle and Abby demonstrated how to tango. Keiko wants to learn—just in case she ever gets a crush on a boy who can tango, though who that could possibly be I don't know, certainly not Henry or Vasudev. Maybe Eric the sixth grader knows how to tango."

They'd now reached the Penderwicks' house. Batty paused, in case Duchess needed a break, but the little dog forged on.

"Tomorrow is Tuesday, which means Mrs. Grunfeld will be at school. I'm going to go in early to talk to her about singing lessons. Keiko says I should just ask Mrs. Grunfeld to teach me, but that seems awfully bold, so I think I'll show her the twenty dollars I'll get from Mr. Ayvazian and ask her if it's enough. And then I hope she'll say 'Twenty dollars a week is just right, and I will be your singing teacher. No need for you to meet someone new who might make you belt.' Then I'll say 'Thank—' Oops, Duchess, are you all right?"

The dog had stumbled, but not until they were well past the Penderwicks' house and the next house, too. Batty gave her some water and sat down on the curb for a few moments of rest. A warm breeze was blowing, and in the sky, fluffy clouds—cumulus!—formed and re-formed into fantastic shapes, a celestial zoo of imaginary animals. Batty thought about songs that had animals in them. "Teddy Bears' Picnic" was a good one.

She started to sing, then stopped abruptly, almost certain that Duchess was trying to sing along with her. "What are you doing?"

Duchess thumped her skinny tail.

"All right, I'll try again," said Batty, and did. "Good grief, you *are* singing along!"

It wasn't exactly singing, more like a soft, happy whining, but Duchess was clearly proud of her attempt. Her brown eyes were bright, and her tail was now going like crazy. Batty pondered this new development. Hound had always been happy to listen when Batty sang, or talked, or whistled, or anything, but he hadn't tried to chime in.

Batty leaned over to talk face to pointy face. "Let's try the key of C."

Duchess gave her an exuberant dog kiss, but Batty pulled away, unwilling to be too easily charmed, and began the labor of loading dog into wagon. It turned out to be much easier than with the stroller. With the wagon tipped just so, Duchess could roll on—then, with Batty leaning heavily on the opposite side, the wagon righted itself, now full of dog. It was a minor triumph for both girl and beast, which they celebrated with a few bars of "Run the World (Girls)."

When they'd gone around the cul-de-sac and back down Gardam Street, they found Mr. Ayvazian outside, waiting for them.

"She walked a little further today," said Batty, tipping Duchess out of the wagon. "And she's still alive."

"Of course she's still alive," he answered, and handed over a twenty-dollar bill. "We'll see you tomorrow, then, won't we, Duchess?"

Duchess yapped cheerfully, and Batty set off home with the money she'd earned, her first solid step toward those all-important voice lessons.

• • •

She was on her way to her bedroom—to stow the money in an envelope she'd already prepared, with *PWTW* written on it in large red letters—when a song exploded out of nowhere. It was that wretched sprite again, bursting out with Dolly Parton's "9 to 5." Batty dove through the nearest door, which happened to take her into Rosalind's bedroom, fell onto the bed, and stuffed her face into the pillow.

Batty was getting used to her sprite, and had decided that it looked Tinker Bell–ish, all sparkly and too pleased with itself. She'd gained little control over it, however. That day at recess, during a game of dodgeball, she'd just barely managed to stop herself from singing after hitting Henry with the ball. True, it was the first time in her life she'd handled a ball that well, but that was no excuse for trying to sing "We Are the Champions" in front of the entire fifth grade.

"Stop, stop, stop!" she pleaded with the sprite, still working on "9 to 5." "Humming is okay, but humming only, please. And a calmer song would be better."

The sprite cycled willfully through several more songs before settling on a Mozart sonata, calm enough to let Batty get off the bed and wander around Rosalind's room while she hummed, though she just couldn't help doing dance steps as she went.

When Rosalind left for college, she'd bravely offered to give her room away to whoever needed it the most, but the family had voted to keep it as hers at

116

least for the first year. Batty was glad they had, glad she could come here to visit. The matching striped bedspread and curtains, the tidy desk and bookshelf, the bulletin boards full of snapshots—all were redolent of Rosalind, as though she could appear at any moment. (Only nineteen more days!)

One bulletin board had been taken down and put in a corner facing the wall. Batty turned it around to look, though she knew what she'd find. Here were photos of Tommy from over the years, starting long ago, when he was still just the goofy kid across the street. Here he was jumping into a kiddie pool with Skye, and here he was, so little he needed two hands to hold his football, and here, going down a sliding board, and here, in his costume for the sixth-grade play. As the photos went on in years, they slowly introduced romance. First Tommy was shoving Rosalind, then holding her hand, then putting his arm around her, then they were all dressed up and ready for prom.

Batty turned the bulletin board back to the wall. At least Rosalind still had it. That gave Batty hope for their getting back together.

Batty drifted over to look at the framed photo on the bedside table. It had held pride of place there for as long as Batty could remember, and had only been left behind because Rosalind had taken a smaller version along with her to college, not wanting to subject the big one to the rough-and-tumble life of a college dorm. The photo showed Rosalind as a very tiny baby being held by her mother—Batty's mother, too, that is. Rosalind looked like most babies, all fat cheeks and no hair, but their mother, how pretty she'd been, so young and happy.

Here's where Skye had gotten her blond hair and blue eyes, the only sister to have them. All Batty's life, she'd heard about how much Skye looked like their mother. And it had been true. But as Skye grew older, it had gotten even more true, until the similarity—at least to this one photo—was startling. If Batty squinted a little, she could almost believe that she was seeing Skye holding a baby.

"Of course, I have our mother's name," she told the sort-of-Skye in the photo.

Because Batty was just a nickname. Her real name was Elizabeth Penderwick, just like her mother's. Batty thought it an excellent name for a professional singer.

CHAPTER NINE
Cilantro?

Ben was in his room gluing rocks to his giant cardboard Minnesota. His mom had helped him mark where all the mountains would go, and these rocks were for the Mesabi Range. Ms. Lambert had said that they could just draw on their states, but it seemed to Ben an opportunity too good to miss for showing off some of his rocks. Plus, Rafael was using pieces of sponge on his to represent swamps, and was even trying to figure out how to keep the swamps wet without them falling right off Florida.

In between gluing rocks, Ben looked out his window at the strange new car, Flashvan, that had arrived the night before. Jane and Skye thought it even more hideous than the photograph had shown, but Ben thought it stunning. Rafael said that when they became famous movie directors, they would ride around in driver-less cars, except when they were in their private helicopters. Until then, though, Ben was delighted with Flashvan.

"Ben!" Batty was outside his door. "Time to walk to school."

Ben looked at his clock. They always left the house at exactly 8:20 a.m. and it was now 8:04 a.m. "No, it's not."

"I need to be there early. Let's go."

Ignoring her, Ben glued another rock to Minnesota. Never had homework seemed so much like play, though he had to admit he wasn't as interested in the cities and lakes as he was in the mountains. The mountains in Minnesota had such great names, like Disappointment Mountain, Toad Mountain, Ghost Hill, and Pilot Knob.

Batty shoved open his door, knocking over two hangers plus a pile of small rocks he'd added for extra security.

"If we leave right now," she said, "I'll carry your backpack to school."

Here was a powerful incentive. "And you'll carry it home, too? Even if I put in rocks I find at recess?"

"Yes, well, up to three rocks, anyway, and not huge ones. Now hurry."

With Ben hurrying, Batty was able to get to school with a precious fifteen minutes to spare for talking to Mrs. Grunfeld. She sent him to Ms. Lambert, headed to the music room, and found Keiko waiting for her outside the door.

"I thought you might need hand-holding," she told Batty.

Batty gratefully took Keiko's hand. "I'm determined to go through with it. *Musica anima mea est.*"

"Right," said Keiko, and knocked on the door.

Mrs. Grunfeld opened the music room door with a smile. "Batty, good morning! And—"

"Keiko Trice," said Keiko. "I'm just here for moral support."

"Mine?" asked Mrs. Grunfeld, surprised.

"No, Batty's. She'll explain."

So Mrs. Grunfeld took Batty into the room. "Why do you need moral support?"

"I've decided I want voice lessons after all." Batty took the twenty-dollar bill from her pocket. "Here's some money I've earned, and I'm going to be getting another twenty every week from now on."

"Good for you, coming up with both the resolve and the money! I'm proud of you."

"Thank you." Batty waited for Mrs. Grunfeld to offer to be her teacher. Maybe twenty dollars wasn't enough. "Do lessons cost more than this?"

"That depends on the teacher you choose. I could put together a list of teachers for you, ones I'm familiar with. Would you like that?"

"Yes, thank you."

"Come see me on Friday, then, and I'll have it ready for you."

Batty thanked her again and walked out, defeated.

"What did she say?" asked Keiko.

"That she'd put together a list of singing teachers for me."

"But what about *her*? Oh, Batty, you didn't even ask, did you?" Keiko knocked on the door again and, when Mrs. Grunfeld opened it, took matters into her own hands. "Batty is too shy to tell you that she wants *you* to be her singing teacher."

"My goodness, that didn't even occur to me."

Keiko pushed Batty back into the room and closed the door behind her.

"I understand if it's because I don't have enough money," Batty told Mrs. Grunfeld.

"My dear, it's not the money. I'm simply not a professional voice coach, just a generalist, at best. And, besides, as soon as school is over, I'm going on a tour of the great opera houses of Europe. I'll see *Così fan tutte* at La Scala and *Fidelio* at the Vienna State Opera. Doesn't that sound marvelous?"

Batty felt herself folding up inside, like an accordion. "Yes, I guess so, but you wouldn't let me belt like the people on television." Tears were starting to come, though Batty fought them. "And another teacher might not like my voice."

"That last part is impossible." Mrs. Grunfeld went into her desk and came back with a box of tissues. "Here, wipe your eyes and let me think."

Batty sat down on the piano bench to get out of the way. Mrs. Grunfeld's thinking seemed to include doing little dance moves while softly humming. When

Batty listened closely, she recognized "Plant a Radish" from *The Fantasticks*, which gave her hope, because she loved *The Fantasticks*.

Mrs. Grunfeld got all the way to the part about planting beanstalks before stopping in front of Batty.

"You must understand that if you're serious about singing, you will need a better teacher than I." She held up her hand before Batty could protest again. "But there's no reason for you not to begin here with me on an informal basis. That is, if you don't mind missing recess one day a week."

"No, no, no, I don't mind missing recess." Batty was ready to run in place and do jumping jacks right then and there to prove how little she needed recess.

"Good. We'll start today, since the weather is so bad. I'll make it all right with your classroom teacher."

"That's Ms. Rho, but she's a little strict. And the weather . . ." The weather was glorious.

"I will take care of all of that," said Mrs. Grunfeld, and Batty believed her. It was hard to imagine anyone or anything that Mrs. Grunfeld couldn't take care of. "And put away your money, Batty. Save it for when you go on to your real coach. The good ones can be expensive."

"Oh, Mrs. Grunfeld, I can't—" gasped Batty, overwhelmed.

"Now, now, none of that. Spending extra time with you will be a pleasure for me. I must confess, I've been thinking of a song that would be just right for your voice. I'm afraid it's a love song, but then so many of the better songs are. Would you mind?"

Batty held tight to the piano bench to keep herself from leaping up and smothering Mrs. Grunfeld with a gigantic hug. "I don't mind about love as long as it's not a duet and I have to sing with one of the boys."

"Agreed. No love duets." Mrs. Grunfeld laughed. "I will work you hard, Batty Penderwick, even though I am just a generalist. You're certain this is what you want?"

"Yes," answered Batty, "this is what I want."

"And, Duchess, by lunchtime it was raining! Not that I think Mrs. Grunfeld can actually make it rain, but you have to admit it was an interesting coincidence. So, anyway, during recess she taught me a song called "Not a Day Goes By," written by Stephen Sondheim, who Mrs. Grunfeld says uses melody to express yearning better than anyone has since Verdi. And she said that Sondheim's atypical tonal intervals are only one example of his genius—which I knew already from listening to A Little Night Music eight million times— and that singing his songs would help me stretch my understanding of melody. Here, Duchess, listen to a little bit."

But Batty could barely get into the song without giggling—Duchess was singing with her again.

"Also, I told Mrs. Grunfeld about Jeffrey and the

Grand Eleventh Birthday Concert. She said it was a great idea and that Jeffrey is my *mentore*, which is Italian for 'mentor.' It sounds better in Italian, don't you think?"

Batty stopped talking to shake the rain from her hair, and to make sure that Duchess hadn't yet worn herself out. While Batty loved this soft spring rain, it couldn't be pleasant for the dog. Because Duchess was so low to the ground, any rain that missed her wide back splashed up to her undercarriage.

"Are you sure you wouldn't be happier in the wagon? I don't want you catching a cold. One arf for yes and two for no."

"Arf, arf, arf, arf."

"Four wasn't a choice. Okay, I'll decide. You're going into the wagon." Batty pulled the wagon alongside Duchess, and removed the plastic bag she'd laid over the blanket to keep it dry.

"Arf, arf, arf, arf, arf."

"Shh," said Batty, tipping the wagon on its side, but Duchess showed no interest in getting into it. "What's going on with you? Why won't you get in?"

"Arf, arf, arf, arf, arf, arf, arf, ARF!"

Batty was amazed that Duchess had the energy for so much barking and pulling. Maybe it wasn't that she was trying to get away from the wagon. They were in the cul-de-sac now, and Duchess was pointed toward Quigley Woods—maybe she was trying to go there. Batty let Duchess tug her a few feet closer to the path.

Yes, that's what she wanted, and while Batty thought the woods too damp and mucky for an overweight dachshund, she couldn't help but wonder what had brought about this sudden burst of life.

"Okay, but I hope you have a good reason. And it had better not be a rabbit, because I don't believe in terrorizing rabbits. Not that you could keep up with a rabbit."

On they went into the woods, with Duchess straining against her halter, her nose to the ground, definitely tracking something. At least Batty no longer had to be concerned for the local rabbits. What with the barking and the clamor of the empty wagon, every animal for miles around would be warned of their approach.

Now they were plunging off the path, with Duchess swerving around trees, and Batty doing what she could to slow her down. All at once the little dog stopped, panting and clearly delighted with herself.

"Not a rabbit," said Batty.

Duchess had led her, in fact, to another dog, an oddly wrinkled—and soaking wet—dog crouching beside a wreck of fallen tree branches, torn down in a long-ago ice storm. While he wagged his tail feebly, seemingly relieved to have been found, Duchess strutted and yipped, as proud as if she herself had created this mournful beast out of the raw clay of nature.

Batty knew about approaching strange dogs, no matter how tame they seemed. She sidled slowly toward this one, being careful not to make eye contact and, when he didn't growl or bare his teeth, held out her fist for him to sniff. Which he did, snuffling sadly, then ducking his head for her to pat. Now she could see the problem. He'd managed to get his leash snarled up in the dead branches and he was stuck.

"Poor guy. What are you doing here?" She read the tag hanging from his collar. The address was on Marsh Lane, two streets over from Gardam. The dog's name was listed, too. "Cilantro, like the plant?"

He cocked his ears, acknowledging that while Cilantro was indeed his name, it wasn't his fault. He did seem to believe, however, that being stuck was his fault, and for this he was apologetic.

"Don't worry, I'll get you out of here. But, Duchess, you have to settle down first."

Duchess's journey through the woods was catching up with her. Obediently, she toppled onto her side, her four legs twitching. Batty tied her leash to the wagon, just in case she miraculously revived and decided to dash off again.

The untangling wasn't easy, and Batty picked up lots of mud and a few scratches in the process, but soon Cilantro was free and saying hello and thanks to Duchess. Now it was time to get him back to Marsh Lane, where she hoped someone was terribly worried about him. First, however, she had to get Duchess back to the Ayvazians, who would certainly be starting to wonder where she was. And with Duchess

127

now looking half dead, it was clear she'd have to be put back into the wagon to go anywhere at all. Embarrassed in front of her new friend, Duchess at first resisted the wagon, but once Cilantro had gravely sniffed it and approved, she allowed Batty to lever her up and in.

Batty started back the way she'd come, now with two dogs. Cilantro followed more willingly than she'd expected, though he did slow them down by continuously changing his mind about walking next to, behind, or in front of the wagon. By the time they emerged onto Gardam Street, he'd switched positions seven times, and Batty was losing patience with having to unwind his leash from the wagon pull. It didn't help that the rain had decided to come down harder, and though they'd all been wet before, now they were drenched, and the blanket underneath Duchess was soaked through and through.

Such a relief, then, for Batty to spot Ben and Rafael running from the Geigers' house to the Penderwicks'. Even from here, they looked wet and muddy, which meant they'd probably been digging for rocks in the rain. But, dirty or not, they could still take Duchess home so that Batty could get this crazy Cilantro back to where he belonged.

"Ben!" she called. "Rafael! Come here!"

They veered toward her, shouting "Eleven o'clock, eleven o'clock!" Batty assumed it was some new code of theirs. Cilantro, however, assumed they were making war cries. He cowered behind Duchess and her wagon, trying to blend into the scenery. It didn't work.

"Where'd you get that dog?" asked Ben.

"Duchess found him."

"Are you going to keep him?" asked Rafael.

"Cilantro? No! He's got a home." Though she wondered what kind of owner would let such a goofy dog run off by himself.

"Good, because he doesn't look normal," said Ben.

"He's not actually abnormal, I think." She looked doubtfully at the wrinkly dog, now peering around Duchess at the boys. "He didn't get this scared until you started screaming 'Eleven o'clock, eleven o'clock.' What's it mean, anyway?"

"Nick!" said Ben. "He's with Tommy now, in Delaware, and he's going to leave after dinner and he should be home around eleven o'clock. Isn't that *great*! Ready, Rafael?"

"Golf-Romeo-Echo-Alpha-Tango, GREAT, Golf-Romeo-Echo-Alpha-Tango!" they chanted together, jumping up and down as they did it.

Cilantro slunk back behind Duchess.

"The boys are happy, not angry," Batty told the frightened dog, but that didn't help. "Ben, I have to get Cilantro back to his house. Please take Duchess home and tell the Ayvazians that Duchess walked really far and I'm sorry she's so wet."

Encouraged by the memory of Mrs. Ayvazian's cider donuts, Ben and Rafael willingly took over

129

Duchess while Batty set off with Cilantro. If she hadn't been certain she'd never see him again, she would have told him about Nick being a soldier, and how good it was that he was coming home, though Batty did hope he'd gotten over his obsession with finding the best sport for everyone—that is, especially for her. But then Cilantro probably wouldn't have listened anyway. He was too busy growling at anything he found unfamiliar, including several trashcans and a bicycle leaning against a garage. When they got too close to a recycling bin, he went all out and barked. His bark was as peculiar as his looks—plaintive and deep, like a lovelorn tuba.

When they reached Marsh Lane, Cilantro pulled Batty in a straight line to his house, where he threw himself at the front door, scrabbling and barking. Batty could hear people shouting his name even before the door opened, and when it did, chaos and happy reunion ensued. There was a man with a baby in a sling, and two other small children at his feet, all of them thrilled, but none as thrilled as Cilantro, who disappeared into the house without even a backward glance at Batty.

The man's name was Mr. Holland, and Batty forgave him for pet neglect as soon as he explained that they were new to the neighborhood and just getting adjusted, and that since Analise—one of the small children—had let Cilantro escape around lunchtime, they'd called the police and the shelters and had driven all round Cameron putting up flyers.

"We were afraid we'd never see him again," he said. "Where did you find him?"

"In Quigley Woods, but I had help," said Batty. "A dog I walk led me to him."

"You're a dog walker? But that's great! Do you want a new client?"

No, no, no. The last thing Batty wanted was yet another dog to walk, particularly a dog as prone to trouble as Cilantro. If she'd been better at talking to strangers, she'd have come up with a firm refusal for Mr. Holland. As it was, she could only stutter about how she didn't think she was qualified to walk more than one dog at a time and how her parents would have to approve and how they might say no and, anyway, there could be an important dusting job coming up any day now. But nothing could discourage Mr. Holland. He offered Batty another twenty dollars a week to add Cilantro to her roster, said he'd call her parents to discuss it all that very evening, and insisted she take another ten dollars right then, as a reward for bringing the dog back to his loving family—especially Analise, who'd been wracked with guilt since letting him go in the first place.

Batty trudged back home through the rain, stunned with this new development. Suddenly she had *two* new dogs in her life, when she'd wanted none? Because her parents would probably say yes— Marsh Lane wasn't so far away. And there'd been no calls from other neighbors with dusting jobs or anything else, so she didn't have that as an excuse.

Soon, though, Batty reminded herself of what was important—*Musica anima mea est*—squared her shoulders, and hummed a little Sondheim to cheer herself up.

Ben had begged to be allowed to stay awake until Nick got home, but to no avail. That Lieutenant Geiger could arrive without being greeted by Penderwicks and without even the Welcome Home signs, which hadn't been put out because of the rain, was too awful for Ben to contemplate. So he didn't. Instead, after his parents had said good night, he crept over to Batty's room.

She was reading *Masterpiece*, about a boy named James and his friend Marvin, who happens to be a beetle. It was high on her list of books she refused to ruin by writing about in a book report.

"You've got to keep me awake until Nick comes home," Ben said.

"That's hours from now. How am I supposed to keep you awake?"

"You can talk to me." He sat down on the bed. "Tell me about Cilantro again and how Dad said you can walk him, especially since he's named after a plant."

Ben knew the whole story already. He and Batty had both listened to their mom's side of the conversation when Mr. Holland called, and again while she and their dad agreed that Batty should be allowed to walk Cilantro.

"You know as much as I do," she answered. "Why would I tell you again?"

"Because I need to stay awake. Or you can hum to me. You hum all the time anyway."

"I don't hum *all* the time." She didn't want Ben noticing such things.

"Then let's play a game. Please, Batty. I really want to see Nick tonight."

Because Batty knew it would indeed be nice to have Penderwicks awake for Nick when he got home, she put aside *Masterpiece* and got out the board game Othello. They played game after game after game while the clock crept much too slowly toward eleven, until finally she stretched out.

"Batty?" said Ben, poking her. "Wake up."

But she wouldn't, so he stretched out, too, just to get comfortable, and the next thing he knew, he woke up with his face planted in the middle of the Othello board. He started up—the clock said 10:55! Furious with himself, and peeling off the game pieces that had stuck to his cheeks and forehead, he ran across the hall and to the window in his room. It was okay. There was no blue truck yet, *and* the rain had stopped. Now he could put out the signs before Nick got home.

Ben crept down the steps but paused when he heard Skye and Jane talking in the living room.

"Now he's sending me music he's written," said Skye. Last week it was 'Pavane for S.P.' and today I got this one."

"'Unrequited in D Minor.' Wow."

"It's not like I can read music."

"You could ask Batty to play them for you on the piano."

"Yeah, right. It's embarrassing enough showing these to you. At least he doesn't put words to them. I don't think I could stomach an entire song about his unrequited love for me."

Most of what had at first sounded to Ben like gibberish—especially the *pavane* and the *unrequited*, whatever they were—now became clear. His sisters were down there talking about Jeffrey. If he weren't so desperate to put out Nick's signs, he would have gone right back up to his room. Ben absolutely did not want to get caught in another discussion of love.

"He wrote music for me once," said Jane. "When I was ten, remember? I thought it the most interesting thing that had ever happened to me."

"So why didn't he fall for you? You would have appreciated him."

"Skye, he's always been nuts for you, ever since the first time you two met."

"I crashed into him and almost knocked him out!"

"Well, now you know not to do that anymore."

Ben heard a sort of half-groan, half-mumble from Skye, which seemed to be the end of the conversation. After a few minutes of quiet, he felt safe enough to resume his way downstairs. He was almost to the bottom baby gate when Jane started up again.

"I was telling Jérôme about wanting to be a writer,

and he said that to be a writer one must have a great heart. At least I think that's what he said."

"It's not necessarily true, anyway," answered Skye.

"I know. I thought of asking him what about Sartre, but then he was off on something else and I got completely lost. He speaks French so quickly."

"Because—he's French."

This time the end of talking was marked by Jane throwing a pillow at Skye. Again Ben waited for a few moments before moving on, but he didn't wait long enough. Just as he started over the baby gate, he heard Skye.

"I just miss Jeffrey, the old Jeffrey, the way he was before he started—"

More love talk! Ben tried to stop himself, but he overbalanced and ended up tipping headfirst over the gate and onto the floor. Both sisters were with him in a minute, picking him up and inspecting him for damage.

"I'm not hurt," he said, trying to regain his dignity. "I just came down to put out the signs for Nick."

"We put them out when the rain stopped," said Skye, "and left on the outdoor lights so he could see them."

"You should go back to bed," said Jane. "Nick might not be home for hours."

"Please let me wait with you," said Ben. "Please."

Skye looked at Jane and shrugged, and Jane looked at Skye and nodded, then they took him back into

the living room and settled him on the couch between them. He was determined that this time he
truly would stay awake all night if necessary, even if
he had to listen to his sisters talking about love stuff
the whole time. But Skye picked up a book, nothing
he could read over her shoulder, unfortunately—too
many long words about something called string theory. Jane started scribbling in a blue notebook, and he
didn't even try to read over her shoulder. What Jane
wrote was always private until she decided to share it.

Despite Ben's resolve to stay awake, soon he'd
slumped against Skye, lulled to sleep by the soft rus-
tle of turning pages. He woke up once when Jane had
murmured she was going to bed and covered him with
a blanket before she went, and another time his eye-
lids fluttered open long enough for him to see Skye
standing by the window, looking out, on guard. After
that, Ben sank deep into his dreams, which eventually turned into a tale of being lifted off a couch and
carried outside. He struggled against that—he was too
old to be carried—until all at once he was awake and
being handed over into the strong arms of Lieutenant Nick Geiger. Ben started to cry, happy this time,
and Nick was laughing and making jokes, and Mr. and
Mrs. Geiger were out there, too, also crying, even Mr.
Geiger, and then Mrs. Geiger was saying that Nick
needed his rest—lots and lots of rest and sleep—and
Skye took Ben back from Nick. She carried him home
again, but once there, he climbed upstairs and into his
bunk by himself.

"Nick remembered me," he said to Skye as she tucked him in.

"Of course he did, you nincompoop. Now go to sleep, and don't tell anybody we let you stay up, okay? Dad and Iantha would be furious."

"Okay. I Lima-Oscar-Victor-Echo you, Skye."

"Lima-Oscar-Victor-Echo you, too, buddy."

CHAPTER TEN
Spring Takes a Holiday

THE PENDERWICKS DID WHAT THEY COULD to help Nick sleep, tiptoeing around and stopping Ben from peering in any of the Geigers' windows. So quiet was Gardam Street that spring itself decided to take a nap. The temperature dropped, then dropped again, and snow clouds started to gather. Mrs. Geiger's daffodils drooped their yellow heads, and the Ayvazians' creamy white magnolia blooms shivered in the unexpected cold. By evening, Iantha was insisting that everyone wear warm sweaters when going outside, and on Thursday morning before school, she bundled them all into the winter coats, hats, and mittens they'd abandoned weeks earlier.

The snow itself held off until that afternoon. Batty and Ben spotted the first flakes as they walked home from school. Ben was celebrating—the snow meant a possible day off from school, a rare treat in late April. Batty was torn. No school on Friday meant missing chorus with Mrs. Grunfeld. But since it also meant missing the horror of the book report chart review, she decided that, on the whole, a day off would be a good thing, and she was singing as she darted through the snowflakes to fetch Cilantro.

For the official inaugural walk with both dogs the day before, she'd picked up Duchess first, and that had been a mistake. The adventure of finding Cilantro in Quigley Woods had taken a severe toll on the fat little dog, and she'd had to spend most of the walk in the wagon, which meant slow going for Cilantro and lots of extra wagon-pulling for Batty. So today she was changing the order of pickup, which would let her give Cilantro a brisk walk before adding Duchess to the mix. But when Batty got to Marsh Lane, Cilantro seemed to have forgotten who she was and refused to leave his house.

"Maybe he doesn't like the snowflakes," said Batty.

"We moved here from Idaho," said Mr. Holland, again wearing his baby in a sling. "He's used to snow."

"Then maybe he won't come out because Duchess isn't here," tried Batty. "He thinks she's in charge."

"I don't care what he thinks. You tug while I push."

Batty tugged on the leash, leaning back with all her weight, until Cilantro made it out the door, which Mr. Holland closed decisively behind him. Bereaved,

Cilantro made his tuba sound and tried to stuff his nose through the letter slot.

Patiently Batty waited until Cilantro remembered who she was and let her take him back to Gardam Street, barking only a little more than normal, mostly at snowflakes that came too close to his nose. Once they'd picked up Duchess, Cilantro did indeed perk up. So it was true. He did see Duchess as the boss of this crew, and Duchess seemed to agree. She'd regained enough of her energy to reject the wagon, instead strutting out in front of Cilantro, showing off the new red sweater Mrs. Ayvazian had run out to buy her for protection against the snow. Batty hadn't the heart to tell either Mrs. Ayvazian or Duchess that the red accentuated the dog's great girth and made her look like an overstuffed Christmas stocking with legs.

Up Gardam Street they went, calmly enough except for Cilantro suddenly forgetting what the wagon was, and barking at it. But Batty got him back under control and was almost feeling good about her dog-walking skills when, just as they reached the Geigers' house, Nick appeared on the doorstep, calling out hello. Duchess, thinking he was calling hello to her, lunged toward him. Cilantro, thinking the same thing, lunged away from him. Then the situation worsened. Ben came flying out of the Penderwicks' house, as though he'd been watching out the window in case Nick appeared—which he had been—and the addition to the scene of a shrieking boy caused Duchess and Cilantro to change directions, but oppositely, until Batty, hopelessly snarled in the two leashes, her legs bound together, toppled over onto the wagon. As she fell, she realized that this was the stupidest possible way to first see Nick, as he would be certain to link her inability to keep upright with her lack of ability at sports.

As Nick and Ben came over to rescue her, it was Cilantro rather than Duchess who Batty feared would have the heart attack, as he tried frantically to run away, tightening even more the leash wrapped around Batty.

Until Nick planted himself in Cilantro's path and spoke quietly but firmly. "Sit. Stay."

To Batty's surprise—and Cilantro's, too, she thought—he sat, and so did Duchess, the whole fat redness of her. And they stayed.

"How did you do that?" asked Batty.

"Talent." Nick gave her the smile that Rosalind always called the irresistible Geiger grin, except when she was annoyed with Tommy (and then she didn't call it anything at all). "Ben, you hold the dogs' collars, and I'll get your sister out of her mess."

"Yankee-Echo-Sierra, Sierra-India-Romeo," said Ben.

"No, no, none of that Sir stuff. Not while I'm on leave. Call me, I don't know, how about Mr. Fabulous?"

"Good grief," said Batty.

"Good grief yourself." Nick unhooked both leashes and unwound them, freeing Batty. "These are your new clients? Mom told me you started a dog-walking business."

"Actually, I wanted to do dusting and companionship, but nobody needed me for that. I didn't think I should walk dogs, because of—you know."

Nick understood. "I'm sorry about Hound. That was a sad day when I heard."

Batty tried to imagine Nick feeling sad about Hound in the middle of fighting a war.

"Weren't you—" She paused, feeling awkward. "I mean—you weren't too busy to think about home?"

"Some days home was all I thought about. Not *you*, necessarily, you understand." There was Nick's grin again, and the air was cleared.

"When can we start playing basketball?" asked Ben.

"Not while it's snowing. We've got lots of time. I'll be home until the first Sunday in May."

"But that's my birthday!" said Batty. "You can't leave on my birthday!"

"You really can't," said Ben, who would have said that about any day if it would keep Nick with them longer.

"I won't leave until after your party, okay? The army can do without me for an extra twelve hours."

"Thank you."

"And for your birthday present, I'll help train you in whatever sport you've selected."

"I've told you a million times that I don't want a sport."

"Sure you do. Sports build character."

Batty thought she already had plenty of character. But there definitely was something she didn't have. "Can you teach me how to make the dogs obey?"

"First you have to believe they will obey you. It's all a matter of self-confidence. Go ahead, tell yourself that you're the boss, then give them a command."

I'm the boss, thought Batty.

"Duchess, Cilantro, lie down," she said.

They ignored her.

"I'm the boss," said Batty out loud. "Lie *down*. No, Duchess, no."

Duchess was jumping up on Ben, trying to lick his face.

"I'm definitely not the boss," said Batty.

"We'll work on it later," said Nick. "Right now I'm getting out of this crazy snow and going back to sleep."

But he wasn't allowed to sleep just yet. While Batty pulled away the dogs, Skye and Jane, with Lydia swinging wildly between them, burst out of their front door and flew across Gardam Street to pounce on him and smother him with sisterly affection.

When Batty got back home after the dog walk, she heard lots of banging coming from upstairs. She ran up and found the source—Lydia's room, where Skye and Jane were assembling the new big-girl bed that had just been delivered by a truck.

"Where's Lydia?" Batty asked them.

"Under the crib," said Jane.

"Did Nick scare her?"

"Of course not. She fell in love with him immediately."

"She doesn't like the new bed," explained Skye. "See if you can talk sense into her."

Batty lay flat on the floor. Yes, there was Lydia hunched under her crib, clinging to the bottom of the mattress like it was a life raft.

"Aren't you excited about your new bed?" Batty asked her.

"Lydia's bed," said Lydia, getting a better grip on the crib mattress.

"*This* is your bed now," said Skye, pointing at the big-girl bed with a screwdriver.

"And it's a pretty bed," added Jane.

The white wooden bed frame sat low to the ground and had violets sprinkled across the headboard. Even better, in Batty's mind, was the long drawer that fit underneath. She dragged a reluctant Lydia out from under the crib so that she could see it.

"Think of what you can keep in that drawer," she said. "Books, toys!"

"Your crown!" Jane slid the drawer out and in as demonstration. "It would be right there with you when you sleep."

"No me gusta," said Lydia.

Jane and Batty both looked at Skye. They recognized Spanish when they heard it, even if they didn't know what it meant.

"Maybe I shouldn't have taught her that one," said Skye.

"And it means?" asked Jane.

"It means she doesn't like it—i.e., the bed. But in my defense, we were discussing Flashvan's bumper stickers at the time."

Batty grabbed Lydia, who was now trying to pull herself up into the crib.

"I didn't know she could climb *in*," said Jane.

"There's so much we don't know about her." Skye took Lydia and hoisted her up high. "You'll rule the world, right, Lydia? King Banana Head! *¡El Rey Cabeza de Plátano!*"

But Lydia wanted only the familiar comfort of her crib. Skye put her there while they finished up with the new bed, hammering and bolting and finally smoothing on fresh sheets and a new lavender quilt. When even these wondrous sights didn't convince Lydia, it was soon clear she wasn't ready to abandon her crib.

"So I guess you have two beds, Lydia," said Batty.

"Lucky princess!" said Jane.

Lydia covered her face with Baby Zingo. It took Iantha coming home to uncover her again, mostly by reassuring her that she could continue to sleep in the crib until she was used to the idea of a big-girl bed. Knowing Lydia's tenacity, everyone agreed that could be never.

Batty went to her piano lesson prepared to stay overnight at Keiko's house. By then, school closings had already been announced for the next day, and the girls had convinced both sets of parents that a sleepover was thus not only reasonable but also a perfect opportunity to get lots of homework done.

They did do some homework that night, a little math, plus making a list of examples of gerunds, trying but failing to top the one Henry had already come up with in class: "Studying grammar isn't all it's cracked up to be." They also read up on Babylon and its famous hanging gardens, on which they'd volunteered to give a brief verbal presentation on Monday.

"Whoa," said Keiko, staring down at one of the books. "Nobody knows if these gardens really existed! This is like studying the Kingdom of Wisdom in history class."

"But that would be fun," said Batty. *The Phantom Tollbooth* was yet another book much too wonderful to wreck with a book report. "Anyway, whatever we do, we'll be better than Henry and Vasudev. They're going to say that beings from other star systems descended to earth to build the Great Pyramid."

"Still, maybe we should have picked Stonehenge."

"Ginevra is doing Stonehenge."

They exchanged woeful looks, picturing Ginevra getting extra points by making a tiny clay model of Stonehenge, with real grass and piped-in birdsong.

"Yesterday Abby told me that Melle told her that Ginevra likes Vasudev," said Keiko.

"That doesn't mean that Vasudev likes Ginevra," said Batty.

"Yes, it probably does."

Keiko had a point. There was a sweet cuteness about Ginevra, plus her extra-good behavior in school, that seemed to draw the boys to her. Batty didn't know why. But she thought it too soon for Keiko to surrender the field, especially since Ginevra had just that day turned in two more book reports—causing Ms. Rho to tape another extension to the chart. While in her heart Batty knew that Ginevra was a nice person, she sometimes couldn't help wondering if nice people could also be show-offs.

"Don't give up on Vasudev," she said.

"I won't, and there's still Henry. Plus, Eric the sixth grader smiled at me in the cafeteria yesterday, except Kait Feldmann was standing next to me, so he could have been smiling at her. She's awfully interesting and pretty, don't you think?"

"So are you. I'm sure he was smiling at you."

"Maybe. I've decided to give up on Ryan. Too much competition for movie stars, like from millions of people." Discouraged, Keiko stared at the ceiling.

"Don't worry," said Batty. "Maybe you won't feel

like getting a crush for years and years, and by then you'll have met lots more possibilities."

"And maybe by then you'll feel like it, too."

"Maybe."

"I know, I know. *Musica anima mea est.*"

"Oh, Keiko, am I obnoxious about that?"

"No, no. It's—I don't know—thrilling. Like you've dedicated yourself to a cause. Like being a Jedi warrior." Keiko jumped up and rushed over to her closet. "That reminds me."

She pulled out an armful of long, glistening dresses of various colors and tossed them on the bed.

"What are these?"

"For your Grand Eleventh Birthday Concert! They're my mom's ancient prom dresses. She said you should wear whichever one you want."

Batty held one up to her, a silvery concoction with poufy sleeves. It was too long and had a few places that Batty wouldn't fill out for several more years. "Keiko! I'd look ridiculous!"

"Maybe they're a little big." Keiko held up a different dress, this one a deep royal blue. "Try this on anyway. Please."

They both ended up trying on several of the dresses, parading around until they tripped on them, which made so much noise that Mrs. Trice arrived and told them to settle down and get into bed.

Keiko fell asleep immediately, but Batty lay awake for a long time, watching the snow and thinking about her birthday concert. It was now only seventeen days until her birthday, which meant sixteen until Rosalind came home, and only nine until Skye's birthday. So nine days until Jeffrey came to visit and Batty could sing for him.

Just thinking about it brought music bubbling up. She put herself to sleep by singing quiet lullabies into the pillow.

CHAPTER ELEVEN
Ninja Moves

THE SNOW FELL THROUGH THAT NIGHT and into the next day, smothering Gardam Street. The moment it stopped, and even while Skye and Jane shoveled the Penderwicks' driveway, Batty was stomping away at the cold wet stuff, determined to get spring back as quickly as possible. She enlisted the dogs to help, coaxing Duchess to shove her way into the snow, her broad chest acting like a miniature snowplow and leaving behind a print that Ben and Rafael hoped was from a wormlike alien out of the Alpha Centauri system. Cilantro didn't need coaxing. He took to the snow as his natural environment, bounding stiff-legged through drifts, except when a snowplow came to clear the street, which made him hide behind Batty.

Then overnight the temperature zoomed up and

water poured off the roofs and into the gutters and downspouts, along the driveways and into the street, where rivulets chuckled into the storm drains. Only the most stubborn snow was left behind, and the warm soaking rain that came next took care of that, and spring was back for real. Teensy mauve budlets appeared on lilac bushes, the forsythia were suddenly all bright, waving yellow, and when early the next week the first crimson azalea blooms arrived, Lieutenant Geiger woke up again and reentered life.

Ben shadowed him, and Rafael, too, imitating the way he walked and asking innumerable questions about basketball and anything else they could think of, until the neighborhood was filled with loud chatter, bouncing balls, and running feet. Nick offered to get Lydia started on basketball, too, but she preferred dancing and thought he'd come home just to watch her twirl and leap. This he did with much patience, though sometimes from behind sunglasses, which made Batty wonder if he was staying awake through each recital. Skye and Jane he persuaded to rise at dawn for early-morning runs, and when they couldn't keep up with him, he put them on a fitness regimen, which he supervised.

Batty resisted all Nick's attempts to get her involved in any sport or fitness programs, but she did work with him on dog-training. She wanted Duchess and Cilantro to be accepting her authority by the time Jeffrey arrived for Skye's birthday, but the week

151

passed and it was now Friday, with only one day left, and Batty had to admit they'd gotten nowhere.

"Heel," she said with little hope as the three of them wandered up Gardam Street, the dogs with their leashes tangled together once again. "But if you can't heel, since you're all twisted up, you should at least go in the same direction."

Yet they tugged and yanked, and Cilantro barked at a mailbox that he was certain had never been there before. At least there was no longer the complication of the red wagon—Duchess hadn't needed it for several days now. If she wasn't good at following Batty's commands, at least she had lost weight. Her funny dachshund tummy was further off the ground, her harness now loose enough to slip and jiggle.

When they reached the Geigers' house, the two dogs finally decided to pull together, toward the front step, where Nick sat overlooking a large percentage of the Penderwick crew. Skye and Jane were doing sit-ups on the lawn, and Lydia danced around them, the sun glinting off her crown. Only Ben was absent, gone to Rafael's house after school to dig up rocks and dream up a movie about basketball-playing aliens.

The dogs gave quick identifying sniffs to Skye and Jane—and Duchess paused to give Lydia a big kiss—but Nick was their goal, their love.

"Sit," said Nick when they arrived, and the dogs sat. "Batty, if you can wait a few minutes, I'll walk Duchess and Cilantro with you. We're almost done here."

"Thank goodness," said Jane, and flopped down flat, done with sit-ups.

"I said *almost* done, Penderwick. Twenty more." Nick rubbed both dogs' heads, sending them into ecstasy.

Jane didn't move. "Nick, you're killing me."

"Your sister hasn't stopped. Get going."

"Aren't you worn out yet?" Jane asked Skye.

"Of course I am." Skye determinedly bobbed up and down. "But I won't give him the satisfaction."

"You'll be glad I kept you in shape when you hit the temptations of college," said Nick. "When Rosalind gets home, she'll tell you I'm right."

"Lucky Rosalind, who won't get home until you're just about to leave again." Jane went back to doing sit-ups.

"Jane didn't mean that," said Batty.

"Yes, she did," said Skye.

"No back talk, grunts," barked Nick, but with a side smile for Batty. "C'mon, let's see you make these dogs obey."

"They won't."

"They certainly won't if you keep up that attitude. Try to make them come to you."

Batty handed him the leashes, then walked ten feet away. Their leashes weren't that long, but she knew they wouldn't listen to her, so it made no difference.

"Duchess, Cilantro," she said. "Come!"

They continued to stare at Nick, but Lydia did dance over to Batty, proudly bearing a bright dandelion she'd plucked from the lawn.

"Flower," she said.

"Is that for me?" said Batty.

"No. Nick." Lydia danced away, on the hunt for more dandelions.

Batty turned back to the dogs. "Come over here, you monsters."

"Make them look at you first," said Nick.

"Duchess, Cilantro," tried Batty. "Eyes to me!"

When they wouldn't even look at her, Batty gave up and went back to sit with Nick, marveling at his easy authority.

"Fifty-eight, fifty-nine, sixty." Jane fell, panting, onto the ground.

Skye also finished her sit-ups, though too proud to pant. "I can't believe we made all those Welcome Home signs for Nick, can you, Jane?"

"We did it because Ben missed him, not because we did."

"They don't mean that," Batty told Nick.

"Yes, we do," said Jane.

"Twenty-five push-ups for insubordination," said Nick.

Groaning, Jane and Skye rolled over and started on their push-ups as Lydia brought Nick a fat handful of dandelions.

"Lydia loves Nick," she said.

"And Nick loves Lydia," he replied. "Give me your crown."

"She won't," said Batty.

But Lydia took off her crown and handed it over, then watched as Nick deftly wove the dandelions around the spikes.

"Lydia is a princess," she told Duchess. "Snow White."

"Woof," said Duchess.

"And Cilantro can be a count," said Batty, so that no one would feel un-royal.

Finished with his weaving, Nick set the crown, now bright with living gold, onto Lydia's glowing curls. "You're definitely no Snow White with that red hair."

"Twenty-four, twenty-five." Jane collapsed. "She's Princess Dandelion Fire."

"Princess Dandelion Fire!" repeated Batty. "That's perfect for you, Lydia. Say thank you to Nick for decorating your crown."

Lydia kissed Nick's cheek. "Lydia thanks Nick."

"Twenty-eight, twenty-nine, thirty," finished Skye, stubbornly doing more than Nick had asked for. "And Skye doesn't. Batty and Lydia, make sure you never, ever let Nick start you on a fitness regimen."

Nick, Batty, and the dogs soon set off, leaving Jane and Skye still recovering, and Lydia again dancing, waving her arms as she thought a princess named Dandelion Fire would. At the edge of Quigley Woods,

Nick took Cilantro's leash from Batty and set off with his swift stride. Batty and Duchess had to run to keep up.

"Not bad, Batty," said Nick after a while. "Maybe running is your sport. Come out with me one of these mornings and see how you like it."

"I. Don't. Want." She slowed down to catch her breath. "A. Sport."

Nick and Cilantro pulled out ahead. Duchess would have stayed with them—her little legs going a million miles a minute, her tongue hanging out—but Batty kept her back.

"You have to slow down," she said. "Come on, let's just walk for a while."

Duchess was willing to reduce her speed to trotting, but any slower than that she wouldn't go. One more example of dogs not listening to Batty.

"I don't seem to have any natural authority," she said. "Ben and Lydia don't see me as a boss, either."

Spring had found its way into Quigley Woods. The first shimmer of lemony green was on the trees, clumps of wild grass pushed up through last year's dead leaves, and here and there an early violet showed itself, a purple glow amid the less regal greens and browns. And on top of all that beauty, the air was sweet, the sun warm.

Batty was happy—Jeffrey was arriving the next day, and Rosalind only seven more days after that—and her sprite was happy, too, coming out with "Tomorrow" from *Annie*.

But in the meantime, Duchess was suddenly on the brink of exhaustion. She'd tried to sing along with Batty, and that, on top of the trotting, had been too much for her.

"Duchess is going to have a heart attack!" shouted Batty.

Nick doubled back to meet them. Duchess fell over onto her side while Cilantro snuffled anxiously at her.

"See, you've pushed her too hard," said Batty.

"She just needs a rest." Nick handed Cilantro's leash to Batty, then swept up Duchess and slung her around his shoulders. Yet more proof that she'd lost weight—the tubbier Duchess would have simply slid off. "Come on. We'll follow the creek, then circle back around. Run!"

It was when they were circling back that Batty heard someone calling her name. She knew it was an older sister, apparently one who'd revived from the workout. Knowing that whoever it was would probably try to hand off Lydia, Batty wasn't in any hurry to reach her. But the voice didn't go away, and all at once Batty knew that it wasn't Skye or Jane out there, but another sister entirely, the one Batty had been missing so very much. Here came her sprite again, wanting to burble whole songs, albums, orchestras full of music, and now Batty was throwing Cilantro's leash at Nick and bolting through the woods, herself a greyhound, until she'd burst out of the woods and found herself wrapped in Rosalind's

157

arms, laughing and asking a million questions. What felt like a joyous miracle turned out to be a normal occurrence—Rosalind had been offered a ride home for Skye's birthday and couldn't resist.

"And Jane told me you were out here, so I came right away—" Rosalind broke off, mid-explanation, her face changing from surprise to pleasure to shyness. "Tommy?"

Batty turned around to look, though she already knew it wasn't Tommy. "That's Nick."

But Rosalind had already started forward. "Nick! Of course it's Nick."

She ran at him full tilt, hesitating only at the last second, when she couldn't figure out how to hug him with a dachshund draped around his neck. So instead she just cried into his shirt.

Nick shook his head and grinned at Batty. "The rest of us are over this part."

"Well, I'm not." Rosalind sniffed and let Duchess lick away the rest of the tears. "I get to cry the first time I see you in months and months, even if you are wearing a dog."

"That's Duchess, one of the dogs I'm walking," said Batty, "and the other one is Cilantro."

Cilantro had his head buried in a bush, unaware that the rest of him was out in plain sight for all to see.

"His IQ isn't his strong point," said Nick. "Unlike you, Rosy, except for when you were dumb enough to let my brother go."

"Nick, you know you've got it backward. He let me go. And the last time I heard, he was seeing some girl named Theresa."

"She was a mere stopgap, a pale substitute. Anyway, that's over and done with. Tommy's down there in Delaware moping for you."

Rosalind tucked her arm through his. "Batty, tell Nick he doesn't know what he's talking about."

"Ha, like he listens to me." Batty took Cilantro's leash and dragged him out of the bush. "It's Rosalind, Cilantro! She's my best sister, and you will like her very much."

As they all made their way down Gardam Street, Batty almost danced with happiness. Not just Jeffrey now, but Rosalind, too. Rosalind! How fun, how lucky, how magnificent, how—

"Well, well, well," said Nick.

"Don't, Nick," said Rosalind. "Just don't."

Bewildered, Batty looked around, and then saw him.

"Rosy, who's that man?" she asked.

He was leaning against a car in the Penderwicks' driveway, giving off an aura of ownership, not only of the car but of all he surveyed. The car, low-slung and gleaming white, was parked behind poor Flashvan, which looked suddenly embarrassed by its own vulgar racing stripe. As for the man himself, he was dressed from head to toe in black, carefully rumpled in all the right places, looking like a picture in a magazine.

"That's Oliver, and he's not a man. I mean, I guess he's a man—he's a junior, anyway. He gave me the ride home."

"Nice car," said Nick.

"Behave." Rosalind squeezed his arm. "I've known Oliver for only a few weeks, so this isn't a big deal. Right, Duchess?"

Duchess licked Rosalind in sympathy, but Batty thought it was a big deal, as did Cilantro, who was trying to head back toward Quigley Woods.

She wished she could let him—her old shyness had descended, *boom*, and she felt five years old again—but the man had walked to meet them, and Rosalind was happily making introductions.

"Oliver, my sister Batty," she said.

"Hello." He nodded and smiled.

Batty nodded back—it was the best she could do. Speaking to such a man was out of the question. Cilantro saved her by tuba-ing. If he couldn't get away from this person who could possibly be a moving trash can, he would bark at him.

"Down," said Nick. Cilantro unwillingly lowered himself to the ground.

"And, Oliver, this is Nick." Rosalind beamed, wanting them to be friends.

Oliver reached out to shake Nick's hand, which forced Nick to unwind his arm from Rosalind's.

"So how did you two meet?" Nick asked.

"Film class," said Rosalind.

"Semiotics and Narrativity in Cinema," said Oliver. "I fell for her when she admitted she hadn't seen any Buñuel."

"Buñuel?" asked Nick. "Plays for the Mets, right?"

Rosalind narrowed her eyes at Nick, silently scolding him for something that Batty didn't understand, while Oliver looked satisfied, as though he'd set up a test for Nick and Nick had failed. Batty hoped she wouldn't be the next to be tested. Like maybe this Boonwell guy played for the Yankees instead of the Mets. Baseball players were definitely not one of her strengths.

Rosalind was back to smiling. "Oliver, Nick is the one who taught me how to play basketball, years and years ago."

"My best student, except for her jump shot. Rosy, how's your follow-through these days? Remembering to snap your wrist?"

"My follow-through has always been excellent. You just needed some reason to criticize me."

Oliver didn't seem to enjoy their banter. "Still play ball?" he asked Nick.

"These days I just mess around a little."

Batty considered "messing around" an inaccurate description of Nick's approach to basketball, or to any other sport. Just the day before, she'd seen him shooting hoops with some of his old high school friends and he'd looked as good as ever.

Cilantro started to pull again, demanding Batty's

attention. When she could turn back to the people, she saw that Oliver had somehow shifted things around. Nick was separated from Rosalind, and now it was Oliver who had possession of her, his arm around her shoulder. Batty wished she'd seen him do it, so she could describe it to Keiko. It was like a stealth ninja move, but for boyfriends. And one Batty hoped never to have done to her.

She left soon after that, needing to get away from this man who made Cilantro tuba so sadly. Nick and Duchess came with her.

"Well, well, well," Nick said again when they were out of earshot of the others.

"I didn't understand all that about the baseball player. Boonwell somebody?"

"Luis Buñuel. He's not a baseball player. He was a Spanish filmmaker, a long time ago."

"So you were—"

"Messing with Oliver, yeah. The guy's a pretentious jerk, exactly the type freshman girls tend to fall for."

"I didn't fall for him."

"No? You're not blown away by his smoldering gaze and sculpted cheekbones?"

"What do cheekbones have to do with anything?" She'd have to tell Keiko.

"What do I know? I'm just repeating what I've been told. Some girls swear that *my* cheekbones are the key to my rugged handsomeness." Nick stood still to let Batty inspect his face. "What do you think?"

"I guess they're all right." Batty was more concerned with Oliver than with Nick's cheekbones. "Do you think he's staying with us?"

"Probably. Don't worry about it, though. He won't be around for too long."

"How can you tell?"

"I'm Nick. I know everything. Besides, any woman who's loved a Geiger has been spoiled for other men."

Batty hoped Rosalind had been spoiled for other men, though without Tommy around, it couldn't be proven. But she trusted Nick. However annoying he could be, he was also practically always right.

The Ayvazians were delighted to see Nick, and pulled him into the house, determined to ply him with coffee and cake. But before Batty could leave with Cilantro, Nick borrowed a pen from Mrs. Ayvazian, rolled up one of Batty's sleeves, and wrote his phone number on her arm.

"If Oliver annoys you too much—starts quizzing you about semiotics, say—call me."

"I don't know what semiotics are."

"I have only the vaguest idea myself, but I'll make something up for you."

"I can call you anytime?" She pulled her sleeve back down, hiding it.

"Yes, but only if it's an emergency, since I'm sharing this evening with a beautiful woman."

"Who?"

"None of your business." He relented. "One of my old girlfriends from high school. I hope to spend time with as many of them as I can get hold of, plus a few new ones."

"Spoil them all for other men."

"You got it." He faked a punch at her nose. "But I'll be at Skye's birthday party tomorrow night, so you'll have me for backup then. And Jeffrey's still coming tomorrow, right? Skye hasn't blown him off again?"

"He's still coming." Batty knew because she'd asked Jane and Jane had said yes, she was certain, because she'd made Skye promise she wouldn't tell him to stay away. And whatever problems Skye had with communication, she never broke promises. But if Skye knew when Jeffrey would arrive, she hadn't told even Jane. Jane said they were probably still negotiating, whatever that meant.

"Sometime," she added.

"He'll get here. The lure of the Penderwick sisters, et cetera. Everything will be fine, I promise."

"I guess so." Batty pulled her sleeve back up, making sure the number was still safely there on her arm. "Thanks, Nick."

CHAPTER TWELVE
Bribery

THE FIRST TIME ROSALIND CAME HOME from college for a visit, she and Batty set up a ritual that they'd stuck to ever since. As soon as Rosalind had given hugs and hellos to the rest of the family, she'd take Batty upstairs to her room, just the two of them, for a catch-up talk while she unpacked. Batty loved these private times, and often found herself telling Rosalind things she hadn't realized she'd wanted to talk about, matters she'd been keeping to herself, fretting over them in secret.

But since Rosalind had never before come home for a surprise visit—and she'd certainly never come home with a surprise guest—Batty didn't know if this time would be like the others. She hoped so, yearning to tell Rosalind about the strangeness and discomfort of walking Duchess and Cilantro—the disloyalty she felt, and the terrible risk that once again she wouldn't take good enough care of creatures under her protection.

When she got back to the house, Jane, Skye, and Artie were outside with Rosalind and Oliver, and from the gaga look on Jane's face, Batty suspected that Nick had been correct about cheekbones and the other thing—oh, right, *smoldering gaze*. Skye didn't seem to be overwhelmed by Oliver's looks, but she was listening intently while he told her about taking time out of a Switzerland ski trip to visit the Large Hadron Collider. Batty was pretty sure that Skye didn't care about skiing, so it had to be the Large Hadron Collider, whatever that was, that had her so interested. It did sound science-y.

Batty lurked, half hidden behind Artie, who now seemed wonderfully normal and familiar. Rosalind and Oliver were pulling their suitcases out of the trunk of the car—so he *was* staying there with them—somehow managing to do it with Oliver's arm still around Rosalind. Then they started toward the house. If Rosalind was going to follow the usual ritual with Batty, this would be when she'd turn and ask to meet her upstairs in her bedroom.

And Rosalind did turn and, spotting Batty, smile, but before she could say anything, she was swept into the house with the others.

For five minutes Batty waited, in case Rosalind popped out again and summoned her for their private talk. But the only person to appear was Jérôme, wandering up the driveway in search of Jane.

Batty ran away, back to Quigley Woods and solitude.

After an hour or so of sweet calm in Quigley Woods, coming home again was a shock for Batty. The front hall was full of people, like a packed elevator. It took her a while to sort them out. In the center were Oliver and Rosalind, his arm again—or still—around her. Ben, back from Rafael's, was next to Oliver—oh, dear, had Oliver managed to charm Ben? By giving him a magic rock or something? Skye was sitting on the steps with Katy and Molly. Jane, Artie, Jérôme, Pearson, and a Donovan were jammed in around Oliver and Rosalind. On the outskirts were Batty's parents—what was going on, anyway? Even Lydia was there, blissfully dancing through the crowd, her dandelion-bedecked crown bobbling past people's knees.

Batty slid around the mob to get to her parents, safe and stable, and tried not to listen as Oliver spoke.

"I always say that the world exists only to end up in a good film. Not that I can take credit for that statement. Rimbaud said it first about books."

"Excuse me, but it was not Rimbaud, but Mallarmé," murmured Jérôme politely. " 'Le monde est fait pour aboutir à un beau livre.' "

Oliver looked like a mosquito had just buzzed past his ear. "Rimbaud? Mallarmé? Does it really matter who said it?"

167

Batty thought that it might matter to Rimbaud and Mallarmé, whoever they were. At least this time she could be pretty sure they weren't baseball players. And she decided to be fond of Jérôme, and hoped he would continue to keep watch over Oliver. But he'd gone back to staring at Jane, which was mostly what he seemed to do these days.

Rosalind had spotted Batty and was waving to her across the multitudes. "Oliver is taking us all out for Chinese food. Come with us, okay?"

Had Rosalind gone insane? She should have known that Batty would rather do anything—walk on broken glass, even—than go out to dinner with all those people.

"Can I go, too?" asked Ben. "I love Chinese food."

"Sorry, Ben," answered his dad. "It will be too late a night for you and Lydia."

"Obviously it's too late for *her*." Ben was appalled to be categorized with Lydia, who happened to be going past him, waving her arms enthusiastically in his face. "Leave me alone, Lydia."

"We'd take good care of Ben, Mr. Penderwick," said Oliver easily.

"And it will be educational, too, Daddy," Ben pleaded. "Oliver's going to teach me about movies."

Batty blanched. So that's how Oliver had gotten to her little brother, by talking about movies. Would Ben soon start talking about Buñuel and—what was that other word—semiotics?

"Definitely educational," said Oliver. "I can tell Ben about the Kubrick course I took last year. Everyone knows that he directed *2001: A Space Odyssey*, but his early career is where the interesting contradictions lie. He went from *Spartacus* in 1960 to *Lolita* in 1962, and though both movies are about power and the dangers of extreme subjugation—"

Iantha interrupted. "Yes, thank you, Oliver. That is indeed interesting."

"Ben, you are staying home," added Mr. Penderwick.

"But—"

"No buts. *Pater sum.*"

All of Mr. Penderwick's children could translate *Pater sum* into "I am the father." But they also knew that in this house it really meant that further arguments were pointless and could lead to unpleasantness.

"Anyway, I'm not going, Ben," said Batty. "We can play Othello if you want."

"Othello." Ben repeated it with bitterness. A board game couldn't match up to Chinese food at a restaurant.

"The children will put on a Shakespeare play this evening?" Jérôme asked Jane.

"Othello isn't a Shakespeare play, *ce n'est pas un drame*. I mean, *c'est vrai*, of course it is a Shakespeare play. But Othello *est aussi un jeu.*"

"A game? About Shakespeare?"

"Speak English, Jane," said Artie. "You continue to confuse Jérôme."

"*Oui!*" said Lydia, exhilarated by all the French being spoken. She spun and dipped, bumping into Pearson and Katy, singing la-la-la-la, and losing a few dandelions in the process.

Rosalind picked up the dandelions and took hold of Lydia as she waltzed by.

"Let me put these back into your crown, honey."

"We should get her better flowers than dandelions." Oliver reached out, not to help put dandelions back but to pluck those remaining from Lydia's crown.

Lydia would have none of that. She made awful faces at Oliver and, to be doubly safe, leaned away until she was almost in a backbend.

"*Non,* Man, *non, NON!*" she said. "Princess Dandelion Fire."

"Nick gave her the dandelions, and she's very fond of him," said Iantha, apologizing for her daughter.

"Of course," said Oliver.

"Nick!" said Rosalind. "I'll go ask if he wants to come to dinner with us."

"Of course," said Oliver again.

Batty watched as Rosalind disengaged herself from Oliver—with a slight tussle—and ran out the front door. If Batty hadn't felt so overwhelmed, she would have stopped Rosy by explaining about Nick's date with the high school girlfriend. Never mind. It was a relief to see that she could still separate from Oliver, if only for a few moments. And now Oliver, outmaneuvered, was pulling Ben into the living room. Batty strained to see through the mass of people—it looked like Oliver and Ben were having a private conversation. She shuddered at the thought of having a private conversation with Oliver.

Moments later, after Rosalind returned without Nick, the mob shuffled out of the house, loaded themselves into cars, and drove off for Chinese food, leaving behind a quiet house and, a grand treat for Batty, an intoxicatingly empty living room.

She made splendid use of it, settling at the piano to play and play, both before and after dinner, and to softly sing, too, when she was sure no one but Lydia was listening. Lydia danced until she was borne away to bed, and Batty's parents wandered in and out, telling her how wonderful she sounded. Eventually Ben was wandering in and out, too, not so much to praise Batty but because it had gotten too dark outside for rock-hunting and he'd decided he would be willing to play Othello after all.

"Since you fell asleep in the middle of our last game," he said, resting the game box on the lower end of the piano keyboard. Batty played around it, transposing to higher octaves when necessary.

"Please," said Ben.

After his fourth or fifth "Please," Batty gave in, and they set up the game on the floor. Soon the room was filled with the clicks of pieces being flipped from black to white and back again. Until their parents started up a conversation in the dining room, just loud enough for their words to drift across the hall and into the living room. It began with Mr. Penderwick.

"Have I ever told you about that arrogant Neil Somebody who dated Claire for a while in college? The one who was always talking about García Lorca— quoting his poems and making it sound like he knew the guy? When I finally pointed out that Lorca had been dead for decades, he asked me what point I was trying to make. Iantha, what? Why are you looking at me like that?"

"If I were to take a guess, Oliver reminds you of this Neil Somebody."

"Well, yes."

"Then out with it."

Batty nudged Ben and put her finger on her lips for him to be quieter at clicking. This could be important information.

"I mean, Mallarmé! Ha! And earlier, Oliver informed me that no one can appreciate films without a deep knowledge of Jean Renoir. He suggested we rent *Grand Illusion* and spend the weekend watching and discussing it." Mr. Penderwick groaned. "Is he wooing our Rosalind, do you think?"

"I'm not sure it's gotten to the wooing stage, if anyone has even used that expression in the last hundred years. What's gotten into you, Martin?"

"*Eheu fugaces, Postume, Postume, labuntur anni,*" he answered. "That is, I'm feeling old."

"You're not old, darling, either in English or Latin."

"Hmm," he said. "So is Rosy wooing him?"

"I don't *know*, Martin. He is terribly attractive, though."

"Iantha!"

"Well, he is. It's just a fact. Something about his cheekbones, I suppose."

Mr. Penderwick groaned again, even louder this time. "Can't we just have Tommy and his normal cheekbones back? I don't like all this change."

"You'll have to get used to change, my poor husband. Rosalind could have lots of boyfriends before settling on one, and then there are the rest of the children to get through."

"It will kill me. I'm not ready to think about potential sons-in-law."

"That's good, because none of your daughters are ready to think about potential husbands. Martin, you really need to calm down."

"It's just that this Oliver—"

"Shh." Iantha interrupted him. "He is our guest. Now, where can he sleep tonight? We could put him on the couch in our study, except that it's covered with your botanical samples."

"That's what my study is for, since I am a botanist. Oliver can sleep on the living room couch. Maybe that will discourage him."

Batty bent her head, hiding her smile from Ben. She felt less awful about Oliver, knowing that both her dad and Nick agreed with her about him.

"So Oliver gets the living room couch," said Iantha. "How about Jeffrey tomorrow night? He was supposed to sleep in Rosalind's room, but with Rosalind home—I suppose we could move Batty into Lydia's big-girl bed and let Jeffrey sleep in Batty's room. I don't think she would mind."

Batty definitely wouldn't mind. She would have hated Oliver sleeping in there, but not Jeffrey.

"Jeffrey, I like. I'd build a new room for him," said Mr. Penderwick. "But if any other young men show up this weekend, tell them they have to sleep in the garage."

That must have been the end of her parents' conversation, for Batty heard no more. She wasn't sure whether Ben had bothered to listen, and when she looked back at the board, the number of white chips seemed to have mysteriously multiplied.

"Did you cheat?" she asked, since the white chips were Ben's.

"Penderwicks don't cheat." He tipped over the board, spilling out the pieces. "Maybe a little. We can start over."

"Last game, though. I want to get back to the piano."

"Batty, what's a son-in-law?" he asked.

So he *had* been listening to their parents. "Whoever marries Rosalind, Skye, or Jane—or me, too, I guess—will be Dad and Mom's son-in-law. Also your brother-in-law."

"What if I don't like him?"

"He will be anyway. Like when Uncle Turron married Aunt Claire, he became Daddy's brother-in-law."

Ben couldn't remember back before Uncle Turron and Aunt Claire were married. Uncle Turron was just Uncle Turron, big, beloved, and father to Marty and Enam. None of that seemed like a possible cause of trauma. Unlike—

"Even Oliver could be a brother-in-law?"

"I hope not. Though I know *you* like him—you were begging to go to dinner with him and talk about movies."

"I thought I liked him, but then he gave me this." Ben pulled a five-dollar bill out of his pocket. "Before they left, he pulled me into the living room—"

Batty interrupted. "I saw that! What did he want?"

"He asked me if I like Nick and I said everyone likes Nick. And he said, Rosalind likes him, too? And I said of course she does. Then he gave me that money and told me not to mention it to anyone."

Batty eyed the money with distaste. Penderwicks didn't need to be bribed to keep secrets. "Then why are you telling me?"

"I didn't promise him I wouldn't."

"But you took the money."

"I know." He let it fall onto the Othello board. "I thought I'd use it for my movie studio, but now I don't think I want it. You can have it to help with Skye's birthday present from you, me, and Lydia."

Jane had helped them pick out the present, a *Doctor Who* sweatshirt with a picture on the front of Skye's favorite Doctor, the tenth. Their parents would have paid for the whole thing, but Batty had proudly chipped in half the cost from her dog-walking money, and Ben had followed her lead, putting in a dollar from his rock-digging money. He thought it was an excellent present and had been dying to give it to Skye.

"I don't want Oliver's money," said Batty. Five dollars was a lot, but this was dishonorable money.

"We could give it to Dad to help with groceries," said Ben.

"He definitely wouldn't want it."

They discussed several other options, including sending it to the president to help him run the government. But they didn't think he would want money meant for a bribe, either. In the end, they snuck upstairs to the bathroom, where they ripped up the five-dollar bill and flushed the pieces down the toilet, laughing so hard they almost woke up Lydia.

Soon after that, their parents made Ben go to bed, and Batty went to her room to listen to music. And to wait for Rosalind to come home, hoping still to get in their talk. For hours Batty waited, cuddling on her bed with Funty and Gibson, the stuffed animals, until finally she turned off the music and went sadly to sleep.

CHAPTER THIRTEEN
Doctor Who *and Bunny Foo Foo*

WHEN BEN WOKE UP on the morning of Skye's birthday, he decided that she should be given her present immediately, a *Doctor Who* sweatshirt being too special to mix in with all the other presents at her party. But he couldn't do it by himself, since the sweatshirt was also from Batty. And Lydia, but she wouldn't know the difference.

He went across the hall to see if Batty was awake, and yes, she already had music on her record player— one of those musicals she liked so much. He gave the secret knock and went in. Not only was Batty awake, Lydia was there, too, dancing to the music.

"Did she escape again?" he asked Batty.

"She showed up two hours ago and wanted to sleep in here with me."

"Lydia doesn't like the big-girl bed," said Lydia.

"But you weren't even *in* it," Ben told her. "You were in your crib. Besides, Batty's bed is even bigger than your big-girl bed."

Lydia put on her you're-missing-the-point face and went on dancing.

"Maybe she'll like the new bed more after I sleep in it tonight," said Batty. "We're having a sleepover, right, Lydia?"

"La-la-la-la-la-*LAAAAA*," sang Lydia too loudly.

Batty turned off the record player, and Ben stopped feeling the need to cover his ears.

"Let's give Skye her present now," he said.

"You know she's probably still asleep. They were out really late. Besides, the present is downstairs in the piano bench." The piano bench was near the couch where Oliver was sleeping.

"I'll go get it anyway. It's my house."

Batty was glad when Ben returned safely with the sweatshirt. Not that she thought Oliver would hurt Ben, but a man willing to bribe children could be capable of who knows what.

"He snores," said Ben.

"Figures."

Since a present is no good without being wrapped, they let Lydia scribble across several pieces of paper, taped them together, and wrapped the sweatshirt in the untidy-but-personalized result. Then they quietly marched to Skye and Jane's room and peeked

178

inside. Both older sisters were dead asleep in their beds.

"We should just leave it for her," whispered Batty. Waking up Skye was not for the timid.

Ben was shaking his head no—he wanted to see Skye's face when she opened her gift—when the decision was taken away from them. Lydia, on her own, had gone boldly into the room and was now touching Skye's nose. Ben followed, and then Batty. At least, she thought, this might give her a chance to find out when Jeffrey was arriving. If Skye weren't too annoyed to share information.

"*Nariz,*" said Lydia, again touching Skye's nose.

Skye opened her eyes. "And where is my *boca?*"

Lydia touched Skye's mouth, then her own. "*Boca.*"

"We're sorry we woke you up," said Batty.

"We brought your birthday present, though," said Ben.

Skye looked at the clock and groaned. "Give it to me, you little monsters."

Yawning, she carefully took off the wrapping, making a fuss about each of Lydia's squiggles, and when she got to the sweatshirt, she loved it as much as Ben had known she would. She put it on over her pajamas and flopped back down onto her pillow.

"So, happy birthday," said Ben.

"Thank you, I love it, now leave."

"*Ojos,*" said Lydia, pointing to Skye's eyes.

"*Sí, ojos.* I mean it, get out of here. You, too, Batty."

"Umm—"

"*What?*"

"Do you know what time Jeffrey is coming?"

"One-thirty," said Skye, and put the pillow over her head.

At one-twenty, Batty guided Lydia through the basketball game spilling out of the Geigers' driveway and onto Gardam Street. All the other Penderwick siblings were involved, including Ben, who was delighted to be playing not only with his sisters, but Nick, Artie, Pearson, Katy, Molly, both Donovans, and even Jérôme, who had no idea what he was doing but was doing it gallantly. Oliver was playing, too. Batty thought that he'd be a better player if he paid more attention to the ball and less to Nick's every move.

"Lydia wants to play," said Lydia.

"No, you don't." Batty kept a firm grip on her little sister, who could get smashed in a basketball game that energetic. "We're going to the corner to wait for Jeffrey, remember?"

"Little Bunny Foo Foo."

"Yes, exactly, good remembering. Jeffrey who sings 'Little Bunny Foo Foo.'" He had a special version just for Lydia, done as bad Italian opera, with the facial expressions and hand gestures to match.

The morning had been a disappointment for Batty, spent lurking around the house just in case Rosalind found time for her. But Oliver seemed always to be in the way, making private talk impossible. Batty almost wished Rosalind hadn't come home this weekend, and she tried to cheer herself up by reverting to her original countdown. Only seven days now until her favorite sister came home from college for the summer—*without* Oliver and his cheekbones. Not long at all.

"Flower," said Lydia, pointing to a dandelion brightening up a lawn. Her own dandelions were now sadly wilted, turning her crown into a flower graveyard, but she continued to resist any attempts to replace them. "Lydia loves Nick."

The disappointing morning had made Batty yearn even more for Jeffrey's arrival. Not that she had false hopes about how much attention she'd get from him. Her plan was to catch him just as he arrived on Gardam Street and before he was swept into the excitement and crowd. Not to sing for him right away—that was impractical, especially with basketball taking up the street—but to reserve a time for later. She hoped for Sunday morning. If she could get him away from the house and everyone in it for just an hour, they could talk and she could demonstrate the miraculous thing that had happened with her voice, and then they would plan her Grand Eleventh Birthday Concert, and life would be perfect.

She and Lydia waved as they passed the Ayvazians' house, in case Duchess was looking out the window, then rounded the corner. Another hundred feet and they'd reached their goal, a glass-enclosed bus stop with its own bench, the best spot for watching for a certain battered little car.

"It's black, with white stripes on the hood," Batty told Lydia. "We'll shout and jump up and down when we see it, okay?"

Over the years, Batty had spent lots of time at this bus stop. When she was small, Rosalind had sometimes brought her down to watch and cheer on the big buses that rumbled by every fifteen minutes. On some glorious occasions, they'd climbed aboard one of the buses heading to Wooton, the next town over, where they'd eaten ice cream at Herrell's or visited Broadside Bookshop, with its entire wall of books for children. And once—the adventure of it was crystal clear in Batty's memory—when they got to Wooton, they boarded another bus that took them all the way into Boston for a day's visit with Jeffrey. Skye and Jane had come along, too (but not Ben, who was deemed too young, or Lydia, who didn't yet exist), and they'd had lunch at a spaghetti restaurant and taken subways here and there, and Jeffrey had treated them to a Swan Boat ride in the Boston Public Garden.

"Black car," said Lydia.

"What? Oh! Jump and yell! Jump and yell!"

They jumped and yelled as the black car zipped toward them, slowing down at the last minute, and there was Jeffrey rolling down his window and waving like a maniac.

"Follow me!" he cried, then putted along as they ran beside him.

But Lydia's legs couldn't go fast enough, and Batty hoisted her up on the run. They caught Jeffrey just as he turned onto Gardam Street, pulled over to the side, and opened his door. Batty tossed Lydia to him for the usual welcoming tummy raspberries, which always made Lydia shriek and giggle. Too old for raspberries, Batty decorously climbed in on the passenger's side and carefully inspected Jeffrey, with his freckles and his smile and his hair with the place that would never lie down, even now, all these years later. This falling-in-love-with-Skye nonsense hadn't changed how he looked.

"I don't think I could have stood it if you hadn't come this time," she said.

"Me neither," he said. "Why are you staring at me?"

"I'm making sure you're still you."

"And?"

"You are. What a relief."

Lydia wriggled to get Jeffrey's attention back. "Goldie put Frank in a box."

"No, Lydia, we're done with Frank," Batty told her.

"But who is he?" asked Jeffrey.

"A dead guinea pig. Change the subject."

183

"Okay, what about you? Written any of those book reports yet?"

"Ugh, no. Change the subject again."

"What about the ongoing research into crushes? Have you and Keiko made any progress?"

"That's Keiko's research, not mine. She's still working on it, but she did drop Ryan the movie star."

"I never thought he was right for her. What else, Batty?"

"Talk to me about music!"

"You want to hear about the Boston Symphony Orchestra?"

"No," said Lydia.

"Yes," said Batty. "Please!"

Jeffrey had been at Symphony Hall that past week to see the Boston Symphony Orchestra perform Berlioz's *Symphonie Fantastique*, which he could describe to Batty in detail, and with such passion and excitement that even Lydia sort of listened. He demonstrated part of the second movement on an imaginary clarinet—and Batty scolded him for not bringing his actual clarinet along. From Berlioz he went on to the local bands he kept track of, the music he was writing, and then to news of his dad, whom Batty knew well and loved, too. A professional saxophone player, he lived in Boston near Jeffrey's school, and they often worked on their music together.

"And, Batty, I've started playing clubs with him, just the small ones, but still. Dad said that when I'm older, we can tour together, even go abroad. He's told me about playing in Germany, how they love jazz over there. Can you imagine how great that would be?"

Batty could imagine that and more. She already saw herself as the singer on their tour.

"And I'll go, too," she said, without thinking.

Restless from lack of attention, Lydia tried to stick her head through the steering wheel, which made her crown fall off, scattering limp dandelions onto Jeffrey and his car. There was a great deal of drama getting her head back out and the dandelions back onto the crown and the crown back onto her head.

"Life will be much easier when she gives up on the crown," said Batty.

"Yet I remember someone who wore butterfly wings when she was even older than Lydia."

"That was different." The wings had been Batty's. "I think."

"Little Bunny Foo Foo," said Lydia.

"Oh-ho!" Jeffrey reached into the backseat and produced a large pink stuffed rabbit. "Little Bunny Foo Foo!"

Jeffrey burst into the song, hopping the pink rabbit around the car and sending Lydia into joyful squeals. Batty sang along in a voice as silly as his, though more Viennese opera than Italian, and was so happy that she wished she could take these moments and store them away to be brought out and relived whenever she wanted.

When they'd gone through all the "Bunny Foo Foo" verses—and they were legion—Jeffrey reached again into the backseat. This time he brought back a record album, *Kiss Me, Kate*.

"Here's some Cole Porter to keep your musical taste sharp and sophisticated. Make sure you listen to 'So in Love,' one of the truly great love songs of the twentieth century. What? *Now*, why are you looking at me?"

"Just, you know, love songs."

"You're scolding me about Skye, aren't you?"

"Sort of. Anyway, thanks for this. You spoil us." She hugged the album. "I have something important I need to tell you."

"Is it about love? Skye's found a boyfriend who isn't me?"

"If she doesn't want you for a boyfriend, why would she want anyone else?"

"What would I do without you, Battikins?"

"You'd miss me terribly. And the something important I need to tell you is about me and it's a special topic and it'll take time and we need to be alone. Also, Jeffrey, I know what you are now! You're my *mentore*!"

"I like that. What made you think of it?"

"That's part of what I need to tell you."

"How about we go out to breakfast tomorrow morning, just you and me? Sylvester's?"

"Yes!" Sylvester's had the most delicious pancakes, almost as good as her father's.

186

"Okay, good." Squinting into the tiny mirror over the dashboard, he tried unsuccessfully to smooth down his hair. "I guess I'd better go forward into battle. Do you have any tips for me?"

"Musica anima mea est."

"Yes, there is that. Anything else?"

Batty shook her head. What else was there, really? "Well, you're arriving in the middle of a basketball game."

"I can handle basketball." That was true. Nick had taught him, too.

"And stay away from Oliver—"

"Who is *not* Skye's new boyfriend?"

"Try to concentrate. Oliver is an annoying person that is supposed to be attractive because of cheekbones. He likes Rosalind and lectures everyone about movies. So stay away from him, and, Jeffrey, do your best not to talk about love to Skye. You know how she is when she doesn't want to talk about stuff."

"Yeah, I know." He made one last attempt with his hair but gave up in disgust. "I guess I'm ready. You two have to walk—no car seat for Lydia. And, Batty, breakfast tomorrow, because we've got a date, right?"

Batty nodded, too full of happiness and excitement to speak, too close to letting her sprite burst out into song. After Jeffrey drove up the street, she hustled Lydia and her new pink rabbit back home for a nap and then shut herself up in her room, planning what she'd say to Jeffrey the next morning, and what

187

she'd sing. And she listened carefully to *Kiss Me, Kate*, coming to the conclusion that "So in Love" was indeed a good song, but she preferred the funnier ones. She had "Brush Up Your Shakespeare" memorized by the time she left to walk the dogs.

CHAPTER FOURTEEN
Still Life with Peacock Feather

WHEN BATTY GOT BACK HOME from walking the dogs, there were teenagers lounging all over the place, some left over from the basketball game, some arriving for the birthday dinner, some who fit into both categories. For once, she hardly cared, too delighted to see that Oliver's sleek car was no longer in the driveway. Hoping that he was gone forever, she rushed into the house and ended up in the kitchen, where dinner preparations were in full swing. Mr. Penderwick was chopping up vegetables for quesadillas, Rosalind was pulling a cake out of the oven, Jeffrey was shredding cheese, and Iantha was cooking up small, plain cheese quesadillas for Lydia, who was to be fed before the big dinner got rolling. Then there were the nonworkers: Lydia in her high chair, wearing both her crown and her lamb bib, her new pink rabbit beside her; Jane sitting cross-legged on the floor, in everyone's way; Ben, strutting around, showing off his new Celtics T-shirt; and Asimov, sticking close to Jeffrey, hoping for falling cheese.

Batty sidled up to Ben and whispered, "Where's Oliver?"

"He left," Ben whispered back.

"For good?"

Ben shook his head. "I don't think so."

Rats. But even for a brief time, it was a treat to have Rosalind on her own, just like it used to be. Batty nuzzled up to her, forgiving the earlier disappointments. "Maybe we can talk sometime before you go. Just the two of us."

"I would love that, Battikins. We'll find time tomorrow," said Rosalind. "Honey, what?"

"Nothing," said Batty, whose singing sprite had just made a mad breakout attempt. She grabbed a piece of cheese from Jeffrey and stuffed it into her mouth, hoping the sprite didn't like cheese. "I mean, the cake smells yummy."

Penderwick birthday cakes were always deliciously homemade and from scratch. Cake from a mix or, even worse, store-bought birthday cake, would have been a sign that the world was coming to an end. Each sibling had her or his own special cake, ritually chosen at the age of five, which the first Mrs. Penderwick had declared the age of reason, at least when it came to cakes. Rosalind's was angel food with

190

strawberry icing; Skye's, chocolate with raspberry icing; and Jane's, lemon with lemon icing and chocolate sprinkles. Those three recipes were all carefully recorded in their mother's handwriting. Batty's recipe, in Rosalind's round, thirteen-year-old handwriting, was for spice cake with cream cheese icing, and Ben's, written down by Iantha, was double chocolate with vanilla icing. Lydia didn't yet have a special cake, not having reached the age of reason.

"I'm starving," said Skye, wandering into the room. "When's dinner?"

"Go away! You can't be in here!" Rosalind flapped her hands at Skye, sending her out of the room. Tradition had it that Skye shouldn't see the cake until it was iced and decked out with burning candles.

She retreated to the doorway and leaned there, sniffing avidly. "Just pretend I'm not here."

"Lydia," said Jeffrey, energetically keeping up his cheese-grating. "Is Skye here?"

"*Sí*," said Lydia.

"Oh, no, she's not! We can say anything we want about her."

"Lydia," said Skye. "Tell Jeffrey he's a *cabeza de plátano*."

"*¡Cabeza de plátano!*" shrieked Lydia.

So Jeffrey must be behaving himself, thought Batty. Skye would be calling him something much worse than a banana head—in either Spanish or English—if he'd been talking love to her.

The back door opened and in strolled Nick,

holding a bunch of dandelions. Now, thought Batty, we're *all* here, which she shouldn't have, because it made her singing sprite want to pop out again. She grabbed something else to stuff into her mouth, this time a cherry tomato.

Nick kissed Iantha's cheek, then Rosalind's—but that was mostly an excuse to look at the cake—and waved cheerfully to the rest.

"Fresh supplies?" asked Mr. Penderwick, nodding at the dandelions.

"I thought Lydia might like to be spruced up for the party," answered Nick. "What do you say, Princess Dandelion Fire?"

"Lydia loves Nick," she answered.

"And me, too, right?" asked Ben, stopping in mid-strut.

"Of course you love Ben," said Batty. "Don't you, Lydia?"

"Okay." But Lydia's attention was now all on Nick and his bright new dandelions.

"So, Rosy," he said while pulling old flowers from the crown and weaving in the new. "I noticed that the Oliver-mobile isn't in the driveway. Have you sent him away?"

Batty nudged Ben.

"Of course not. He's just gone on an errand. I think he's picking up a gift for Skye."

"A car just like his, I hope," said Skye. "That would be a good present."

"Nick, do you think Rosy *should* send Oliver away?" asked Jane from the floor, her gimlet eye expression taking over her face.

"Don't encourage Nick, Jane," said Rosalind. "I don't care what he thinks."

"I care," said Mr. Penderwick. "Nick, would you like some pretzels?"

"Daddy!" Rosalind elbowed her father, protesting.

"Nick, if you're done with that crown," said Iantha, coming to the aid of her eldest, "give this quesadilla to Lydia."

Nick put it on Lydia's tray. "Here you go, Lydia-McBydia-Bob, eat, eat, it's good for you."

"*Gracias*," said Lydia, and took a big chomp.

"But back to Oliver," said Nick. "I think he's a show-off."

"What?" Rosalind exploded, and Skye and Jane exploded with her—the three were a team for this.

"*You*, Nick Geiger, dare call someone a show-off?" Jane asked while Skye howled with laughter.

"I am not a show-off," he replied. "I simply can't help being good at everything. A show-off is—"

Skye had abruptly stopped laughing and was waving her arms frantically at Nick, trying to shut him up. Not just Nick, but the entire kitchen went silent, staring at her, because she seemed to have gone mad without any obvious explanation. And now she was flattening herself against the doorjamb, making way for a tall copper vase loaded with—it took a while for

193

Batty to identify *what* the vase held. Bare branches, several plumes of dried grass, a peacock feather, and was that a bird's nest on one of the branches?

"A still life for Skye's birthday," said Oliver, handing over the gargantuan thing to Skye, who disappeared behind it. "I was going to get her flowers but wanted something less ordinary."

"That's very thoughtful of you, Oliver," said Iantha, stomping on Nick's foot to keep him quiet—Batty saw her do it—and putting her arm around Rosalind, who had gone a bit red in the face.

"I have two more in the car, one for you, Iantha, because you're such a kind hostess, and one for Rosalind, because she's Rosalind." Oliver left again.

"I don't understand," said Ben.

"It's supposed to be like art," explained Jane. "Sort of."

"I mean the part about Rosalind being Rosalind."

"Later, son," said Mr. Penderwick.

"Jeffrey, are you laughing at me?" Skye was trying to peer around the peacock feather, but the branch kept jabbing her in the face.

"Never," he said, though he had been. "Would you like help with your present?"

"It's just that this feather—" Skye blew on it.

Which was a mistake, because the resultant fluttering caught Asimov's attention. He made a flying leap across the kitchen and onto Skye, attempting to scale her to get to the—wait, a feather *and* a bird's nest? Asimov had never experienced such riches here in his own kitchen. When Skye's yelps of pain didn't discourage him, Jane and Jeffrey raced across the room to peel him away, but only after they'd bumped into each other. Using the uproar as cover, Ben stole a fingerful of the cake icing, and Batty blocked Lydia, just in case Asimov came flying in a different direction this time.

But Lydia was undisturbed by the bedlam.

"Another quesadilla," she said.

"Say please," replied her mother automatically, plopping one onto Lydia's plate. "The rest of you, pull yourselves together. Ben, stay away from the icing. Jeffrey, help Skye put that down in the dining room, then go with Oliver to bring the other . . . still lifes inside. Martin, looks like we'll need yet another leaf for the dining room table to make space for them, and, Nick—"

"Yes? Anything, Iantha."

"Please don't tease Rosalind anymore tonight."

"Yes, ma'am."

"And help Martin with the dining room table. Rosalind, you and I can figure out how to organize the table. Go, all of you. Jane, Skye, go."

As all the grown-ups and teenagers scattered, Iantha herding them ahead of her like a flock of naughty chickens, Batty sent out a silent apology to Ginevra for ever considering her a show-off. Even fifty book reports—even one hundred—wouldn't be as obnoxious as three massive and probably expensive bunches of weird stuff.

"Do *you* understand that part about Rosalind being Rosalind?" Ben asked Batty.

"I think Oliver was saying how much he likes her."

"Yuck." Ben swiped another taste of icing to get over that bad news. "I wish she would send him away, like Nick said."

"I know."

"Uh-oh," said Ben.

"What?"

Batty turned to follow her brother's gaze—and there was Oliver coming back into the kitchen with a handful of roses. What was he doing *now*? With only the three youngest Penderwicks in the room, who would he be giving—

"For the crown," said Oliver, advancing determinedly on Lydia, who looked up from her quesadilla, startled.

"*Non,*" she said.

Both Ben and Batty overcame their distaste for Oliver enough to grab at him on his way to Lydia, but he easily shook them off and kept going.

"Roses are better than dandelions." He brandished them like a sword.

"*Non, non,*" yelped Lydia, stuck there in her high chair, unable to get away from the unwanted roses.

Batty and Ben went for Oliver again, and Jane, attracted by Lydia's cries, rushed back into the room, but no one was quick enough to stop the first of Nick's dandelions from being yanked and dropped to the floor.

"*No me gusta, no me gusta,*" sobbed Lydia, ducking and weaving. And when she couldn't avoid Oliver, she fought back with the only weapon she had, smashing the remains of her second quesadilla onto his heretofore spotless shirt.

Pandemonium erupted, with people running in and out of the room, some trying to clean up Oliver, who could only stare down in disbelief at his cheese-smeared shirt, and some trying to calm Lydia, who was now wailing about both the insult to her crown and the loss of her quesadilla.

Batty was not one of the people concerned with Oliver's shirt. If she had disliked him before, now she loathed him.

"Maybe I should take Lydia upstairs," she told Iantha.

"Batty, Batty," wailed Lydia, holding out her arms to her sister.

"Would you, honey? That would be very helpful." Iantha was hauling Lydia out of the high chair. "Shh, sweetheart, you're safe. Oliver didn't mean to upset you."

Batty thought that was much too generous. Oliver may not have meant to upset Lydia, but he didn't seem to care that he had. But then Iantha hadn't seen his attack on the crown.

"Mom, I'll put her to bed and stay with her," she said.

"And miss the dinner? You wouldn't mind?"

Batty would mind. She'd planned to find a quiet corner from which to watch the crowd and the gaiety—and Jeffrey. But her loyalty was to Lydia, whom she should have better protected from Oliver and his roses.

She retrieved the fallen dandelion from the floor, tucked it into the crown, then took Lydia from Iantha. "No, I don't mind."

"Thank you, sweetheart. I'll bring some dinner for you when I come up to say good night to her."

The part about not minding became truer when Rosalind ran into the hall to catch Batty and Lydia before they could start up the steps.

"I'm so sorry," she said, kissing Lydia.

"The man hurt Lydia's crown," sobbed Lydia.

"I know, honey. He doesn't understand little girls, because he doesn't have a Lydia at home to help him." Rosalind kissed Batty, too. "What a good big sister you are. We'll talk tomorrow, okay?"

"Okay. I mean, yes!"

Next came Nick, who wrapped his arms around both Batty and Lydia, told them they were the best of the bunch, and that Lydia would always be his princess.

"And, Batty, you're a champ," said Nick.

"I know," she answered. "Even without a sport."

"No, you still have to get a sport."

Then, just as Batty was unlatching the bottom baby gate, Jeffrey appeared bearing Lydia's new pink rabbit, rescued from the high chair.

"Little Bunny Foo Foo," he sang.

"Little Bunny Foo Foo," Lydia wailed back at him. There was no cheering her up.

"Don't forget our breakfast tomorrow morning," Batty told him.

"Never." He put his hand on his heart. "Penderwick Family Honor."

"And, Jeffrey, *musica anima mea est.*"

"I know, I know." He kissed the top of Lydia's head, then did the same for Batty, and as he went back to join the others, Batty decided that missing the dinner was nothing after all—the last few marvelous moments had made up for it.

Getting a sobbing two-year-old ready for bed was no easy task. The removal of each piece of daytime clothing was a misery, as was the putting on of each piece of nighttime clothing. But all of that was nothing compared to what happened during face-washing and teeth-brushing. Batty, however, patiently persevered, and eventually Lydia was clean and in her polka-dotted pajamas. And still hiccoughing with occasional sobs.

Batty plumped her down onto the big-girl bed. "Do you want to talk about it?"

"Lydia doesn't like the man."

"Neither does Batty, and neither does Ben. We're all in this together." Batty held up her hand for a high five, which Lydia managed in between sobs. "Did you know that I'm going to sleep in your big-girl bed tonight?"

"*Batty's* bed?" Lydia's last sob dried up at the possibility that the new bed had after all not been meant for her.

"No, I'm just borrowing it for the night. It's your bed."

"No, no, Batty's bed," said Lydia, then pointed to the crib. "Lydia's bed."

"Okay, fine. So what do you want tonight, stories or songs?"

"Songs," said Lydia.

"Excellent choice. Songs, songs, lots and lots and lots of songs."

CHAPTER FIFTEEN
Into the Woods

THE VOICES WOKE BATTY out of a sound sleep. She couldn't figure out where she was until she saw the glowing stars—the Hound constellation—on the ceiling. Yes, of course, she was in her old bedroom, with Lydia curled up nearby in the crib. The clock said midnight, and the voices, Batty realized, were Skye's and Jeffrey's. They had to be in the upstairs hall near the top of the steps—anyone talking there could always be clearly heard in here. Batty had loved this trick of the room when she was small, listening to her father and her sisters out there, keeping her safe from loneliness and monsters.

She had a moment of wondering if she should warn Skye and Jeffrey that she was eavesdropping, but she was too comfy to get out of bed, and anyway, it didn't sound like a private conversation. First they were laughing about how Pearson had got his shirt-sleeve caught on one of Oliver's still lifes and almost pulled the whole thing down onto the birthday cake. Then they were laughing—but not as hard, because this part of the evening had been embarrassing for poor Jérôme—about how in the middle of the present-opening, as Jane chattered away in her usual broken French, trying to describe her great passion for books, Jérôme, hearing instead that her passion was for *him*, had erupted into an effusion of *amour, amour,* and more *amour*. Confusion had reigned until Molly called a friend named Lauren, who was much better at French than Jane, to handle the translation and hurt feelings.

Batty was glad to hear that Lauren had been successful, so much so that Jérôme left the birthday party to go meet her. But mostly Batty was glad she'd missed the hoopla, and rolled over to go back to sleep. She was almost dozing off again when Skye's voice cut back into her consciousness, sharper now, stripped of laughter.

"What is *that?*"

Jeffrey answered her. "What do you think it is? Your birthday present."

"That's a small box. If it's jewelry, I'll kill you."

"Skye, do you really think I'd buy you jewelry? Just open it."

Batty shifted restlessly in the bed. It was too late

now to warn them that she'd been listening, and besides, she needed to hear what happened next. If this present were about love, they were all in trouble.

But now she could relax, because Skye was laughing again.

"It's a calculator watch! I love it!"

"Water-resistant and capable not only of telling the time but of advanced mathematical calculations, according to the saleswoman," said Jeffrey.

"Thank you. I do love it, and I deeply apologize for accusing you of buying me jewelry."

"I forgive you. Notice, please, too, that this calculator watch has a sky-blue wristband to match your sky-blue eyes. But not in a romantic way, just aesthetically, you understand."

"It had better be just aesthetically, because you promised no romance. You've been fine up until now. Don't blow it."

"I know I promised, and I'm sticking to it."

Good, thought Batty. They'd gotten past the tricky part and still weren't arguing. If they could just say good night now and part, there would be no risk of Skye getting upset.

There was silence, and more silence, and Batty was almost back to sleep when Jeffrey started up again.

"It's just that it's hard for me to be with you and not want—" He paused. "You're so beautiful, you know."

"No, no, no, Jeffrey, no."

"And there's no one else? You're certain?"

"You just promised—"

"I know, but—"

"I hate this. It's like my best friend has been taken over by an alien." Skye's voice caught. "You have to go back to Boston now. I don't want you here anymore."

In Lydia's room, Batty sat up, wide awake now. *Please, please*—she sent out silent messages—*please don't go back to Boston, Jeffrey. Say that you've promised to have breakfast with me. Say anything, but don't go.*

"If I have to leave, I will," he said, and Batty softly moaned into the darkness.

"Not forever," said Skye. "Just until you calm down."

"What if I don't ever calm down? Okay, forget I said that, and I will leave tonight if you need me to. But smile for me first, Skye, so I know that you'll forgive me someday." Jeffrey waited. "No? I really can be your best friend and love you, too, you know."

"No, I don't know. Obviously you can't."

Silence again. Batty was still, frozen in place, loneliness pressing on her like a too-heavy blanket. She wished that if Jeffrey were going to leave, he'd get it over with, so that she could figure out how to make it through the next morning without singing for him.

And now he was talking again. Dumb, dumb, dumb.

"Do you ever think about falling in love? I mean, not with me necessarily, but anyone."

Skye groaned. "No, I don't. Not yet. Not now."

"Ever?"

"Jeffrey, my best friend wouldn't be torturing me like this. How many different ways do I have to explain it to you that I don't want to talk about this?"

"I just want to understand."

"You want to understand? You really want that?" Skye's voice was rising in pitch, and Batty, having a hundred times seen Skye lose her temper, could picture her now, eyes darkening and hands clenched, thumping together in frustration. "Then listen to me. This is what happens when people fall in love. They get married, right? And they're really happy and have great jobs, and then they have babies and they're still happy and love the children, and then with no warning—out of absolutely nowhere—the mother's suddenly going to have another baby even though she already has three perfectly good daughters. And that would be bearable except that it turns out she also has cancer. . . ."

"Skye, you don't need to say all this," said Jeffrey. "I'm so sorry. I'll just go now."

"But if you want to understand, I *do* need to say all this."

And maybe she did need to say it—Batty didn't know—but Batty did know that she didn't need to hear it. She knew this story already. It had a very sad ending, and she couldn't bear the way Skye was telling it. She tried to scramble away, diving underneath the covers, jamming her hands over her ears, but nothing could block that voice, so full of pain and anger.

"The mother has cancer and she's pregnant and because treating the cancer could hurt the baby, she has to make a decision. And she never asks her daughters what they think—or even her husband, for all I know—and she decides to protect the baby and let the cancer kill her. So she dies. She *died*. And in exchange—"

"Don't say it, Skye," Batty heard Jeffrey say. "Please. I know you don't mean it."

"Why wouldn't I mean it? It's true. In exchange for our dead mother, we got another sister, just what we didn't need. We got Batty."

Batty's world turned black and void of sound. If the two in the hall were still talking, she could no longer hear them. She was floating somewhere far away in a thick fog of desolation, with shreds of old explanations tumbling around, around and around, slipping away before they could be made sense of. If only she could put the shreds together properly, Batty thought, maybe the fog would lift. But try as she would, all was confusion and misery.

After a very long while—how long she didn't know—another argument started up, but this one was inside Batty's thoughts. One voice, the louder one, told her that she was a fool. Had she never considered that her mother needn't necessarily have died of cancer, not with the treatments available these days? Why, Keiko's grandmother had survived cancer, and Mr. Geiger, and Jane's French teacher. Had Batty never been smart enough to put those facts together? The other voice in her head, the quieter one, tried to say that no one had ever told her the whole truth. They'd said her mother had died of cancer, but they'd left out the part about her refusing treatment, about sacrificing herself, and about . . . about Skye being so angry.

And what of Rosalind and Jane? Were they angry, too? And her father?

No wonder her family never talked about her guilty role in Hound's death, not with this so horribly more calamitous, more tragic, death in her past.

The quiet voice wept.

Of course they're all angry, said the loud voice, scorning tears. And they thought you knew. How could you be so stupid as to not figure it out on your own?

Well, now she knew, thought Batty, both voices speaking together. But she wouldn't tell anyone that she knew. No one, not her family, not even Keiko. Her father and sisters had chosen to keep their secret, and she would keep it, too, locking it into a box and burying it deep. It was the least she could do for Skye—for everyone—for replacing the lovely woman they'd adored and lost.

●　●　●

Some secrets buried away in boxes are peacefully forgotten, just as we hope they'll be. But some refuse to stay in their boxes, popping out at the worst possible times. And then there are those—Batty's was one—that linger and fester, gnawing away from the inside out. So when she next woke up, hours before dawn and still entangled in half-remembered dreams, she at first wondered how one of Ben's rocks had gotten lodged inside her. Not until she'd shaken off sleep did she realize that it wasn't a rock—of course it wasn't—but a hard knot pressing up against her lungs, as though her insides had twisted themselves together while she slept. It was her secret, horrid and uncomfortable, and already Batty couldn't remember what it felt like not to have it there. She couldn't unremember what she'd heard in the night, what she already thought of as The Conversation. It had divided her life into two parts, a "Before Batty" and an "After Batty." The Before Batty had been young and naïve. The After Batty—she wasn't sure about her yet.

But still, she allowed the tiniest, weakest ray of light into her unhappiness. Maybe Skye had relented about Jeffrey going back to Boston in the middle of the night. Hoping, hoping, Batty swung out of bed and went down the hall to her own room. It was empty, and the bedcovers were too neat for anyone to have slept there that night. But she wasn't yet willing to give up, not until she'd gone outside to look for the little black car. If it was gone, Jeffrey was truly gone, too. She made her way past all the obstacles, the baby gates, Oliver's horrid snoring coming from the living room couch, the front door lock—

The little black car was gone.

Trembling in the pre-dawn chill, Batty sank down onto the front steps. Her eyes burned from too little sleep, the awful stomach knot squeezed in on itself, and here came that thick fog of misery, threatening to engulf her. No, no, not again.

She stood back up, determined to outrun it, to flee the hopelessness. Where could she go so early in the morning? She looked at the eastern sky, over the Ayvazians', and saw dawn hinting its arrival. Soon there would be light, even in Quigley Woods. That's where she'd go. Not in bare feet, though, and not in her pajamas printed all over with porpoises. She went into the garage, remembering a pile of old shoes and scrubby work clothes heaped in one corner, and found a pair of red rain boots only a few sizes too big, plus an old sweater of her father's. The sweater was huge on her and had holes and paint stains, but it would keep her warm, and cover some of the porpoises.

Before reaching even the cul-de-sac, Batty knew the boots were a mistake. They chafed at her bare feet and kept trying to slip off—it was like wearing buckets. But she had to keep moving—there was no peace behind her—so on she plodded into the woods, lured by the promise of privacy and by the eerie chorus of the spring peepers, those tiny frogs that sing loudest and most insistently at dawn and dusk. The peepers were too small and secretive to be spotted, but the birds swooped down to greet this early-morning human interloper, and a baby rabbit found itself sharing the path with two huge red-rubber feet previously unimaginable in its green-and-brown-wooded world.

Batty wouldn't go to her special place by the willow, not this morning. It was too forlorn and empty without Hound, and not far enough from home. But what if she crossed the creek into the wilder half of Quigley Woods? She'd been there several times under Rosalind's protection, though never on her own. The rules of Gardam Street forbade it for anyone under twelve, and those who didn't care about rules were usually discouraged by rumors of quicksand.

Today Batty didn't care about rules—or rumors, either. She followed the nearest path to the creek, then determinedly set off upstream to where it widened and ran shallow enough for fording. She could have headed downstream instead, to the small wooden bridge, which would have been safer—and had always been Rosalind's choice—but Batty wasn't in the mood for *safe*. And when she reached the shallows and waded across, she was almost pleased that the water wasn't quite shallow enough for her boots, which needed to be emptied when she reached the other side. The way on from here required climbing a hill that turned out to be steeper than it had looked, and after several slips backward, Batty took off the boots and went on with bare feet. By the time she made it to the top, her pajamas were torn and muddy, and her feet and ankles scratched, grim marks of her struggle. She didn't care.

The woods were denser and darker on this side of the creek, and the paths less defined. Sometimes there were no paths at all, just areas with slightly less underbrush. Nevertheless, Batty put her boots back on and tromped into the trees, soon surprising a red fox out for a morning amble. Neither knew who was more startled, but the fox broke eye contact first and slid away into the shadows.

Maybe because the fox was the same color as Ben's and Lydia's hair, or maybe because, in her troubles, Batty had forgotten how to be sensible, she decided to follow the forest creature. She struck out in the direction it had gone, although it was already out of sight—and whatever would she do with a fox if she managed to catch up with it? But she didn't think of that until there had been nothing that looked like a path for five minutes. And then she remembered the quicksand—that would suck her in and never let her go—and how, if it lay in wait anywhere, it would be off the paths. Forgetting the fox and also that quicksand can't actually chase people, Batty panicked, racing through the woods until she tripped over a fallen log hidden under years of dead leaves.

She thought about crying then, but managed to

fight it off by concentrating instead on standing back up, only to discover that she'd wrenched her ankle. Not so badly that she couldn't walk, but enough so that she'd never make it back down the big hill to the creek. Which really didn't matter anyway. Chasing the fox had befuddled her sense of direction, and she no longer knew how to find the hill again.

Batty looked around for something to head toward. There, over to her left, she caught a glimpse of white, far off through the trees. That was as good a choice as any. Limping, she pushed her way toward the white, which turned out to be a birch tree, then she picked a pile of gray boulders to head toward, and from there, she reached a small clearing, and on and on, until with great luck she managed to stumble upon a path that took her out of the woods and back to the real world—that is, to an unfamiliar backyard with a sliding board and battered swing set.

Batty dragged herself over to the swings and lowered herself onto the one that looked the sturdiest. It was still quite early—no one was around to mind her resting there while she figured out how to get home from wherever "here" was.

But it turned out there *was* someone there, peering at her over the top of a bush. No, wait, two someones. Batty blinked, wondering if her misery was producing double vision. But when the someones crept out to see her, they stopped being hallucinations and became a set of twins, identical in looks and dress, nervously holding hands. She recognized them now—they were kindergartners at Wildwood.

Batty realized how peculiar she must look to them, with her huge sweater and boots and her poor, wretched pajamas. And what about her hair? She reached up to check.

And with hair a gigantic mess, full of twigs and leaves, and with a face that possibly reflected the desolate truths she'd learned in the last dozen hours.

"I hope you don't mind that I sat on your swing," she said. "My ankle hurts."

"Do you live in the woods?" asked one twin.

"We're not allowed to talk to strangers," said the other.

"I'm not a real stranger. My name is Batty Penderwick, and I go to Wildwood, just like you do."

The twins turned to each other, communing wordlessly before facing Batty again.

"You're Ben's sister," said one. This seemed to make them think Batty was safe to talk to and also added to her stature in their eyes.

"He's in second grade," said the other. "And he's friends with Rafael."

"Yes, that's right," said Batty. "Do you know where we are? What your address is?"

"Massachusetts."

"Anything more? Your street?"

They didn't know their street, but they thought that their mom would know it. And also, their names were Tess and Nora, and could Batty please say hello to Ben for them when she got home? When she promised, reluctantly, they took her inside, where their mother politely hid her shock at the sudden apparition of a bedraggled fifth grader. More important, she told Batty the street address.

Now Batty knew where she was and how to get back to Gardam Street. Not through Quigley Woods—she'd only get lost again—but along the roads. It was quite a long walk, though, much too long for her in this state, especially with a sore ankle.

She had to call someone, wake up whoever it was, and expose her pathetic adventure. Not Iantha or her dad, who would need explanations she couldn't give, and not Rosalind, who would need almost as many explanations, and who, besides, probably would bring Oliver along. And not Jane, either, because if she called Jane, Skye would find out. And Batty didn't want to see Skye, or for Skye even to know anything about all this.

So when the twins' mother handed her a phone to call home, Batty pushed up the sleeve of the ancient, wrecked sweater, and instead dialed the number still written on her arm.

Ten minutes later, Batty was climbing into Nick's truck, laden with drawings Tess and Nora had made for Ben, folded up into tight little squares for privacy. Nick hadn't been happy with her when she'd called, and he wasn't happy now.

"When I said you could call me for an emergency, I didn't mean that you should create one of your own. What made you think it was a good idea to take a dawn stroll through Quigley Woods?"

"I guess I didn't really think."

"You *guess*? And you crossed the creek! Do you know how dangerous that is?"

She fought back. "Well, I didn't get stuck in quicksand!"

"Of course you didn't!" He shook his head. "I made up the quicksand a long time ago to discourage Tommy from following me."

"Then maybe it wasn't so dangerous."

"You could have broken a leg and no one would have known where to find you." He glanced at her, then went on more calmly. "Are you all right? Because you look terrible."

"My ankle hurts a little. I tripped over a log."

He pulled over the truck and made her take off the boot so that he could inspect her ankle, bending it gently this way and that. "Doesn't seem too bad. I'll give you an ice pack for it when we get back."

He started up the truck again. "Did Oliver upset you? Is that why you ran off?"

She shook her head, wishing she could pin everything on Oliver. "Don't ask me any more, okay? I don't want to talk about it."

"Whether or not you talk about it, your family is going to know something's wrong. Because it's written all over your face."

"I'll change my face!" she cried. "And they won't notice. Oliver will distract them."

"Finally, a use for Oliver." He concentrated on driving while she stared out the window at the spring morning, bleak and meaningless like everything else in her life. "Batty, I can't help being concerned about you. I've known you for too long."

"There's nothing to be concerned about."

He frowned. They both knew she wasn't telling the truth. "I'll stop asking questions if you promise to stop running around the wild parts of Quigley Woods by yourself until you're older, and I mean much older, not just eleven."

"I promise I won't cross the Quigley Woods creek by myself until I'm at least twelve."

"I guess that'll do for now." They pulled onto Gardam Street and then into the Geigers' driveway. He told her to stay where she was while he put together an ice pack for her. Staying in the truck was easy. Batty wished she could hide there for the rest of her life.

He came back with a plastic bag full of ice cubes. "Put this on your ankle, and with a little rest, you should be fine."

"Thank you, Nick. And for rescuing me."

"You're welcome. Wait, before you go, one more question. Don't give me that look. This is a good question. What do you want for your birthday?"

Her birthday! How had she managed to not consider her approaching birthday? Suddenly she couldn't bear the idea of celebrating that day in May, almost eleven years ago, when she'd come into the world and her mother had started to leave it. The birthday that was supposed to have been so much fun, a triumph of surprises, had turned into a nightmare.

The anguish that Batty had been trying to outrun caught up and took over. She slumped in her seat, and the tears she'd fought off poured out of her, buckets and rivers and oceans of tears. If only Nick would have gotten out of his truck and left her alone, she could have cried forever. But there he was still, waiting patiently.

"I'm sorry," she gulped when she could get herself under control.

"You *will* tell me what's upsetting you before you get out of this truck."

"It's nothing. I just don't want anything for my birthday. Maybe I won't even have a party." She wiped her nose and eyes with her father's holey sweater. "And don't tell anyone about this morning, or about me crying, or about anything. Please, Nick, please. Not my parents or my sisters. Nobody. Please."

Nick refused to make promises, and Batty refused to explain her tears. It was a standoff, and soon there was nothing left but for Batty to get out of his truck and sneak back into the house. She used the kitchen door and saw no one but Lydia, perched in her high chair, happily moving spoons around.

"Lydia loves Batty," she said, waving one spoon in greeting.

This got Batty crying again. She ran upstairs, stuffed the most obvious evidence—sweater, boots, the twins' drawings—into her closet, and threw herself into bed between Funty and Gibson.

CHAPTER SIXTEEN
Dreaming

DREAMING, BATTY WAS IN MAINE. Hound was chasing a flock of cardinals across the beach, bright flashes of red against gray rocks and blue water. And Skye was there, too—no, an older version of Skye whom Batty knew and yet didn't know. There! The cardinals were safely away, and Batty reached for Hound—

"Wake up, honey, please."

With a sickening lurch, she crashed awake. No ocean. No Hound. No mother.

"No," she said into her pillow.

"Batty? Are you all right?"

Batty rolled over, blinking away her sleep. The person talking to her was Rosalind, but a different Rosalind from the one Batty had last seen, the one to whom she could tell anything. All that was changed now. Batty shut her eyes tight, stuffing her sad secret back into its box, way down deep.

"Do you realize it's afternoon already? Every time we looked in on you, you were out cold. Do you feel sick?" Rosalind put her hand on Batty's forehead. "No fever."

Batty restlessly jerked her head away. "No fever."

"Your stomach?"

Batty gently kneaded her stomach. Yes, the giant knot was still there. "It's okay."

"You must be hungry, though. You slept through breakfast and lunch. Should I make a sandwich for you before I leave? Eggs and toast?"

"No, thanks. I'll get something later." She was hungry—the stomach knot hadn't affected her appetite—but first she needed to be left alone to deal with her ankle and the dirty, ripped pajamas.

"Do you know that Jeffrey went back to Boston?" Rosalind asked.

"Yes." Batty waited for Rosalind to say more, like that she knew how much Batty must mind, or simply to reassure her that everything would work out. But now Oliver appeared in the doorway, looking pointedly at his watch.

"Rosy," he said. "Time to go. Long drive back to school."

So now he was calling her Rosy. That was a name for family and close friends only. Batty had a quick fantasy of Rosalind standing up to him, telling him never to call her that again.

"Just a few more minutes, Oliver." Rosalind once again put her hand on Batty's forehead. "You're sure you're okay? I don't like going away with you not feeling well."

"I feel fine."

"We didn't get our chance to talk, I know, but I'll be home again on Saturday. Iantha's going to drive down to bring me and my stuff back," said Rosalind. "Only six days. Barely enough time for a new countdown!"

Batty tried to smile, knowing that's what Rosalind wanted.

"And then it's your birthday!"

In what was already an instinctive gesture, Batty put her hand on her stomach, trying to soothe the writhing knot. "I'm not sure I want any presents," she said.

"That's crazy," laughed Rosalind. "Of course you want presents."

"Rosy!" said Oliver.

"I've got to go, honey." Rosalind kissed her goodbye and left, taking with her Oliver, whom Batty hoped never, ever to see again for the rest of her life and beyond.

She pulled back her covers and cautiously examined her ankle. It was only a little sore, and when she stood up, she found she could walk normally. This was a big relief. Limping would have made it hard to keep her morning misadventure a secret. She also needed to get rid of the ice pack, but that was easy. She emptied it out the window—by now it was only water—and threw the plastic bag into the closet to join the sweater and boots. Her pajamas were a bigger problem. Dirt could be washed out, but the rips were gaping, far beyond Batty's small mending skills. Briefly she considered taking them to Jane for repair, but she'd have to make up a story to explain how they'd gotten that way, and lying wouldn't make her feel any better about herself. The pajamas went into the closet, too.

Anything else? Socks would cover the telltale scratches on her feet and ankles until they healed. But wait, those drawings from Tess and Nora! If Batty didn't hand them over to Ben, and then those twins approached him with a story about his sister appearing in their backyard with leaves in her hair, he would go berserk. Batty had to give Ben the drawings, along with some sort of an explanation, and bind him to secrecy. She would call a MOPS.

The tradition of the MOPS, originally standing for "Meeting of the Penderwick Sisters," had been started long ago by the three oldest sisters. Batty had attended plenty of these as she grew up, and so had Ben, although when he was added to the family, "Sisters" had been changed to "Siblings" to accommodate his boy-ness. A MOPS was always a private meeting, with built-in rules about honor and secrecy. Secrecy! Batty was thoroughly sick of secrecy.

Taking the drawings with her, she snuck to the bathroom, hoping a shower and clean clothes would give her the sense of a fresh start. And afterward, when she scrutinized her face in the mirror, she couldn't find any traces of her new burden. Maybe she could pull this off. Holding her head high, she went downstairs to test out this new Batty—"After Batty"—on the family.

Parents first, she decided, and found them in their study, peacefully preparing for the coming week at work.

"You're up!" said Iantha. "How are you, sweetie? Feeling okay?"

"I'm good. Hungry."

"Hungry is excellent." Her father got up from behind his desk. "Plenty of quesadillas in the fridge. I'll reheat some for you."

"I can do it, Daddy. Honest."

And she fled, because right now that was all she could handle. Cursing herself for weakness, she pressed onward. Next up was Skye, not by Batty's choice, but because there she was at the dining room table, under the shadow of Oliver's absurd still lifes, and working on her computer. She looked sad but was wearing the calculator watch Jeffrey had given her. That was something, Batty supposed.

"Hi." Batty stopped beside Skye's chair. She had to get this over with sometime.

"Hi." And Skye glanced up, one second, two seconds, then bent over her work again.

That done—and who *cares* if Skye is sad, thought

223

Batty—she soldiered on, into the kitchen for the quesadillas. She got down two of them, and the food propped her up enough that she hardly noticed when Jane breezed through looking for pretzels. Now to tackle Ben about the twins. She went outside, hunting for him.

She heard him before she saw him, from somewhere behind the hydrangeas.

"You can play with the Chinook," he said. "And this is the sound it makes: *schwoof, schwoof*."

"*Schwoof, schwoof, schwoof*."

Batty peered through the stalks. Good grief, it was Lydia back there, waving Ben's Chinook in the air. Ben never, ever let her play with his action figures.

"Lydia, are you bothering Ben?" she asked.

Ben answered, with a shade of embarrassment, "No, she's okay. The Chinook is already missing some rotor blades. I won't let her touch the Black Hawk."

"Lydia is the army," said Lydia.

Batty's surprise at this cooperation between her two younger siblings must have shown in her expression, because Ben offered an explanation.

"You know, the quesadilla smashed on Oliver," he said. "Plus that Spanish thing she yelled at him."

"*No me gusta*," said Lydia obligingly.

"It was cool." Ben beamed proudly. "When Oliver left, neither Lydia or I said good-bye. I thought you'd want to be there not to say good-bye, too, but Rosalind said you were still in bed. Why were you in bed all day, anyway? Everybody thought you were sick, and I called Rafael and he said maybe you were bitten by a tsetse fly and dying of sleeping sickness."

Batty pushed her way through the bushes and sat down with them. "You can see that I'm not dying. Anyway, there are no tsetse flies in Massachusetts."

"Are you sure?" Ben was used to her being healthy. Except for that time a few years ago when she'd gone into the hospital to have her tonsils out—he hadn't liked that at all.

"Yes, I'm sure. We learned about them in science." They'd studied bugs that March. Vasudev had done his report on tsetse flies, glorying in the details of their lethal bite. Keiko had chosen crickets, and Batty, ladybugs. Strange, she thought, how that ladybug report seemed to have happened a very long time ago. Right, because that had happened to Before Batty.

"Then why did you sleep so much? You missed lunch and everything."

"I'll explain, but I have to call a MOPS, but just us. No Skye or Jane."

"Then it's not a MOPS," said Ben. Among the MOPS rules was one about not leaving people out.

"You're right. But since it's just for you and me, and Lydia, since she's here, I guess we could call it a Meeting of the Younger Penderwick Siblings. A MOYPS."

"What can you tell me that you can't tell Skye and Jane?" asked Ben, suspicious.

"I can't tell you until we swear secrecy. Obviously."

"This better not be about dying, because you already said you weren't. Anyway, Lydia doesn't know how to do the swearing part. Or how to keep secrets."

"We'll teach her the swearing part, and I'm not worried about her and secrets. Nothing she repeats ever makes sense," said Batty. "Lydia, put down the Chinook and face this way. Good. MOYPS come to order."

"Second the motion," said Ben with a marked lack of enthusiasm.

"All swear to keep secret what we say here, even from the parents, and also from the older sisters." Batty made her right hand into a fist and held it out toward Ben, who put his fist on top of hers. "Now you, Lydia. Make a fist."

It took a while to persuade Lydia to make a fist and then, once she'd made it, not to punch it in the air like a winning athlete—no one knew where she'd learned *that*—but eventually her little hand ended up on top of the pile, and Batty and Ben could chant the oath.

"This I swear, by the Penderwick Family Honor," they said, then broke apart the fist pile.

"Here's why I slept late," said Batty. "I woke up really early this morning, took a walk in Quigley Woods, got lost, hurt my ankle a little bit but it's much better now, found a way out of the woods, called Nick, he picked me up in his truck, and I came home and went to sleep again. The end. Except there were these twins—"

Ben interrupted her. "You're going too fast. Why did you get up so early?"

Batty hadn't counted on questions. How could she possibly explain her pre-dawn madness? "I had a lot on my mind."

"Like what?"

"Like—" She picked up the Chinook and flew it around for a while, but her thoughts weren't coming together. "Ben, do you ever think about your dad, you know, not Daddy, but the one whose genes you have?"

"Jeans." Lydia pointed to Ben's denim-encased legs.

"*Genes*, not jeans," said Ben.

"*Jeans*," repeated Lydia happily.

"No, Lydia, you don't understand," said Ben. "My first father died in a car accident before I was born, and then Mom and Dad got married and Dad adopted me. And I do think about my first father. Mom's told me lots of stories about him."

"Right." Batty used putting the Chinook down—slowly, carefully—to get control of the tears that threatened to spill.

"Why are we talking about my dad? And what's wrong with your stomach? You keep touching it like this." Ben put his hand on his own stomach, where his knot would be if he had one.

"Nothing's wrong with my stomach." Batty sat on her hand to keep it from betraying her. "So I was lost in Quigley Woods, hurt my ankle, and called Nick to come get me, and there were these twins."

"*Twins*." Lydia loved this game.

But Ben was still trying to catch up. "How did you know Nick's number?"

"He gave it to me." Batty rolled up her sleeve to show him. "In case we needed help with Oliver."

"Oh." Ben really wanted Nick's number written on his arm, too.

"So there were these twins"—Batty paused to let Lydia say "twins" again, but this time she just stared, unheedingly—"named Tess and Nora, and, Ben, they know you."

"Me?"

Batty got the twins' drawings out of her pocket and handed them to Ben, who laboriously unfolded them. "What are these *hearts*?"

"*Hearts*," said Lydia gaily. She'd gotten hold of the Dexter (also known as Spike) action figure and was having him climb up the side of the house.

"And is this supposed to be you?" He handed one of them back to Batty.

The drawing indeed contained lots of red hearts and lots of flowers, plus one unattractive stick figure with wild hair, huge boots, and BATI written beside it.

"Yes, that's me. I looked a little strange. And I don't know why there are hearts. Maybe she likes you."

"There are hearts on the other one, too. How can they like me? I don't even know them."

Batty thought of Keiko and Ryan the movie star. "It happens sometimes."

"Here, Lydia, you can tear these up if you want to."

Ben passed the drawings to Lydia, who jabbed them to pieces with Dexter and buried the results under a rock.

"Okay, good," said Batty. "Thus ends the MOYPS."

"What?" Ben protested. "We're done? This was the weirdest meeting ever."

"I'm sorry, Ben. It's the best I can do right now."

This time the dream was about school. Nick was visiting the fifth grade to explain that book report charts were an accurate measure of one's inner worthiness. The class gave three cheers for Ginevra and her inner worthiness and three boos for Batty, who Nick said had the worthiness of a worm. When Batty tried to stand up for herself—but mostly for worms, because worms were as worthy as anyone else—Nick interrupted to announce that they would now sing "The Itsy Bitsy Spider," in French, which everyone but Batty could speak.

Halfway through the song, Batty managed to fight her way out of French spiders and into wakefulness, which at first presented another confusion, since she wasn't in her own room, but in Lydia's. And then she remembered that Lydia had pleaded for her to stay another night, in the apparent belief that she would be able to hold on to the safety of the crib as long as Batty slept in the big-girl bed.

So here Batty was again, awake while everyone else in the house slept, just like she'd been the night before, or actually that morning, or—she looked at the clock and it was almost two a.m.—since this was morning again, that had been *yesterday* morning. With all these extra wakings and sleepings, she was losing track of which day was what.

"This is very early Monday morning," she told herself. "Which means I need to get back to sleep so I can get up again in five hours to get ready for school."

Sleep, however, was not so easily bidden. Not after bad dreams and not with the awful ache in her middle. Batty let her gaze drift around the room, hoping for distraction from her woes. The Hound constellation, Lydia on her back, clutching Baby Zingo in one arm and Jeffrey's pink rabbit in the other, a duck night-light casting strange shadows across the walls and onto the framed photographs on Lydia's dresser. One photograph showed Lydia's class at Goldie's, with a beaming Lydia surrounded by her friends Tzina, Jordy, Gradie, and Lucy. A second was of Asimov trying to remove the doll's sweater Lydia had just put onto his head. And a third—Batty got out of bed to look more closely at this one, her favorite of the three—was from when Lydia was only a week old. Still just a tiny lump of person, she was being held up to the camera by Iantha. They were in the front yard, under the maple tree, and the sun was shining and Iantha was smiling and her red hair was blowing. Batty leaned in and looked more closely, noticing something she never had before. What was that, just where the picture went into the frame? She turned on the bureau lamp for more light. Why, it was a hand. And though it was only a hand, cut off at the wrist, Batty suddenly remembered that day, and how she'd been standing off to one side, waving at the new baby. It was her own hand.

She turned off the light and turned away then, her stomach throbbing. Stupid girl, she told herself, to be upset because she'd been left out of a photo. She'd been left out of plenty of photos before.

"And I've been in plenty, too," she told the room.

Batty waited, listening, but the room offered nothing back, not from the sleeping Lydia, the duck light, or even from the Hound constellation.

"All right, I'll prove it to you."

She turned off the bureau light and made her way downstairs to her parents' study. There were her father's bookshelves, crammed with hundreds of biology texts with impossible titles, and way up, at the end of the top shelf, was a box. To reach that high, she dragged over a chair, and even with the chair, she had to stretch up on her toes. There were a few seconds of uncertainty, the box wobbling at the tip of her outstretched fingers, but Batty's determination won out, and soon she and the box were down on the floor, sitting in a pool of light cast by her father's desk lamp.

PICTURES. That's what was written on the lid. More recent family photographs—ones taken since Iantha's arrival—were neatly stored in albums. The opposite of those albums, this box was a delirious jumble of the four sisters' years before Iantha. Batty had looked through it several months earlier for pictures of Hound, especially for that perfect one she remembered but had probably made up. But tonight she was looking for something different, though what it was she wasn't exactly sure.

She dove in, at first scanning each picture carefully, leaping higgledy-piggledy from one year to another, summer to winter, Christmas to Fourth of July, first days of school to last. Many of the pictures did include her—Batty with paint on her face in kindergarten, Batty dressed as a clam for the third-grade play, Batty with Hound and Funty in the red wagon.

"See that?" she said to herself. "You weren't always left out."

But something kept her digging into the box, though after a while, she went more quickly—she was getting tired and there were so many pictures. And maybe she wearied of seeing her mother with Rosalind, her mother with Skye, her mother with Jane—but wait, here was one of Hound as a puppy. Batty held it up for a long look, just as she'd done the last time through the box. In the photo, Hound was still so tiny that Skye could hold him in her arms—a young and pigtailed Skye clutching him and beaming. Then, just like the last time, Batty decided she wouldn't take this one up to her room. It belonged to Skye, not Batty, if Skye ever wanted it.

Batty went even more quickly now, past vacation pictures, sports pictures, on and on, until there, at almost the bottom of the box, finally, she found what she now knew she'd come looking for. A photograph of her mother in a hospital bed, looking so thin and weak that the resemblance to Skye was almost gone. But she was smiling and proudly cuddling the baby who had been brought into the world at such a great price. Who was to say if the price had been too great? Batty, alone in the night, staring at the only photograph she'd ever seen of herself with her mother, couldn't know. And she had no one to ask.

Exhaustion swooped in and she needed to return to bed before falling asleep right there on the floor. Batty piled the pictures back into the box, except for the most precious one—that was hers now—and maneuvered the box back onto its high shelf, and the chair back to her father's desk. She would leave the study just as she'd found it, so that no one would know she'd been searching. Then she took the purloined photograph upstairs to her room, and slid it under Hound's canvas bag at the back of her closet. Another secret, carefully hidden.

She was caught as she left her room to go back to Lydia's. Ben, who could usually sleep through anything, must have heard her, because suddenly there he was in the hall, only half awake.

"What are you doing?" he asked.

"Nothing. Go back to bed."

"You're sleepwalking, aren't you?" Ben's look of alarm filled her with guilt. "Maybe you do have that tsetse fly thing after all."

"Ben, don't be silly. I'm fine, really I am."

"But—"

"Go back to bed. Now."

His face scrunched with concern, Ben disappeared back into his room.

CHAPTER SEVENTEEN
Silence

Bᴇɴ ʜᴀᴅ ɴᴇᴠᴇʀ ʙᴇꜰᴏʀᴇ seen someone sleepwalk, and now that he'd caught Batty doing it, he definitely didn't like it. As confused as he'd been about her Quigley Woods adventure, at least that had been within normal behavior. Sleepwalking wasn't. He went back to bed hoping that when he saw her in the morning, she would laugh and tell him it had been a joke. But the Batty he ate breakfast with was pale and sleepy and not in the mood for jokes. Both parents asked how she felt and she said fine, but Ben didn't believe her. And then when he tried to bring up sleepwalking on their way to school, she said she didn't want to talk about it. So they talked about nothing.

Ben fretted over it all through school on Monday—except during the exciting touch football game at recess—and decided to discuss it with Rafael. He waited until the end of the day, when they were waiting for Batty outside the big Wildwood front doors.

"You know how Batty slept so much yesterday? I caught her sleepwalking last night."

"Definitely sleeping sickness," said Rafael.

"No, because the right flies don't live in Massachusetts. Uh-oh." Here came two little girls who looked exactly alike. Ben took hold of Rafael and dragged him across the sidewalk and into the middle of a cluster of sixth graders.

"What are we doing?" asked Rafael. Usually they avoided sixth graders, especially these extra-big ones.

"An evasive maneuver." Ben wished he could explain the twins to Rafael, but they were tied up with stuff he'd sworn to keep secret at the MOYPS. He risked a glance backward through the sixth graders. The twins had disappeared. No, there they were, getting onto a bus. Whew.

"Alpha-Lima-India-Echo-November-Sierra?" whispered Rafael.

Ben didn't think it was a big stretch to call those twins aliens. "Yes, but they're gone now."

He pulled Rafael back to the safety of a sixth-grader-free zone. There were several fourth graders nearby, but not big ones, so that was okay.

"What did they look like?" asked Rafael. "Blobs or tentacles? Or like robots?"

236

"Who?"

"The aliens."

"Oh, you know." Ben wanted to get back to the oddness of Batty. "So, it can't be sleeping sickness. And she keeps putting her hand on her stomach."

"Maybe she has a hernia," said Rafael. "My uncle Albert had a hernia and needed an operation."

"It's not a hernia." Ben had never heard of a hernia—she couldn't have that.

"Maybe a giant stomach tumor, then. Or maybe she has an alien implantation!"

"*Who* has an alien implantation?"

Ben jumped. Somehow Batty had snuck up behind them. He'd dropped his guard once those twins got onto their bus.

"Well, obviously not you," he answered. "Rafael, tell her it's not her."

Rafael was too busy staring at Batty. "How *are* you?" he asked.

She frowned at them both. "I'm fine, and everybody better stop asking, if they know what's best for them."

"Sorry," said Ben, though he wasn't, because she didn't look any better than she had that morning, maybe even worse.

"Sorry," said Rafael, though he wasn't, either, because he thought Batty looked terrible, and he was very curious as to which mysterious disease she might be suffering from.

"That's better. Now let's go, Ben."

• • •

The walk home was even quieter than the one in the morning. Batty didn't ask Ben about how his day went, or what Ms. Lambert had taught his class, or even about his homework. He hated it. And as soon as he got home, he ran across the street looking for male companionship, particularly with a male who wouldn't talk about sisters having alien implantations.

Ben found just what he needed behind the Geigers' house: Nick working out with weights.

"Can I do it, too?" he begged.

"You're too young for weight training." Nick put down the forty-five-pound dumbbell he'd been using for bicep curls.

"But I'm strong." Ben leaned down to grab the dumbbell with one hand but could just barely lift it off the ground. When he tried with two hands, Nick took it away from him.

"If you touch that again, I'll have you running laps until you're in the fourth grade."

Being scolded by Nick was somehow more fun than being praised by anyone else. Content, Ben sat on the grass and watched as Nick went through his workout. The very last part was push-ups, and for a special treat, he did them with Ben sitting on his back, proudly pretending to be an army pack crammed with gear.

"Enough," said Nick finally, tumbling Ben onto the grass. "So what's the news in Penderwick land?"

"Batty doesn't have sleeping sickness, like Rafael thought."

"I'm glad to hear it. Why did Rafael think that?"

"Because she slept for so long yesterday." Ben thought for a minute about the nature of the MOYPS secrecy oath he'd taken, and decided that he didn't have to keep secret what Nick already knew. "But you know why she slept so long—because she was in Quigley Woods and hurt her ankle. Her ankle is better now."

"That's good."

"But she's acting weird. Different. And she was sleepwalking last night."

Nick picked up his dumbbell and started lifting again. "Maybe she's worried about something."

"But what?" The MOYPS hadn't explained anything at all. "You know my father's dead, right? My first father, not Dad."

"Yeah, I know that."

"That's what I told Batty, that everybody already knows."

"Huh," said Nick, and switched his dumbbell to the other hand. "Just keep a watch on her. Consider it collecting data, what we in the military call intel."

"Intel." Ben liked that word.

"Not that you're spying on her, because you and she are on the same side. It's more like you're on a reconnaissance mission, keeping the area safe for your unit."

"Only Batty is my area." Ben liked this idea. "And I can report to you."

"If you discover anything you need help with, report to me. In fact, promise me you will."

"I promise. And now I need your phone number, too."

"Oh-ho! You know about that, do you?"

"Yes, and I want it on my stomach, not my arm, so that no one else can see it."

Nick laughed, but he went inside and came back with a pen. Ben found that having his stomach written on tickled, but he bore it like a soldier.

"It's upside down," he said when Nick finished.

So Nick wrote it again, but this time upside down so that it was right side up for Ben. "Anything else?"

"Tommy's number?"

"Why not?" Nick wrote Tommy's number, too. "Anything *else*? The phone number for the secretary of defense, maybe? Or the woman I'm taking to dinner tonight?"

"No, thanks." Ben looked happily at his stomach.

"And how was school today for you?"

"Good. We played football at recess. But then after school some twins showed up."

"The twins I saw yesterday when I picked up Batty? The ones who made drawings for you?"

"Did you see those drawings? They had hearts and flowers all over them."

Nick whistled. "Maybe the twins like you."

"I don't want them to like me."

"Just tell them you already have a girlfriend. Remy, right?"

"No!" He couldn't believe it. Even Nick thought this awful thing about him. "Remy isn't my girlfriend!"

"Sorry." Nick did look sorry. "I can remember the time when I, too, would have been horrified. These days, I'm delighted when women draw hearts for me."

"Well, I'm not delighted. No way."

"This is not a big problem. If the twins bother you, tell them, 'I'm sure you're nice people—'"

"I'm *not* sure they're nice people!"

"You don't have to be sure. You're just softening the blow," explained Nick. "Repeat after me: 'I'm sure you're nice people, but I'm not interested in developing a relationship with you.'"

Although Ben felt that so tame a statement would be powerless against crazed females, he obediently repeated it until it rolled off his tongue. Then he asked Nick to teach him a few military self-defense moves, just in case Tess and Nora got too aggressive.

"No, I will not," he answered. "Use words instead."

"Then could you teach me to jump out of a Black Hawk?"

"Do you see a helicopter here in the backyard? Because I don't." But Nick picked up Ben and threw him out of a "helicopter" a half dozen times. "Enough? Because you're beginning to wear me out, and I thought that was impossible."

"One more time," pleaded Ben, who'd landed in a different country each time and had a few more he wanted to try.

"No more times, but we can shoot hoops if you want to."

Ben did want to, even more than he wanted extra jumps, so they went into the garage for the basketball. Just before they got started playing, Ben thought of another thing that had been bothering him about Batty.

"She's quiet now," he told Nick.

"What do you mean? Like not talking?"

"Yeah, she doesn't talk much." Ben thought for a while. "And she's not humming at all."

"Huh," said Nick, and tossed the ball through the net.

Batty knew she wasn't humming. Her sprite had deserted her, been driven out, vanished, since The Conversation, the one that echoed over and over through Batty's memory. *In exchange for our dead mother, our dead mother, our dead mother, we got Batty, Batty, Batty, just what we didn't need, didn't need, didn't need.*

She was taking Duchess and Cilantro on an extra-long walk through Quigley Woods, her escape from home and the pretense of not being thoroughly unhappy. If she'd hoped that her sprite would be waiting for her in here—and she hadn't quite dared to—she'd been mistaken. Batty had nothing inside her now but regular old human parts, plus a painful knot that gave no indication of wanting to leave.

Cilantro whined and snuffled at her, as though he'd sensed her misery.

"I'm okay," she reassured him, though she knew dogs could always spot a lie.

Maybe she had to encourage her sprite to return, lure it back with music. Batty had never felt less like singing, but maybe the singing would make her feel better. It was worth a try.

"Sit," she said to the dogs, neither of whom did. But at least for this one moment they weren't pulling on their leashes. "Good enough, I guess. Keep it up. I'm going to sing now."

She planted her feet, stood up straight, took deep breaths, and—broke off, horrified at the dreadful rasping noise she'd made. So it wasn't just that her sprite had gone, it had taken Batty's very voice along with it, to who knew where and for how long. Forever? She sank onto the ground beside the dogs, overwhelmed with this new grief, piled on top of her already impossible burden of sorrow.

So now what was she if not a singer? Batty no longer knew.

Cilantro pressed up against her, showing his concern.

"It's just that my voice is gone," she told him. "You'll still like me even if I can't sing, won't you?"

While Cilantro seemed okay with that, Duchess gave out a low whine, then barked.

"You can still sing on your own, Duchess," Batty told her. "Whoa, calm down."

For it seemed that Batty's lack of singing wasn't the problem. Some scent or another had gotten Duchess's attention, and she was ignoring Batty, straining against her harness to get at whatever it was. Her excitement stirred up Cilantro, who went into a crouch, tuba-ing his distress.

Batty gathered up the voice Nick had tried to teach her. "Duchess, stop it! I mean it! Sit!"

This time Duchess glanced at Batty, but with a look that meant she had no intention of sitting—now or maybe ever—then suddenly went rigid. The scent had done something marvelous. Duchess pulled toward it. Batty pulled back. Duchess pulled again, harder, and this time pulled herself right out of her harness.

For Batty, it seemed as though the whole forest went silent, waiting to see what would happen next. Hardly breathing herself, she crept slowly toward Duchess, hoping that the little dog hadn't yet realized she was free. It was a vain hope. After an apologetic bark, Duchess gaily dashed off into the trees, determined to follow the scent, and all the scents—rabbits, foxes, bears!—to the ends of the earth. The ends of the earth came soon enough, what with Duchess's ridiculously short legs, and even with Cilantro trying to pull Batty in the wrong direction. In those few short moments, though, Batty started to cry, and by the time she'd tackled Duchess and was rolling on the ground with her, both of them tangled in Cilantro's leash, she was sobbing. No one was safe with her. Not dogs, not people.

"What would I have done if I'd lost you, Duchess? The Ayvazians would never have forgiven me."

A contrite Duchess licked away the tears and Cilantro tuba-ed his sympathy until Batty had cried herself out. She hooked Duchess's leash to her collar—she couldn't risk the harness again—untangled Cilantro, and stood up. Time to take the dogs back before she messed up anything else.

The Ayvazians, rather than being upset with Duchess's near escape, were delighted.

"She got out of her harness? That fat dog slid right out of it?" Mr. Ayvazian was so impressed, he bent way down to give Duchess a hug and an extra biscuit.

"Don't you see what this means?" Mrs. Ayvazian asked Batty. "That means she's lost a great deal of weight. You've done such a good job with her!"

"We'll buy a smaller harness tomorrow," said Mr. Ayvazian, and gave Duchess yet another biscuit, and two to Cilantro.

"Stop feeding her, Harvey," said Mrs. Ayvazian. "Batty, come into the kitchen and bring the dogs with you before Duchess has gained back all her weight."

In the kitchen, the dogs rushed to the corner where the Ayvazians kept two water bowls, for moments like this when Duchess and Cilantro were both thirsty.

"Mrs. Ayvazian, you're really not angry at me?" asked Batty.

"Why would I be angry at you? It was our fault for not noticing that the harness had gotten too big."

"But maybe I can't be trusted. Maybe I shouldn't walk Duchess anymore."

"You would break Duchess's heart. Your walks are her favorite part of the day. Have a cookie."

The cookies were large and cinnamon-y, and Batty was glad for them, and glad for an excuse to duck her head away from Mrs. Ayvazian's scrutiny.

"Are you feeling all right, dear?"

"Oh, yes." Batty smiled to prove it, hoping her eyes weren't still red from weeping. "May I take some cookies home for Ben and Lydia?"

"That's a nice idea." Mrs. Ayvazian piled cookies into a paper bag.

"Mrs. Ayvazian, you've lived here for a long time, right?"

"Thirty-four years."

"So you remember my mother? Not Iantha, I mean my birth mother."

"Of course I do. She was lovely. Skye looks so much like her, you know."

"Yes."

"Though Jane has more of her personality, I think. Always laughing." Mrs. Ayvazian put a few more cookies into the bag. "Take these for Skye and Jane, too. Never too old for cookies, right?"

"Right."

"I always looked forward to Halloween when your

sisters were little. One year your mother dressed them as the Three Little Pigs. And once, as the Three Musketeers, with plumed hats and tinfoil swords. They loved those swords."

"Three Little Maids from School!" called Mr. Ayvazian from the living room.

"Oh, yes! That was the year she had them in kimonos and had tried to teach them the song and to wave fans around. Rosalind sang the song as best she could." Mrs. Ayvazian sang a few lines for Batty. " 'Three little maids from school are we. Pert as a schoolgirl well can be.' But Skye refused to sing because she'd broken her fan, and Jane, who must have been only three, wanted to sing 'Twinkle, Twinkle, Little Star' instead."

I would have liked a tinfoil sword, or a kimono, thought Batty dully.

"Are you sure you're all right?" Mrs. Ayvazian put her hand on Batty's forehead. "Do you have a fever?"

"No fever." Batty smiled again. "Just a lot of homework to do. Thanks for the cookies, Mrs. Ayvazian."

"You're welcome, and I'll see you tomorrow."

Batty got Cilantro out of the house before she started crying again.

That night, Batty went to Lydia's room to say good night and to tell Lydia that once again she'd spend the night there. To her parents, Batty had said it was for Lydia's sake, but Batty knew that she was the sister most in need of comfort.

"So that's great, right?" she asked Lydia. "That I'll sleep in your big-girl bed?"

"Batty's bed."

"I really am just borrowing it."

"Sing," said Lydia.

"No singing. Stories tonight."

"Sing," said Lydia again. "Itsy bitsy."

Batty wrapped her fingers in Lydia's curls—so soft they were, so springy and sweet. And Lydia was looking at her with such trust.

"I'll try. " She swallowed hard. "The itsy bitsy spi—"

But it was just as bad as earlier, maybe worse. Lydia reached up to touch Batty's lips, as if making sure they still belonged to a human being.

"Frog," she said. "Again."

"I can't. I'm sorry." With great effort, Batty kept back the tears. She would *not* cry in front of Lydia. "I'll tell you a story instead. Once upon a time—"

"There was Princess Dandelion Fire."

"Once upon a time—"

"Lydia was the princess!"

Weakened, smashed on the shoals of life, drawn as fine as spun glass, Batty pulled herself together for one final attempt of the day.

"Once upon a time, there was a Princess Dandelion Fire named Lydia. . . ."

CHAPTER EIGHTEEN
Beethoven

WHEN BATTY KNOCKED on Mrs. Grunfeld's door the next day at recess, she was determined not to cry.

"Welcome!" cried Mrs. Grunfeld, opening the door. "And how was your weekend with your *mentore?*"

Batty started to cry. She stumbled to the piano bench and cried and cried, and when Mrs. Grunfeld handed over tissues and hugged her, Batty cried more.

"I've lost my singing voice," she finally managed to say.

"Lost it? In what way?"

Batty croaked out a few words of "The Itsy Bitsy Spider," then started crying again.

"You have a sore throat?"

Batty shook her head. "No, it's not that."

Mrs. Grunfeld gently massaged Batty's throat. "No swollen glands."

"No." Batty shook her head again.

Mrs. Grunfeld now held her at arm's length and inspected Batty's face with great attention. "Perhaps you'd better tell me about your weekend."

Batty told her as much as she could, leaving out, of course, The Conversation. Even without it, it was a sad tale.

"Your Jeffrey abandoned you," said Mrs. Grunfeld when Batty had finished.

"Yes, I know. Though it wasn't completely his fault. My sister made him leave."

"He could have stood up to her. Teenage boys are not the most reliable of creatures."

"He used to be," said Batty sadly. "What if he doesn't want to be my *mentore* anymore?"

"Has he told you that? No. Until then, you must not be concerned. Anyway, one doesn't need a *mentore* to sing. One needs only the talent and the will, and you have both."

"But my voice!"

"Yes, let's see about that. Stand up and breathe for me. Deep breaths." Mrs. Grunfeld watched as Batty breathed. "Fill your lungs all the way to their bottom."

Batty tried to fill her lungs—oh, how she tried— but when she got to the bottom of her lungs, there was that knot in her stomach, pressing up against them.

"That's the best I can do! Oh, Mrs. Grunfeld!" And here she was, crying yet again.

250

Mrs. Grunfeld didn't fuss, which helped greatly. She simply handed Batty another tissue and said, "Now you see how unhappiness can affect our breathing. Try again; take in a breath slowly, slowly—that's right, relax, think only of your breathing—yes, that's better."

And Batty indeed felt the tension ease up a tiny bit. Not enough, though, not nearly enough. "I can't stand this," she said.

"Yes, you can stand it, because you must," said Mrs. Grunfeld. "Let's not even try to sing today. Instead, we'll discuss the rhythm of breathing—how different singers choose when to take a breath. Does that sound interesting? Yes? Then let us begin with a song of great yearning, written by Anthony Newley and Leslie Bricusse. I will speak the song line by line, you will repeat what you hear, including the breathing. After that we will listen to how Mr. Newley sings his song. Are you ready?"

"Yes."

"'Who can I turn to—'" Mrs. Grunfeld nodded at Batty. "Now you."

But Batty had started to cry again. Mrs. Grunfeld wrapped her arms around the sobbing girl and kept hold of her for a long time.

When Batty got home after school, Jane said that a large box had come for her in the mail and was waiting on the kitchen counter. Batty's first inclination was to turn around and leave again, hoping the box would disappear on its own while she walked Duchess and Cilantro. It was sure to be a birthday present from someone, and the closer Batty got to her birthday, the more it horrified her. However, the box would still be sitting there when she got back. Besides, this one might possibly be from Aunt Claire, Uncle Turron, Marty, and Enam. While she didn't deserve a present from them any more than from anyone else, sometimes Marty and Enam drew pictures of tigers and turtles on the outsides of packages, and that would be nice to see.

But the return address was Jeffrey's.

Tentative, she touched it, then pulled back. Did she really want anything from Jeffrey right now?

The doorbell rang, and Jane was letting people into the house—Batty heard Artie and both Donovans. In a minute Jane would be in here looking for pretzels and asking what was in the box and when Batty was going to open it, and if Batty did open it, Jane would want to discuss Jeffrey's present, and then maybe Skye would come in, too. Batty picked up the box—it took both hands—and ran upstairs with it to her room.

Asimov was waiting for her, stretching and yawning in his spot between Funty and Gibson, and wondering what all the fuss was about. He wondered more as Batty struggled to get through the layers of tape Jeffrey had used to secure the box. Then came the opening of the box, and the digging through the crumpled newspaper used for cushioning, and then—

there were two smaller packages inside, each covered with gift wrap and, again, lots of tape. Each had a note attached. The note on the larger one, which was shaped exactly like record albums, said OPEN ME FIRST. The note on the smaller one, shaped something like a book, said OPEN ME SECOND.

Another struggle with tape, and Batty revealed the bounty inside OPEN ME FIRST. It was indeed record albums, a pristine set still in its original box and plastic wrapping. Batty traced with her fingers the words on the cover: LUDWIG VAN BEETHOVEN, 9 SYMPHONIEN, BERLINER PHILHARMONIKER, HERBERT VON KARAJAN.

"Von Karajan!" Batty told Asimov.

Jeffrey had once wanted to be an orchestra conductor—long ago, when he first met the Penderwicks. He'd since moved on from that, saying that while a conductor couldn't make music without a whole bunch of musicians agreeing to be conducted, a pianist needed only his piano. But he'd retained his fascination with the breed and had taught Batty about the famous ones, Bernstein and Muti, Klemperer and Previn, Solti and Ozawa, and about this very Herbert von Karajan, one of the twentieth-century greats.

This had to be an old recording—decades and decades old. Batty marveled at how such a treasure could stay untouched for so many years, waiting for someone to release its magic.

Jeffrey had taped—lightly, thank goodness!— a card to the box. The picture was of a cat playing the piano, which Batty liked very much, although

Asimov swatted at it when she showed him. But the note inside was even better.

> *Battikins: Some consider this the finest recording ever of the symphonies. We'll listen to it together (especially the <u>Eroica,</u> which you know is my favorite) someday when—um, you know— I'm allowed back into the fold. Until then, Happy Birthday from Ludwig, Herbert, and Jeffrey. P.S. Fine <u>mentore</u> I've turned out to be, missing our breakfast. Hope you can forgive me.*

"I do forgive you," she breathed.

But wait, what about the second package?

She groped around the bed and found it, buried under the wrapping paper from the symphonies. This one had its card on the outside, taped underneath OPEN ME SECOND. Another cat, another piano—Batty didn't bother showing this one to Asimov—and another note.

> *Do you remember giving this to me on <u>my</u> eleventh birthday? A long time ago—you were only four. Because it was your favorite photo, you said that maybe I'd let you "borrow it back" someday. This seems like the right day to me. Yours, Jeffrey.*

Trembling, Batty ripped away the wrapping. It wasn't a book—she was almost certain, because she was starting to remember. Yes, she was right. It was a framed photograph, the one she'd been looking for everywhere, the one—it came back to her now—that she'd kept beside her bed when she was small, until she'd given it away to Jeffrey.

Hound.

That evening after dinner, Ben put the final touch on Minnesota, gluing a final Monopoly hotel to St. Paul. It was due the next day, and Ben couldn't wait to show it off. His would be the best state in the second grade, except for Rafael's, whose Florida would be just as good, because best friends don't compete with each other.

There was this problem, though: Minnesota now held so many rocks that Ben could no longer pick it up by himself. Actually, he hadn't been able to pick it up since gluing on the Sawtooth Mountains. Batty had told him that she'd help him carry it to school, but Ben thought he'd better remind her.

Her bedroom door was closed and loud music was blasting through—classical music played by an entire orchestra. He knocked hard, and then harder, but when she didn't answer, he tried pushing the door, but it wouldn't budge. Something was blocking it.

That was nuts. Blocking doors was what Ben did, not Batty. He pounded on the door until it flew open and Batty yanked him into the room. One glance at her and Ben was ready to leave again. She had an air

255

of recklessness about her, reminding him of how Rafael had been that time just before he leapt off the jungle gym and broke his arm.

"Changed my mind, good-bye," he said.

But Batty was already blocking the door again, wedging a chair under the doorknob. Then she turned down the music so that they could better hear each other. "I'm glad you're here. I'm calling a MOYPS."

"Another one? We just had one."

Now Ben saw the pile of money on Batty's bed, lots of bills. Something big was happening, and he didn't like it. Maybe the reason Batty had been so strange lately had to do with money. Maybe their parents really had gotten poor—way beyond being-careful poor—and Batty was going to give them her dog-walking money. Ben still had three dollars left from his rock-digging money, which he'd been saving for his first movie camera. But he couldn't let Batty have all the nobility.

"Are you giving that money to Mom and Dad?" he asked. "Because I have some, too, if they need it."

"No, I'm using it for myself." Batty picked up her backpack and dumped it, schoolbooks and pens clattering onto the floor. Then she slid the money into an inside pocket and zipped it shut.

"Then you're sure you're not dying? Because you look kind of crazy right now. This is awful."

"How many times do I have to tell you I'm not dying, you goop? Calm down so that we can start. MOYPS come to—"

"What about Lydia? She should be here if it's a meeting of the younger Penderwicks."

"This is really just for you. We'll call it a MOBAB, Meeting of Batty and Ben, okay? Please?"

Ben shrugged his reluctant agreement, feeling the heavy weight of Penderwick Family Honor.

"Thank you," said Batty. "MOBAB, Meeting of Batty and Ben, come to order. Both of us swear to keep secret what is said here from everyone, including parents, older sisters, Nick, and even Rafael."

They bumped fists and swore, and Batty turned the music back up a little, just in case anyone was lurking in the hallway. "I'm taking the bus to Boston tomorrow to see Jeffrey, and no one else knows but you. Not even Jeffrey. I'm going to surprise him."

Ben had been to Boston. It seemed very far away to him—not so far as Maine, where they went in the summer, but still really far. "You can't. You'll get lost or kidnapped."

"No, I won't. I have to see Jeffrey."

"Why?"

Because he'd asked for her forgiveness, and she wanted to give it to him in person. Because he'd sent her a perfect set of Beethoven's symphonies. Because not only had he kept her photo of Hound safe for years and years, he'd known just when to give it back to her. But Ben wouldn't understand any of that, except maybe the part about the photo, and Batty had already hidden it away in her closet, where no one could see it and pry into her feelings.

"I just have to," she said. "Skye might never let him come here again, and I want to see him."

Ben was learning a painful life lesson about secrets. He'd gotten sucked into keeping Batty's Quigley Woods adventure a secret, and now she was expecting him to hide a much more dangerous adventure. Not only that, but he'd just promised Nick to report anything he needed help with, and oh, boy, he needed help with this but couldn't report it because he'd just sworn an oath of secrecy.

"My head is going to explode," he said.

"There's no reason for your head to explode."

He tried reason. "Mom and Dad will be furious. Just think about the trouble you'll get into, especially if you're kidnapped. They might not be poor, but they don't have enough for ransom money."

Batty didn't like the idea of making her parents worry. She was almost certain that she could make it into Boston and back home before they noticed. Or so she told herself, in order to keep her courage high.

"Ben, I promise I won't get kidnapped, and Mom and Dad—I'll call them if I'm going to get home later than they do. Does that make you feel better?"

"No, it does not. What about school? You could get thrown out for cutting."

"Not for doing it just once. Anyway, let them throw me out," she said, and almost meant it. "Then I won't have to write those stupid, horrible, idiotic book reports, never, ever—"

Batty paused, listening, and now Ben heard it, too,

over the music. Across the hall, Skye was knocking on Ben's door and telling him it was time for his bath.

"Tell her you're going to Boston," he whispered urgently to Batty.

"Haven't you been listening?" she hissed. "Skye is the last person I'd tell, and if you tell her, you have no honor, Ben Penderwick."

Skye was now knocking on Batty's door. "Ben, are you in there?"

Ben looked at Batty, who nodded, but with a face full of warning.

"Yes, I'm here," Ben called back. "I'll have my bath soon. Thank you."

They listened for more—but Skye had gone away.

"Tell Jane, then," said Ben. "Or Rosalind. Call Rosalind and tell her."

"No," said Batty. "And no. They'd try to stop me, and I won't be stopped."

Ben suddenly remembered what had brought him here in the first place.

"If you cut school," he wailed, "how will I carry Minnesota?"

Batty had this already worked out. "I'll walk you to school like normal, then not go in. Someone else can help you get Minnesota inside, and I'll run back to the bus stop. But in the afternoon, you'll have to ask Rafael to walk home with you. He's as goofy as you are, but between the two of you, you should be okay."

Ben felt like he was aiding and abetting a great crime. "I wish you wouldn't go."

But she plowed on, relentless. "If something goes wrong and I don't get back in time, you might need to help with Lydia. Like telling her a bedtime story."

"Batty! What story would I tell her?"

Here Batty's planning had failed her. Everything else she'd figured out in detail: bus schedules and ticket prices, how to get from the bus station to Jeffrey's school (subway and trolley), and whether or not the Beethoven symphonies would fit in her backpack so that she and Jeffrey could indeed listen to the *Eroica* together. (No, they wouldn't fit.) She'd even already informed Duchess's and Cilantro's families that she wouldn't be doing a dog walk tomorrow. But it was painful to think of leaving Lydia behind, more so than her parents, even. Lydia was now used to having Batty sleep in the big-girl bed in her room. If Batty didn't get back in time—

"If you don't know any stories, just sing 'The Itsy Bitsy Spider' for her." Batty reflected that it might even be a treat for Lydia after having witnessed the wreck of Batty's voice. "But I'll do everything I can to be back home in time."

"You'd better," he said. "Because if I end up having to sing 'Itsy Bitsy Spider' to Lydia, I'll never forgive you."

She looked at him sadly. There was a lot of that going around in their family.

"All right," she said. "Thus concludes the MOBAB."

CHAPTER NINETEEN
Bus Stop

WHEN BATTY WOKE UP TO RAIN, her courage almost failed her. This wasn't just normal rain, but the kind of driving rain that comes at you sideways and drenches you in an instant. Suddenly the journey to Boston seemed more difficult and scarier than she'd planned. She had to go today, though, rain or no rain. It wasn't fair to expect Ben to keep such a big secret for too long, and if he did end up telling someone, their parents would find out and talk to her and she'd end up promising never again to even think of going to Boston alone, and she'd never see Jeffrey—or not until Skye decided she could, which could be forever.

So after breakfast she stuffed an extra shirt and pair of jeans into her backpack, just in case she got soaked and had to change, hoping no one would notice that the pack was fuller than usual. And for the thousandth time, Batty made sure she still had the address of Jeffrey's school—torn off the box her birthday presents had come in—though by now she had it memorized. And the money—yes, it was still in the zippered pocket. It was every penny she'd earned so far from walking Duchess and Cilantro, except for her share of Skye's *Doctor Who* sweatshirt, and it was enough for bus fare to and from Boston—she'd sneaked onto Iantha's computer to look up bus fares—plus plenty left over for subways, trolleys, and food. Yes, she was ready. She went into her closet to kiss the photo of Hound good-bye and—gently and shyly—touch the photo of her mother, then slung her backpack over her shoulder and went downstairs.

Ben, too, was upset about the rain. Minnesota would never survive it, and after all his hard work, this seemed almost as awful as Batty running away to Boston. He went to his dad for help.

"No, you're right, we can't take the chance of drowning the Land of Ten Thousand Lakes," said Mr. Penderwick as he carried Minnesota downstairs.

"Not lakes, mountains," said Ben, wishing that his dad were paying more attention.

"We can cover Minnesota in plastic, Ben, and then we'll figure out who can drive you to school. How's that?"

Ben saw Batty waiting at the bottom of the steps, already in her raincoat and holding an umbrella. She was frantically shaking her head at him—she meant that he should turn down the ride to school, because the driver could end up being Skye, and Batty couldn't stand getting into a car with Skye this morning. But Ben didn't know why she was shaking her head— he didn't understand anything she did anymore. His hope was that the head shake meant she'd changed her mind about going to Boston.

"That's good, Daddy," he said. "Thank you."

Mr. Penderwick set down Minnesota and went to the kitchen to discuss driving schedules with Iantha.

"It better not be Skye driving us," Batty told Ben. "Because then you're on your own and I'm walking."

"Walking to school, right?" asked Ben with one last gasp of hope. "Batty, don't go to Boston."

"I have to. I *have* to."

Ben groaned.

"What's wrong?" asked Jane, coming out into the hall.

"Nothing," answered Batty before Ben could say something stupid.

"So you guys need a ride to school? We'll take Flashvan."

The good part was that Batty had no problem getting into Flashvan with Jane. The bad part was that Jane wasn't yet used to driving Flashvan, which had something called a clutch. Neither Batty nor Ben understood anything about clutches, and since neither did Jane, there was lots of jerkiness and muttering and lots of inching this way and that to get Flashvan pointed the right way out the driveway. At least Jane didn't stall during that part, but she did stall at the bottom of Gardam Street in full view of the bus stop, where Batty had a wild impulse to flee right then and there, throwing caution and Minnesota to the winds. But she refrained and stuck out the entire uncomfortable, lurching ride to Wildwood. With this one benefit: that when Jane took a look at Batty's pale, anxious face and asked if she felt all right, Batty could answer truthfully that she might indeed be a little carsick.

The rain and fresh air drove away the car sickness, but Jane and Flashvan sat stubbornly in front of Wildwood, waiting to see that Batty, Ben, and Minnesota got safely inside. Since Batty couldn't walk right away from the school with Jane watching, she had to change her plan on the fly and go with Ben into the building. It turned out not to be as great a risk as she'd feared. Because they'd made it to school early, there wouldn't be many people around to see Batty and then wonder why she wasn't in class. So she helped Ben lug Minnesota not only into school but all the way to the second-grade wing. They stopped outside his classroom.

"I'll leave you here," she said. "And I'll go out the side door. Less chance that way of being caught by anyone from my class."

"Promise you'll come back home," said Ben sadly.

"I promise I'll come back home. Now put Minnesota down on my count: three, two, one." As they lowered Minnesota to the floor, Batty spotted a possible threat to her plan—Texas lurching down the hall toward them. "Ben, intruder alert."

"Those twins again?" Ben had been forced to dodge them several more times the day before.

"Not the twins. Remy," she whispered to Ben. "Distract her so that I can get away."

Ben couldn't believe that even more was being asked of him. "Distract her how?"

"I don't know, talk to her."

"*Talk* to her? About what?"

"Please. Please, Ben."

"I could talk to her about Minnesota, I guess." Of all the things his sisters had ever asked of him, this was one of the worst.

"I don't care what you talk to her about. Just do it."

Batty put her hand on Ben's back, shoved him toward his fate worse than death—and also Texas— and slunk away toward the side door, willing herself into invisibility. Then she was outside, sprinting across the parking lot, around the hedge, and flying back toward Gardam Street. In five minutes she was sheltering in the bus stop, wet, yes, but exhilarated. She'd made it this far, and soon a bus would arrive to carry her away to Boston and Jeffrey. Eagerly she watched through the glass, wanting to spot the bus the moment it came into view.

Oh, no. She closed her eyes and hoped she hadn't

seen whom she thought she'd just seen. This would be so much worse than Remy with her cardboard Texas. This would be worse than the entire actual state of Texas. She opened her eyes again and peered out through the rain. Instead of a bus, a man was heading her way, a man running through the rain, a man, she saw as he got closer, who was wearing shorts and an ARMY T-shirt. Which proved that it was exactly the person Batty least wanted it to be: Nick, out for his morning run, and right on target for the bus stop.

But here came the bus! Now it was behind Nick, and now it was passing him. Everything was all right. The bus would reach Batty before Nick did, and she'd get on, and he'd never know the difference. *Hurry, bus, hurry, hurry, hurry.* Using her backpack to shield herself from Nick's view, Batty stepped out of the shelter just as the bus roared to a stop, brakes squealing, wipers hammering, doors banging open.

Batty lunged forward to board but was blocked by a woman getting off the bus, slowly, one careful step at a time. And on came Nick, closer, ever closer . . . but *now* the way was clear. Batty leapt on, paid her money, and ran to the very back, as far as she could get from Nick. She heard the bus doors bang closed again. She'd made it!

The bus's engine revved up, but what was this? The driver was opening the doors up again, and here came Nick, sopping wet Nick, climbing onto the bus, dripping all over everything.

There was one last possible reprieve. He had no money. Batty watched, breathless, as he patted his empty pockets and smiled winningly at the driver, who wasn't going to let him on for free, smile or no smile, army or no army. *Bang* went the doors again, opening to expel Nick, when a young woman near the front got up from her seat to pay the driver what Nick owed, perhaps hoping that he would sit with her and light up the gloomy day with that Geiger smile of his.

But if the young woman was disappointed when Nick headed toward the back of the bus, it was nothing to what Batty felt, with her intricate plans, her necessary escape, in ashes around her. She slumped against the window, refusing to look at him.

"Okay if I sit with you?" he asked.

"No."

"Thanks," he said, and plopped down beside her. "Where are we headed?"

"The bus goes to Wooton."

"So that's where you're going instead of school? Wooton? I'm assuming your parents have no idea where you are." When she didn't answer, he went on. "I thought we had a deal. No more running off."

"I promised not to cross the creek in Quigley Woods. I didn't say anything about buses." She knew she sounded petulant, like Lydia in a bad mood, but she couldn't help it.

"Batty, I can't let you go on, you know that, right? Let me take you to school."

"I can't go to school now. It's already started." She began to cry.

"I'll talk your way in, late or not," said Nick. "Mrs. Thompson still works in the front office, right? She'll remember me. I used to give her flowers to make up for the trouble I got into. Flowers I swiped from my mom's garden, naturally. Stop crying, and tell me what's going on."

"Nothing's going on," she gasped through her tears. "I can't tell you."

"Who can you tell?"

"No one. Besides, they all know. Only I didn't know." She wept and wept.

"You're not making any sense."

"There's no sense to make. Everything's fine."

"Which is why you're crying, I guess." Nick looked out the window. "Listen to me. We're coming up on the next stop, where we're going to get off and wait for another bus to take us back to Gardam Street. Then you'll have two options. You can let me take you to school, where you belong, or I'll take you home to your parents."

"They're not home, they're at work."

"I'll call them. I have to call them anyway, to tell them I found you trying to leave town. I'm also going to tell them about your Quigley Woods stunt, as I should have done before. Now stand up." He got out of the seat and waved to the bus driver that they wanted to get off. "I'm warning you. You're either walking off this bus or I'm carrying you off, and you know I can."

"I hate being too young for anything important," she sobbed. "I hate it, I hate it!"

"I know, buddy. Let's go."

The stop where they got off had no shelter—it was just a pole with a sign that said BUS. Silently they stood together in the rain, Batty with her sobbing and Nick with his determination to get her back to safety. Which he finally did, after a bus ride back to Gardam Street—Batty paid both fares. When she refused to return to school, he walked with her to the house and ordered her into dry clothes, called her parents, then waited dripping on the kitchen floor while they rushed home.

By the time they arrived, Batty had gone upstairs to bed and would answer none of their worried questions. She wouldn't explain where she'd been trying to go, or why. Neither would she agree to be taken back to school that day. Was she sick? No, just tired, she guessed, and proved it by staying in bed for the rest of the day, coming downstairs only for dinner, which she ate quickly and quietly before slipping away to her room.

When Batty refused to go to school again the next day, Iantha took her to the family doctor, who couldn't find anything wrong, but drew some blood to make sure. No one likes having blood drawn, but Batty didn't mind it all that much. The now-familiar

fog protected her from the rest of the world, muf-
fling lights, colors, sounds, and sensations. Batty had
stopped fighting the fog, wrapping herself in it like
a quilt, taking it with her to her room when she got
back from seeing the doctor.

Again, she stayed up there, refusing not only to
walk the dogs—thanking Jane politely but distantly
for taking over the responsibility—but even to go to
her piano lesson that evening. Batty's parents, confused and desperate, tried to cheer her up by talking
about her upcoming birthday and even invited Keiko
over to try to make plans. They had no way of knowing they were only making things worse. The more
people talked about Batty's birthday, the more her
stomach hurt and the more the fog around her thick-
ened, leaving her alone in her dim quiet.

Only for Ben and Lydia did it lift a little, though
she refused to listen to Ben's relief about her not making it to Boston. She would listen to anything Lydia
wanted to say, grateful for this small sister who knew
nothing of dead mothers. But Batty wouldn't sing, no
matter how many times Lydia asked her to.

The few times Skye appeared, Batty pretended to
be asleep.

Mr. Penderwick and Iantha didn't want to upset
Rosalind, not at the very end of her freshman year
of college, not when she was already planning to be
home on Saturday. But when Batty didn't get up for
school on Friday, either, Mr. Penderwick called Ros-

alind, hoping Batty would talk to her on the phone. "No, thank you, Daddy," she answered, and rolled over and buried her face in the pillow. This sent Rosalind into a frenzy, just what her parents had wanted to avoid. Mr. Penderwick reassured her as best he could, but that afternoon, Rosalind called back.

Ben answered the phone—he'd just gotten home from school and was about to eat a bowl of chocolate ice cream. He was supposed to have only healthy snacks after school, but no one was watching, and besides, he'd finally gotten rid of those twins, Tess and Nora, so he wanted to celebrate.

"Ben, it's Rosy," she said when he picked up.

"I know." He put a giant spoonful of ice cream into his mouth.

"How's Batty?"

"Awful."

"What? I didn't understand you."

Ben swallowed the ice cream. "Batty's awful."

"That's what I heard. Listen, Ben—"

Ben listened, and what he heard made him forget the ice cream. With Batty in such bad shape, Rosalind couldn't wait even one more day to be with her. She was coming home that very night—this was good, Ben thought—because Oliver had offered to rent a trailer for his car, pack up both his and Rosalind's college things, and drive her home.

This was bad.

"Batty's not that awful, not really," he said.

"Even if she's just a little awful, I want to see her."

"Can't Mom and Dad come get you instead?"

"They're both still at work, and Oliver's already on his way to pick up the trailer. Just tell everyone I'm coming, okay? Love you, bye."

"How long is Oliver going to stay here?"

But Rosalind was already off the phone. Ben hung up and went back to the ice cream, thinking furiously. Life in this house was hard enough with Batty acting so weird. And now Oliver was coming back? If he upset Lydia all over again, Ben would end up with two cuckoo sisters.

There was only one way he could figure out to stop Oliver. Batty had to call Rosalind back, tell her to wait in Rhode Island until the next day, when their mother could pick her up as planned, because Batty had gotten better and wasn't going to stay in bed anymore, and Oliver should drive his stupid trailer to wherever he lived when he wasn't staying at the Penderwicks' house.

Ben finished the ice cream, marched up the stairs, marched down them again because he'd forgotten the cookies Keiko had sent home with him for Batty— because she was just as upset and worried as all the Penderwicks—marched up again, and used his private signal on Batty's door. She didn't answer, but he went in anyway. She hadn't answered the last four times, either. It was as though she'd forgotten what the signal meant.

Batty woke up when Ben sat down on her bed.

She'd spent the whole day drifting in and out of sleep that gave her no rest, full of endless dreams of searching, searching, searching, sometimes for Hound, but sometimes Hound was with her and they were searching together, weeping, for someone else.

"But dogs don't weep," she told Ben.

He stared unhappily at this listless and pinch-faced girl who'd stolen his sister Batty.

"Are you going crazy? Because Rafael says that if you don't have a hernia or an alien implantation, maybe you're having a full-out wacko breakdown."

Batty shook her head to clear away the dream cobwebs. "No, I'm not crazy. Stop worrying."

"Stop worrying!" That was too much to ask of him. "Everybody's worried. That's all they talk about."

"I'm sorry." She *was* sorry. If she could just disappear, it would be so much easier on everyone.

"That's okay." He held up the bag of cookies, hoping they would give Batty the strength she'd need to agree with his plan. "These are from Keiko, and she said she followed a recipe carefully, so you don't have to make me eat them first. But I ate two on the way home anyway, and they're regular chocolate chip and really good."

Batty took a cookie and ate it slowly. Like all her senses, her taste was dulled. But the chocolate came through with a teeny jolt of pleasure, and she sent out a quiet thank-you to Keiko.

"They are good," she told Ben.

She looked a little better to Ben, but not yet alert

enough to hear about Oliver. He'd give her the Tess and Nora update first. "I finally got those twins to stop bugging me."

"I didn't know they were actually bugging you. You said they would just look at you and then you'd run away."

"I never ran away." That sounded cowardly. "I evaded them."

"Okay." Batty finished one cookie and took another.

"Anyway, I was tired of *evading* them, so today when they looked at me, I went right up to them and said: 'Tess and Nora, I'm sure you're very nice people, but I'm not interested in having a relationship with you.'"

Ben wasn't going to tell Batty that he'd been repeating what Nick had taught him. It seemed more grown-up if he'd made up that statement on his own. But if she asked, he would tell her how the twins had reacted—agreeing that they didn't want a relationship, either, and calmly walking away. Which had convinced Ben that girls were even odder than he'd suspected and that he was wise to steer clear of any he wasn't related to.

She didn't ask. But she'd finished the second cookie and was sitting up straight instead of slumping. Time to hit her with the big news.

"Rosalind is coming home tonight," he said.

Batty held on to that information for a while, trying to feel something. No, one extra day of Rosalind would make no difference. Not now. "Why?"

"Because she thinks you're dying or something. I don't know what Dad and Mom told her. But, Batty, because she's in a hurry to see you, Oliver is driving her."

"Oh, no." More Oliver—and this, too, was her fault.

"We have to do something about Oliver."

"There's nothing I can do." All the things she'd done so far had just caused trouble, and she saw no reason for this to change.

"Yes, there is, Batty, you can call Rosalind and tell her you feel better." Inspired, Ben expanded his plan. "Maybe you can explain everything to her, too, like how you were trying to get to Boston—"

"No! And you can't tell her, either, Ben, you swore."

"Then just tell her you're okay and you'll get out of bed soon. Tell her that, Batty, please."

The news about Oliver had made Batty's fog denser than ever, and she very much needed to be alone. "I'm going back to sleep. You can eat the rest of the cookies."

"Think of Lydia and how much she hates Oliver!" Ben was pleading. "And he could be an in-law and we'll never see Tommy again."

"Ben, you know Rosalind's much too sensible to marry Oliver."

Ben felt like pointing out that he'd always thought Skye too sensible to banish Jeffrey from the house, and Batty too sensible to try to go to Boston, then stay in bed for days, and look where they were now. But the conversation was over. Batty was already lying back down and closing her eyes.

"I'm sorry, Ben," she murmured, and buried her face in Funty.

When Rosalind got home that night, she ran upstairs to Lydia's room to see Batty. But Batty was either asleep again or pretending to be—she barely knew the difference herself anymore—and Rosalind went away disappointed.

CHAPTER TWENTY
The MOOPSAB

Early Saturday morning, Ben crept out of his room to make sure that Batty was where she was supposed to be. He didn't really believe she'd try to run away to Boston again, but he wanted to start the day *knowing* she hadn't.

He pushed open Lydia's door just enough to see that yes, there was Batty asleep in the big-girl bed, curled up with Funty and Gibson. Quietly, carefully, he closed the door again, went back to his own room, and sat down on the floor with his rocks. Putting them into piles sometimes made him feel better.

Oliver had returned even more Oliver-ish than when he'd left, still talking about movies no one had heard of, including one called *The Discreet Charm of the* something—*Boogie-Woogies*, maybe?—the story of how some people couldn't get any dinner. Ben had taken himself to bed a half hour early just to get away from it, and to fret over Batty, and to think of the movies he and Rafael would make someday in which people always got plenty to eat, even when under attack by aliens.

Ben piled his three geodes on top of one another and moved the obsidian into the pile with the rose quartz. He was hungry, and breakfast wouldn't be for a while, not with the rest of the house still asleep. Maybe he'd sneak down to the kitchen for a bowl of cereal. Except that would mean getting past the living room where Oliver was sleeping on the couch, and hearing that yucky snoring.

And how long would that snoring be in the house, anyway? Ben still didn't know when Oliver planned to leave. Soon, he hoped, very soon.

He was putting his chunks of feldspar into a pile— the pink one, the yellow one, the brown one, the other pink one—when someone knocked on his door. It couldn't be Lydia. She didn't try to escape from her room when Batty was in there with her. He crawled across the room to peer through the space under the door. Bare feet, grown-up-size. Definitely not Lydia.

"Identify yourself," he said.

"It's me, Rosalind. Open up, Ben."

"Why?"

The door swung open with no help from him, knocking over his hanger alarm system, and there was

Rosalind in her pajamas, looking very much like the oldest sister who must be obeyed.

"Just come with me. And without any noise."

Cowed, Ben followed Rosalind on tiptoe down the hall to Skye and Jane's room. This was very peculiar and mysterious. His teenage sisters never got up before Lydia did. And when he got into the room, he saw that Skye and Jane weren't exactly up. They were both still in bed, yawning, and not exactly pleased.

"Can't this wait, Rosalind?" said Skye.

"No, we have to talk before the whole house is awake. Get out of bed, both of you, and form a circle. Ben, sit here next to me."

In this house, the only reason to sit in a circle was for a MOPS or some version of one, and Ben had no intention of undergoing another official meeting, with its swearing and secrecy.

"No, I don't think I will, thank you," he said.

"Why not?"

He shuffled his feet and decided to tell the truth, or part of it. "I can't handle any more secrets."

"What secrets are you keeping?"

"He can't tell you, obviously," said Jane. "This is interesting."

"I'll go back to my room now." Ben started back to the door.

"No, you won't." A quick lunge from Rosalind, who had a surprisingly strong grip, and he was in the circle and sitting beside her. "MOPS come to order.

That is, MOOPSAB, Meeting of the Older Pender-wick Sisters and Ben."

"Second the motion," said Skye, "though I wish we could have slept longer."

"Second *that* motion," added Jane.

Rosalind continued. "All swear to keep secret what we say here."

The sisters formed a pile of fists, and Ben reluctantly added his to the top. He was starting to think that *secret* was the most uncomfortable word in the universe. When everyone had sworn by the Pender-wick Family Honor, Rosalind turned to Ben.

"I'm very concerned about Batty," she said. "She's never cut herself off before, not like this. Do you know what's upset her?"

So that's why they wanted him here. Not to tell him more secrets, but to pry out the last secret he was keeping for Batty. They already knew about her Quigley Woods adventure and about her getting on that bus—Nick had told their parents and they had told the older daughters. But no one knew she'd been trying to go to Boston, no one but Ben, and he'd sworn not to tell. Which he wished he hadn't—that secret was a great burden to him—but it was too late for wishing. And now he had three wily and dangerous sisters trying to get it out of him. He was going to have to be strong.

Quickly Ben reviewed what he knew about Batty—things she was upset about that he didn't have to keep secret. He would start there and make it last as long as he could.

"She doesn't want Nick to go back to war," he said.

"None of us want that," said Rosalind.

"Especially since he's going away on her birthday." He knew by his sisters' expressions—Skye was yawning—that he wasn't convincing them. He took another stab. "Batty misses Hound. We should get another dog."

They didn't fall for that, either. They all just kept looking at him. Ben knew from Rafael, who watched lots of television shows with police interrogations in them, that there were many ways to pry information out of people. Rafael had never mentioned how to behave if you were the one with the information.

"How's she doing in school?" asked Rosalind.

Aha! Batty had never told him to keep the book reports secret.

"She does have a million book reports to write before the end of the year and she hasn't done even one," he said.

"I hate book reports," said Skye.

"Everyone does," said Jane. "If it's just book reports, that's not a problem. I'll write them for her."

"Jane," said Skye. "Remember the Aztecs."

She was referring to their distant past when she and Jane had swapped homework assignments, with disastrous results. Even Ben knew this story.

"We never swore we wouldn't do it again," protested Jane. "I mean, poor, tortured Batty."

"Yes, but remember the guilt," said Rosalind. "We'll do it a different way. Batty can dictate reports to us while we type. Maybe it will seem more like talking and less like reporting. But not a word to Dad or Iantha—all swear."

They swore, even Ben, who had zero interest in typing fifth-grade-level book reports. This interrogation wasn't so tough, he thought. Rosalind's next set of questions changed his mind.

"This is good information, Ben, and maybe the book reports would make Batty cut school, but why did she get onto a bus? Do you know why? Do you know where she was trying to go?"

He clamped his teeth shut and covered his mouth with his hand, two layers of protection to keep either *Boston* or *Jeffrey* from slipping out by mistake.

"He knows," said Skye.

"I'll bet Batty made him promise not to tell," guessed Jane. "Am I right, Ben?"

He nodded. That was true. He was pretty sure that it wasn't giving away a secret to admit you had one. Honor was infinitely more confusing than he'd ever thought possible. But he knew his sisters. None of them would ask him to break his promise outright. Still, they might trick him with a stealth attack. He had to stay on his guard.

Rosalind sat for a while, pondering. "What's our evidence? When did Batty start acting strange?"

"The day after Skye's birthday," said Jane. "She ran off into Quigley Woods and then slept most of the day."

"So what happened on Skye's birthday?"

"Oliver arrived the day before my birthday," said Skye. "He happened."

"Oliver didn't *happen*. He just visited," protested Rosalind.

And just like that, Ben saw an opportunity. He felt like a general who spots a weakness in the enemy's battle plan. If he could keep his sisters talking about Oliver, he would not only steer them away from Batty, he might even be able to figure out how to get Oliver out of the house.

"Yes, Oliver visited," he said. "And now he's visiting again. How long is he staying, anyway?"

"A few days, probably," answered Rosalind. "He doesn't have to be home for another week."

"Where is home?"

"Minnesota."

How could such a person as Oliver come from a state with so many great rocks? Would Ben have to rethink his devotion to Minnesota? While he was recovering from that shock, his sisters had gone back to the previous weekend.

"So Oliver visited," repeated Skye. "And then Lydia stabbed him with a quesadilla."

"Quesadillas are one thing. Getting on a bus is another," said Jane. "*Très beau* Oliver wouldn't make anyone get onto a bus."

Ben pulled himself together. He couldn't let them near that bus.

"I didn't stab him with a quesadilla," he said, "but Oliver upset me, too."

"Really?" asked Rosalind, shaken. "You don't like him, Ben?"

"No, and Nick doesn't, either."

"I already knew about Nick." Rosalind turned to her sisters. "Anyone else? Skye? Jane?"

"Well—" started Skye.

Jane cut her off. "Hold on. What about our NIWB oath?"

"NIWB was only for truly awful boyfriends, Jane," said Rosalind, "beginning with that Belmonte kid you fell for in ninth grade."

"Who wore a leather jacket and led a dirt-bike gang," added Skye.

"It wasn't a gang," objected Jane. "And he wasn't awful. Just irreverent."

Ben had never heard of either a Belmonte kid or an NIWB oath, which meant he was hearing his sisters' secrets again, just what he didn't need. At least they weren't talking about Batty. Maybe he should abandon his anti-Oliver scheme and escape now, while they weren't looking at him. If he could just reach the door, he'd make a break for it, grab some food from the kitchen, and go hide in the basement. He'd already ooched a few inches without being caught, and now he ooched a few more.

This time it was Skye who caught him and pulled him back into the circle.

"An NIWB—or No Interfering with Boyfriends—oath," she told him, "is supposed to keep us from criticizing each other's romantic choices."

"Oh. *Please* can I leave now?"

"No," said Rosalind. "NIWB temporarily canceled. Skye, you were saying?"

"Well, remember when Oliver was talking about visiting the Large Hadron Collider and the exciting research that's being done there? I asked him a few questions later—he has no idea what the thing does."

"Neither do I," said Rosalind. "Jane?"

"Nope."

"But, dodos, you aren't *pretending* to," said Skye. "You know how I am about phonies."

"Yes, we do know." Rosalind frowned. "What about you, Jane? Do you like Oliver?"

"He's gorgeous. That smoldering gaze."

"But—"

"I'm not sure I exactly *like* him. Sometimes he makes me wonder whether or not I should go to college, if that's what it does to boys. But, Rosy, if you like Oliver, what does it matter what we think?"

"You're right. Of course it doesn't matter. I'm the oldest and should know what I'm doing," said Rosalind. "Back to Batty."

"Uh, no, um, um," stuttered Ben, caught off guard. He'd stopped listening at *smoldering gaze*, trying to figure out what it was and if it was supposed to be good or bad, and more determined than ever to stay away from girlfriends for the rest of his life. This inattention could have been his downfall in the conflict of wills if Skye hadn't unexpectedly come to his assistance.

"Rosy, isn't the real question whether or not *you* like Oliver?" she asked.

"I thought I did." Rosalind stared out the window. "But this past week I did find myself looking at him more than listening to him. He kept wanting to talk about Ingmar Bergman films and the politics of depression."

"What does that even mean?"

"I don't know—I couldn't listen. But why do we keep talking about Oliver? We're supposed to be figuring out what's wrong with Batty. What else happened that weekend of your birthday, Skye?"

"Basketball, cake, Jane breaking Jérôme's heart—"

"I did *not* break his heart," protested Jane. "I merely caused a bit of painless confusion, which has been straightened out. Jérôme and his new translator, Lauren, are going out to dinner tonight. Besides, I might put Jérôme into a book someday."

"Not everyone is fodder for books," said Rosalind.

"For me they are. I can't help it, you know. But if we're talking about messing up with boys, let's talk about Skye."

"Ugh." Skye lay down on the floor and shut her eyes. "Let's not."

"Jane's right, Skye," said Rosalind. "This whole thing with Jeffrey is a disaster."

"We all miss him," Jane added, "and wish you'd do something."

"What do you suggest?" Skye tugged at her hair. "A frontal lobotomy? I can't force myself to fall in love!"

"Whatever happens, you simply can't make him stay away forever," said Rosalind.

They were getting much too close to Batty's secret for Ben's comfort. Time to change the subject again, and this time he was ready. "Rosalind, you made Tommy stay away forever."

"True," said Skye.

"And that is *way* off-topic," said Rosalind. "Please, let's get back to—"

Jane interrupted. "Rosy, you know you want Tommy back. Honestly, I don't understand why you even bother with people like Oliver."

"I never said I wanted Tommy back!"

"You don't have to say it," said Skye. "Even I can tell you're still nuts about him. Why don't you just admit it?"

Rosalind flushed. "Because. Just because."

"If you want to call him, I've got his number." Ben pulled up his shirt and showed them. "Nick's, too."

"Why are they on your stomach?" asked Jane. "And upside down? Oh, right, they're not upside down for you. Rosalind, let's call Tommy—this could be a sign from fate."

"No, let's not," she said. "Besides, I don't need Ben's stomach for Tommy's number. I know it by heart."

"More proof of your undying love," said Jane.

"No, it is not. *Please* can we get back to—"

"And another thing," said Ben. "Tommy never did anything dishonorable, never, ever. But Oliver asked me if you liked Nick, then gave me five dollars not to tell you he'd asked, but I didn't promise, and anyway, Bat—and anyway, I ripped up the five dollars and flushed it down the toilet."

Never had he seen looks of such astonishment—well, not since Rafael had told Ms. Lambert and the whole class about how his aunt had wrestled a giant octopus while deep-sea diving. Ben almost stood up and cheered. He *was* a general, and he was winning.

And then, just to top off his victory, the meeting was interrupted by a knock. Ben leapt up and opened the door—maybe it was someone in a crisis that only he could solve. But even better, it was his dad in his bathrobe, looking not very awake and not happy, either.

"I'm looking for Rosalind, and I heard voices—ah, yes, there you are, Rosy. Am I interrupting something important?"

"No," said Ben.

"Yes," said Rosalind. "That is, it would be important if we could stick to the subject. So far, all I've learned is that no one likes Oliver and that he tried to bribe my little brother. Why were you looking for me, Dad?"

"I don't like to heap coals on your head, but Oliver waylaid me on the way into the kitchen for coffee—and also to look for my glasses, because they're quite lost this time—and for the last ten minutes he's been telling me the plot of *Last Year at Marienbad*."

"*Last Year at Marienbad* doesn't have a plot."

"I know that, and yet . . ." He let his voice trail off.

"Oh, Daddy, I'm so sorry." Rosalind looked like she was going to be sick. "Do you dislike Oliver as much as my siblings do?"

"Does it matter, *filia mea?*"

"Yes."

"Then, darling daughter, I'll tell you that I'm not fond of Oliver."

"So it's unanimous," said Rosalind bitterly. "I feel like a fool. Unless Iantha happens to be crazy about him."

"You know Iantha—she's very accepting."

"Thus, unanimous." She stood up. "I guess I'd better go downstairs and tell Oliver it's over, whatever *it* is."

"Do you need our help?" asked Jane.

"No, you and Skye go back to sleep. I can't have all three of us breaking up with him. But if anyone knows how to break up with someone you're not exactly with, I wouldn't mind a hint."

"I know, I know," said Ben, raising his hand like he was in class. "It's this thing Nick taught me."

Fifteen minutes later, Ben and his dad were at the kitchen table, feasting. Mr. Penderwick was wearing his glasses—Rosalind had found them behind the toaster—and was on his second cup of coffee and his first plate of scrambled eggs and toast. Ben was also eating eggs and toast, but only after downing the bowl of cereal he'd needed to get him through waiting for the eggs to cook. Both father and son were studiously not listening for any conversation drifting in from the living room, where Rosalind was trying to get rid of Oliver.

"Need more toast?" asked Mr. Penderwick.

"Yes, please." The battle of wits with his sisters had made Ben extra hungry. "With jam this time."

His dad went over to the toaster to pop in two more slices, then asked, in a casual sort of voice and with his back to Ben, "So, was that one of your sisters' famous secret meetings?"

Ben looked suspiciously at his dad, but, unlike a person's face, a back doesn't give up much information. "Maybe."

"They make you go to lots of them?"

"I don't think I'm supposed to tell you." Ben took a drink of orange juice. "But if I had brothers instead of sisters, I bet I wouldn't be going to any."

"That would probably depend on what kind of brothers they were."

"Huh."

The toast popped up and Mr. Penderwick made a great display of slathering it with butter and jam. "Does Batty ask you to meetings, too?"

Ben couldn't believe it. After fighting off his older sisters, now he had to skirmish with his dad? His dad, who was even smarter than his sisters? Stalling, Ben drank the rest of his orange juice and went to the refrigerator for more. Briefly he considered dropping the carton onto the floor—that would distract his father for a while.

But Mr. Penderwick was talking again. "Your mom and I are awfully worried about Batty. If you know anything that would help us—"

"Maybe she has sleeping sickness."

"No, there aren't any tsetse flies in the United States. Anyway, sleeping sickness wouldn't make Batty get onto a bus." Mr. Penderwick put the plate of toast on the table. "I've been thinking about that bus and how it goes into Wooton and how once you're in Wooton, you can take a different bus that goes to Boston. And how Jeffrey is in Boston."

Ben dropped the orange juice carton onto the floor. "Uh-oh."

"I'm close to the truth." His dad barely noticed the mess. "Aren't I?"

Ben shoved the carton with his toe, thinking, thinking, but his thinking had run out. He was weary of thinking. And he didn't want to fight with his dad. He started to cry.

"I hate secrets," he said.

"Me too." Mr. Penderwick hugged his son. "That's all right, you've been a good and loyal brother. You didn't tell me. I guessed."

Rosalind came in, took in the crying boy and the spilled juice.

"What happened?"

"I pushed him too hard," answered her dad, gently steering Ben back to his chair. "Eat up, son of mine— get your strength back."

"Okay." The new toast helped dry his tears. "Is Oliver gone, Rosalind?"

"Yup, and I used that 'I'm sure you're a nice person' thing you taught me." She picked the carton off the floor and wiped up the juice. "Even with that, it took me a while to convince Oliver he wasn't wanted. Apparently no one's ever tried to get rid of him before."

Knowing that Oliver was gone dried the rest of Ben's tears. He could be proud of his role in that, anyway.

"And he told me to thank Jane and Iantha for the hospitality," continued Rosalind, "making the point that they were the only ones who seemed to welcome him. If I hadn't felt a little sorry for him, I would have told him that Jane will tolerate anyone she thinks she might write about someday, and that Iantha is just extraordinarily polite. But then he also said we need to work on Lydia's social skills."

Even without understanding what social skills were, Ben was offended. "Oliver needs work, not Lydia."

"You know, Ben, that's exactly what *I* told him. And then he left," said Rosalind. "Dad, why couldn't I see all along what a jerk he is?"

"*Arcanum est,* my dear, a mystery of the human heart. Have I ever told you about Neil Somebody who dated your aunt Claire? He was always going on about García Lorca—"

He paused. Somewhere Lydia was shrieking.

"BEN, BEN, BEN!"

All three rushed out into the hallway and looked up the steps. There she was, launching herself at the baby gate, determined to get either through it or over it.

"Lydia! No! Stop!" Mr. Penderwick was over the bottom gate and halfway up the steps when Iantha appeared behind her youngest and pulled her to safety.

"I've got her, honey!" she called down cheerfully. "Falling-down-steps injuries averted for now."

Ben hadn't been so worried about Lydia falling down the steps, but something else was bothering him.

"Why's Lydia looking for me," he asked, "when she has Batty right there in her room?"

CHAPTER TWENTY-ONE
The Secret Comes Out

DESPITE EVERYONE'S ATTEMPTS to be quiet early that morning, the activity outside Lydia's room—Rosalind's trips back and forth to Ben's room, Mr. Penderwick's climbs up and down the steps—had woken Batty. It took little now to yank her awake, so restless and dream-haunted was her sleep, more exhausting even than her lonely, anxious days. The dreams she'd left behind this time had been the worst yet, teeming with dark pits of dread, and when there seemed to be a break in the commotion, Batty fled to her own room and into the closet, where she huddled alongside Hound's canvas bag. She'd been sneaking in here a lot over the last few days and doing the same thing each time—taking her two cherished photographs out from under the bag and studying them with her flashlight. She did it now, too, for whatever small comfort she could get. First, the dying woman with her brand-new daughter, that tiny baby who had caused endless pain to the people Batty loved. And then Hound, lost and beloved Hound, whom Batty had also let die.

After a while, she turned off the flashlight, rested her head on the canvas bag, and let herself fall asleep again, hoping that here she would be safe from dreams, in this place where no one would think to search for her. But too soon she was yet again jerked awake. Someone was out there in her room, moving around. If she stayed very still, they would go away. There was no one Batty wanted to talk to.

"You're in the closet, aren't you." It was Rosalind.

How did she know? Batty wondered. It didn't matter. She kept still and said nothing.

"I thought you'd want to know that Oliver's gone for good," said Rosalind. "Ben helped with that, actually."

This raised a spark of curiosity in Batty, a tiny pinprick of interest, but not enough to help her move or answer her sister.

"May I come in?" Light flooded into the closet. Rosalind had opened the door.

There was no room for her back where Batty lay, but Rosalind was pushing her way in, determinedly burrowing through boxes and games to get to her sister. Batty stirred just enough to hide the photographs underneath the canvas bag. And still Rosalind pressed on, shoes, stuffed animals, golf balls, and shells bending to her will, until she was crouching next to Batty.

"Honey, everyone's so worried about you. They've told me that you're not going to school. Can you talk to me about it?"

No.

"Has someone hurt you?"

No.

"Is missing Hound making you ill?"

Not just that.

"Move over, Battikins. I'm getting a cramp."

One part of Batty wanted Rosalind to go away, to leave her alone with her wretchedness. There was another part, though, that wanted Rosalind to stay with her, to comfort her, and this part forced Batty to uncurl herself and scrunch over to one side, but still there wasn't enough room, so Batty scrunched over a little more, and this time, by mistake, she dislodged Hound's canvas bag, and there in plain view were the photographs. Batty tried to cover them again, but Rosalind was already crowding in beside her, and there wasn't enough room, and—

Rosalind spotted the photographs.

"My goodness," she said. "Is that Hound? Isn't that the photograph you gave Jeffrey for his eleventh birthday? And—wait a minute, what's this other—"

Rosalind cut herself off, with a face so sad that it broke Batty's heart all over again.

"I'm sorry, Rosy," she said.

Rosalind came back as from a dream. "What did you say?"

"I'm sorry. I'm sorry. I'm so sorry. I'm—" Batty gasped, suddenly out of air. The big secret was slipping out of its box, choking her. "I didn't mean—I didn't know—I wish I hadn't . . ."

Rosalind put her arms around Batty, trying to soothe her. "What are you sorry about, Batty? I don't understand."

Breathe, breathe, Batty heard Mrs. Grunfeld say. "That Mommy died because—that you lost your—I'm so sorry. . . ."

The secret was almost ready to burst free now, bringing with it all of Batty's desolation, her guilt, her fear. It was tearing her apart—she wasn't sure she'd still be there at the end, but there was no stopping this explosion, not even when she realized how much she was frightening Rosalind, even when she heard Rosalind telling her not to move, *please don't move, promise you won't move, Batty,* because she would be gone for just a minute, and then Rosalind was gone. Batty was smothering, drowning in anguish, and then her father came for her, shoving aside anything that got in his way and somehow carried her out and laid her gently on the bed. Iantha was there, too, covering Batty with blankets and asking calm questions, trying to understand, but Batty could only babble about killing her mother and how they should ask Skye about it because only Skye told the truth—to Jeffrey, anyway,

Skye had told the truth to Jeffrey—and that she understood if they didn't love her, because who could possibly love a girl who brought death with her, and that she knew she'd been a terrible bargain, a pitiful exchange for her mother.

With that, the secret was released from its box, dissipated, confessed, its power stripped away. And somehow Batty, still alive and in one piece, hadn't been abandoned. Because here was her father, holding her and telling her how much he loved her, how much they all loved her. And now, at last, she could slip away into a sleep free of nightmares, into the healing rest she so badly needed.

When she finally woke back up that afternoon, Asimov was at the bottom of the bed, heavily asleep on her feet, and her father was in a chair beside her with an Agatha Christie mystery, the kind he read whenever he needed to relax.

"How do you feel?" he asked.

How did she feel? Something was strange. Oh! Her stomach didn't hurt anymore.

"I feel good," she said.

"Hungry?"

"Yes, hungry."

"Excellent news. Stay right here." Mr. Penderwick left, and shouted down the steps. "Iantha, she's awake and wants food!"

Iantha soon arrived with a tray full of food: a

cheese-and-tomato sandwich, an apple, a glass of lemonade, and a bowl of chocolate mint ice cream.

"I know it's too much," she said. "But I wasn't sure what you'd want."

"Thank you, it looks good." Batty took a bite of the sandwich. "You're not going to both stare at me while I eat, are you?"

"Maybe," answered her dad.

"We're just so glad to have you awake."

"And not crying," said Batty. "I'm sorry."

"Shh, shh," said her father. "You've done nothing wrong. It's I who should be fired from parenthood. But eat up first, and then we'll talk."

"Can you stand a few more visitors?" asked Iantha. "Ben and Lydia have been waiting for you to wake up."

When she brought in Ben and Lydia, they were holding hands and staring solemnly at their sister. Lydia had brought Baby Zingo along, whose striped ridiculousness suddenly made Batty very happy. After all, it was nice to be alive and in this particular family.

"I helped get rid of Oliver," said Ben. "It was really cool."

"I know," answered Batty. "You did great."

"Are you going to eat all that ice cream?"

Batty handed over her spoon and let him dig in.

"Lydia has some big news for you, Batty," said Iantha. "Tell her, Lydia."

"Goldie put Frank in a box."

"Not that news. Tell Batty what you just told me about the big-girl bed."

Lydia put on her I-don't-care-about-that-right-now face. "I want ice cream."

"Whoa!" said Batty. "She said—"

Her father interrupted. "*Ego*. We know. We're trying not to make a fuss, afraid we'll cause her to revert to the third person for the rest of her life."

"But there's more," said Iantha. "A few minutes ago, she said 'I want to sleep in the big-girl bed tonight.'"

"I want *ice cream*," repeated Lydia, since they were missing the important points of the conversation.

"And you'll sleep in your big-girl bed tonight?" asked Batty.

But Lydia and Baby Zingo were already heading out on the hunt for ice cream, so Iantha gave Batty a kiss and went after them. Ben lingered for one last question.

"You're sure you don't have sleeping sickness?" he whispered.

"Positive!" Batty grabbed back her spoon. "And go get your own ice cream."

"Where did he get this idea about sleeping sickness?" Mr. Penderwick asked when Ben was gone.

"Rafael."

"Ah, yes, Rafael. I should have known."

When she'd eaten all she could, she set the tray aside.

"Good girl," said her father. "Now I have a lot to explain, something I should have done a long time ago. Do you feel well enough to listen or do you want to rest more?"

"You don't have to explain, Daddy." She didn't think she could stand hearing the details of how she'd killed her mother. Not just when she was starting to feel better. "I understand everything."

"But you don't understand," he said. "And neither did Skye."

"Skye?" She picked up both Funty and Gibson, settling them in with her for company.

"We've managed to put it together, you see, through hints you gave us while you were . . . upset, and some detective work. It seems that you overheard a conversation between Skye and Jeffrey on her birthday? Is that true?"

"I didn't mean to." She felt her eyes well up. "I know it was my fault for eavesdropping."

"Maybe or maybe not. As a rule, I don't recommend eavesdropping, but it turns out that good has come out of this."

Batty shook her head no. Although she didn't like disagreeing with her father, no good had come, only guilt and sorrow.

"In that conversation, Skye suggested that you're alive because your mother sacrificed herself by not treating her cancer. That she died to save you. Is that what you heard and what you believe?"

"Yes, Daddy. I'm so sorry. I'm so—"

He put his finger on her lips to shush her. "No more apologizing. Now I just need you to listen for a little bit. Can you do that?"

"I think so."

"Good. Your mother and I—" He took his glasses off, cleaned them, and put them back on. "It might be easier for me to tell this as a story. Okay?"

Batty nodded, and he began again.

"Once there was a man named—well, me—and a woman named Elizabeth, but mostly we called her Lizzy, and they fell deeply in love and got married. They both wanted children, and Lizzy wanted four of them. We also wanted the children to be close in age. I'm three years older than your aunt Claire, not all that far apart, but still we didn't always get along when we were kids. Once I tried to give her away to the people who lived two doors down. Did I ever tell you that story? No? There's way too much I haven't told you." He took Batty's hand, kissed it, then kept hold of it. "Lizzy and I planned on having four children, one every two years, but when Skye showed up so soon after Rosalind, we decided we might as well just keep going, and then there was Jane. Three healthy, delightful babies, all in a row, and we were certain that the fourth would be along soon to join them. But when she didn't come and didn't come, we decided to be content with our three. And we were content, for more than five years, until—it seemed

302

almost miraculous at the time—Lizzy discovered that she was pregnant again."

"With me." The hard part of the story was coming up.

"Yes, you. And we were very excited and happy."

"But you didn't know Mommy was sick yet, right?"

"No, but we found out soon—that is, her doctor discovered it during an exam."

"And that's when—"

"Shh. This is where you have to listen carefully, because this is where Skye was confused. She and I had a good, long talk—though I don't know if I'll ever forgive myself for letting her get confused in the first place and stay that way for so many years. I talked it through with Rosalind and Jane, too, and it turns out that somehow they understood—but Skye, well, children can get things wrong, can't they? I should have been paying more attention." He sat quietly, looking out the window, before going back to his tale. "After the cancer was discovered, we took Lizzy to many doctors and got many opinions, but the consensus—I should say, the hope—was that the pregnancy could outrace the cancer, maybe even slow it down. That the cancer could still be treatable after you were born."

"Oh!"

"Yes. Are you starting to understand?"

"Then Mommy didn't . . ."

"She didn't decide to trade her life for yours, no.

It wasn't the way Skye saw it, poor kid—she was only seven at the time, remember. No, it wasn't so black-and-white. We knew that waiting until you were born before treating the cancer would be a gamble, but it was a gamble Lizzy needed to take. She already loved you, you see."

"But she lost." Batty clung to her father's hand, to his strength. "She lost the gamble and died. Skye was right. She did sacrifice herself."

"You must believe me, Batty—if Lizzy had been given the chance to do it again, she'd have made the same decision, taken the same risk, over and over until the end of time. She told me so, the day you were born."

Batty had to turn away from her father now, unwilling to watch him as she asked what she most needed to know. "Didn't you mind, though? Didn't you resent me?"

"Resent you? I railed against fate, and cancer, and the universe. . . . Look at me, sweetheart. That's better. No, I never once for an instant resented you. You were a gift, a part of your mother left behind. You must understand that there are never guarantees with a disease like cancer. Lizzy could have undergone every treatment available and still died. And then we wouldn't have had you, either."

Again Batty turned away from him, but this time it was to cry in her pillow for a while. They were not misery tears but ones of relief, and her father stayed with her, keeping hold of her hand until she was done.

"Thank you, Daddy," she said, sniffing but smiling.

"You're welcome, daughter of mine. Now, your birthday is tomorrow. I know you've been reluctant, shall we say, to discuss your party."

"Reluctant?" She had to smile even more at that understatement.

"Yes, well, I think I understand now what was going on. What do you think about making it a joint party for Nick, because of his going away tomorrow night? Would you like that?"

"I would like that very much."

"You've forgiven him for taking you off the bus?"

"Yes, Daddy. Maybe I've grown up a little since then."

"Humph. We can hope."

She stuck out her tongue at him.

"Despite that attractive face you're making, I'm sure Jane and Rosalind want to see you, too, so I'll send them in soon. Skye has gone over to Molly's house for the rest of the day—she said she needed to get away to think, and it might take her a while to work this out for herself. By the way, she also knows that you were trying to get to Boston and Jeffrey when you boarded that bus."

"Did Ben—"

"He didn't give up your secret, though I have the feeling your sisters tried to force it out of him. No, I made an educated guess, and I'm embarrassed at how long it took me to get there."

"Is Skye angry that I tried to get to Jeffrey?"

"I don't think so. She needs to think about that, too—how banning him affects the rest of us. You know, Lizzy told me that Skye would have the most trouble coping with her death. Maybe because the two of them were so much alike, with their crazy, stubborn—" He broke off and smiled at Batty. "But you inherited your mother's love of music. You know that, right? She always said that if she could be anything in the world, she would choose opera singer. Not that she had the voice—it was sweet but not strong, and not always quite on key, either—but she loved singing, anyway. She sang to you in the hospital, whenever she had the strength."

"Maybe I remember," said Batty, tucking away this nugget of information to marvel at later.

"Maybe you do." He leaned over and kissed her cheek. "Ready for some more company?"

When he'd gone for Rosalind and Jane, Batty got out of bed, eager to try something now, in these few moments when she was alone. Standing up straight, she took several deep breaths, and several more for luck—then tried to sing.

A croak. It was still an ugly croak.

"Can we come in?" called Rosalind from the hall.

Batty got back into bed and made sure she was smiling before saying yes.

CHAPTER TWENTY-TWO
Another Birthday

By mid-morning on Batty's birthday, her room was buzzing with activity. Jane had taken over the desk with her computer, typing as Batty arduously composed book reports out loud. Ben was standing guard by the door to keep parents from entering unannounced and discovering the book report scheme, though truly there was nothing dishonorable about it. Lydia was dancing to *Camelot*, which Batty had put on the record player just for her. And Keiko was there, too, in better shape than when she'd first arrived. Then, seeing Batty glowing and healthy had sent Keiko into tears of relief that bedewed the flaxseed pumpkin brownies she'd brought along. Ben ate them anyway, tears and too much flaxseed and all.

"Batty, anything else on this one?" asked Jane,

who could type book reports more quickly than Batty could think about them. "Here's your last sentence: '*The Dragonfly Pool* ends, like all of Eva Ibbotson's books, with hope, and with one of the most comforting words in the English language: home.'"

"No, that's the end, but didn't I say 'one of the nicest words in the universe'?" protested Batty. "Don't edit, Jane. Ms. Rho will know I didn't write it."

"Sorry, bad habit. We're on a roll—go find another book." They'd finished six reports so far, and Jane was determined to get as close to ten as they could. "Though it could be fun to do a report on a made-up book. Let's say . . . *Ella and Her Uncle*, which could be about a girl whose uncle is some kind of animal. A kangaroo, maybe? And she should have a younger sister. 'Clara,' that's a good name. What do you think, Batty?"

"No, no, and no," said Batty, inspecting her bookshelves.

In the midst of all this, Keiko was getting caught up on the recent romantic dramas. Jane had already told her about Jérôme—he and Lauren were now officially a couple—and had moved on to, as Jane dubbed it, the Ouster of Oliver the Oaf.

"So then Oliver said . . . ," prompted Keiko.

"Then Oliver said 'You'd be a fool to cast me aside, Rosalind. I can take you away from your vulgar family, they who drive the vulgar Flashvan and know nothing of the art of film.'"

"You don't know what he said, Jane," protested Ben from his position by the door. "You weren't there."

"I'm sure it's what he was thinking," said Jane. "Lydia, stop bumping into me."

"Tra-la, la-la, la-la-la-la-la-la," sang Lydia along to *Camelot*. By now she'd bumped into everyone in the room, thinking it part of the joy of dancing.

Someone on the other side of the door was knocking out the secret code they'd established. *Bang, bang, tap, tap, bang, bang, tap.*

"Who's there?" asked Ben.

"Me, Rosalind. Let me in, let me in." She sounded terribly excited, and when Ben opened the door, she almost fell into the room.

"Guess who's come home! Tommy!"

"To win you back, right?" cried Jane.

"I don't know! Iantha's gone across the street to see him." Rosalind ran out again.

Ben tried to follow her because he was dying to see Tommy, and Keiko tried to follow him because this was an amazing opportunity for research, and Batty wanted to follow both of them, because it was exciting to see Rosalind so excited, but Lydia got in the way, and several people fell onto the floor. And, anyway, Jane had closed the door to keep them all where they were.

"Slow down, everybody," said Jane. "Let's wait to see what Iantha finds out. Batty, next book."

"We can't think about book reports with possible love reunions going on!" cried Keiko.

"Next book," repeated Jane firmly, setting Lydia upright, then going back to the desk to type.

"*Cosmic*." Batty decided to stay on the floor to avoid being knocked over again.

"Excellent choice. We love Frank Cottrell Boyce," said Jane, typing. "I'm ready. Go."

"*Cosmic* is a funny book—"

"Touching and uproariously funny," said Jane.

"Stop it!" protested Batty. "*Cosmic* is a funny book about what happens when you get what you think you want, in this case, going into space. Um . . ."

Jane typed, then turned back to Keiko. "So Rosalind, naturally furious and offended, said to Oliver 'How dare you criticize my family, you snotty snob who isn't as smart as he thinks he is. Go from here and never again darken our door, for I have always loved but one man, and his name is Sir Thomas Geiger of Gardam Street.'"

"Jane, you should write this story down," said Keiko.

"Maybe I will."

Rosalind fell into the room again without even trying the secret knock. "He came home to be with his parents! Mrs. Geiger's really upset about Nick leaving, so Nick called Tommy and he said he'd drive home just to be with her and their dad. Isn't that sensitive and wonderful of him? Isn't that just what you'd think he'd do?"

"I guess so," said Keiko. "Don't you mind that he didn't come for you?"

"How could I mind that he's noble and cares about his family? It makes me lo—like him more." She rushed out again but was back before anyone could try to follow her. "But how do I make sure I get to see him while he's here?"

"Have Iantha invite him to Batty's birthday dinner," said Jane.

"Is that okay with you, Batty?" asked Rosalind.

"Yes! Yes, Rosy!"

"Thank you, I love you all, bye." She almost left but then turned back. "I don't think I should see him until I can be calmer, right?"

"That sounds like a good idea," said Jane.

Rosalind left again.

"And just when Rosalind," said Jane, "rid herself of the snooty knave Oliver, Sir Thomas—"

They were again interrupted by the secret knock.

"Who's there?" Ben leaned hard on the door, determined to reassert his authority as gatekeeper.

But whoever was out there shoved it open anyway, and into the room rushed Duchess and Cilantro, with Skye at the other end of their leashes. This was the first time the dogs had ever been inside the Penderwicks' house, let alone inside what they could sniff out as Batty's den, and the thrill of it made them wild with excitement. Though they'd seen Batty the day before—when she'd resumed responsibility for their walks—they were still getting over the shock

311

of her previous vanishing. Plus, apparently Jane had tried to teach them French, further scrambling Cilantro's poor brain.

Duchess launched herself at the bed and amazed everyone by nearly scaling its heights, while Cilantro howled the room's trash can into submission.

"Sit, you numbskulls," said Skye. After knocking over a stack of books and also Lydia, the dogs did sit, pleased at having established domination over a bedroom. "Batty, I thought you might want to take a walk."

"Take a walk, clear your head," said Jane. It was one of their father's favorite sayings, and one of the few he always said in English.

"Yes, the walk was Dad's idea." Skye righted Lydia, who tried to get Cilantro to dance with her. "The dogs were mine."

"If you want to go, Batty, we can do more of these reports later," said Jane. "And I've still got lots to tell Keiko."

Keiko was delighted—any excuse to spend time with Jane and hear more stories of love. So Batty shyly agreed to go with Skye, grateful to her for thinking of the dogs. This would be the sisters' first time alone since Batty had been feeling better, and the dogs would help them through the silences.

"But before we go," said Skye, "I've brought news. Tommy told Iantha he'd come to the party tonight, and Rosalind has gone out 'shopping,' to make sure he doesn't think she's waiting around for him. She also asked that the rest of us stay away from Tommy, too—apparently she doesn't trust us not to blow it. Jane, especially you."

"Well, *excusez-moi*," said Jane. "But she's probably right."

"Except for you, Ben," said Skye. "You can go see Tommy if you want."

That was the end of Ben as gatekeeper—he was out of the room and down the steps in a flash. The sound of the front door slamming behind him echoed through the house.

"Why Ben?" asked Keiko.

"He earned it, I think," said Batty. By now Ben had told her about teaching Nick's getting-rid-of-unwanted-suitors speech to Rosalind. Batty had been impressed that the same declaration had worked on both collegian Oliver and the kindergartner twins—more proof of Nick's broad-based world knowledge. She'd even memorized it in case she herself ever needed it, but mostly for Keiko. "I'll explain later."

"So, Bats, you ready to go?" asked Skye.

During Batty's darkness, she'd forgotten spring and its joyous advance. Suddenly cherry trees were dripping cotton-candy flowers, and the lilacs were coming into bloom, perfuming Gardam Street with May magic. In Quigley Woods, where Skye and Batty headed with the dogs, the trees were in full leaf, their greens deepening every day, and the wild crab apples had thrown out white flowers, declaring that even in the forest one could flaunt fleeting beauty. Instead of a shy violet here and there, great clumps of them now dotted the paths. And here was Batty's old friend the red cardinal come back, but only to scold the dogs and race away again.

On and on the sisters went with neither saying a word, until Batty couldn't stand it anymore.

"Stop a minute," she said to Skye, and pulled on Cilantro's leash to make him stop, too.

"I'm no good at this, Batty."

"Actually, you're terrible at it," Batty surprised herself by saying. She'd never before spoken that way to Skye.

"I know. And I'm still confused about everything."

Cilantro tugged, but Batty wasn't yet ready to move on. She had a particular confession to make, and she wanted to get it over with. "Skye, I apologize for listening to your conversation with Jeffrey. I didn't plan to. I was in Lydia's room and I heard you by mistake, and then it was too late."

She trailed off, embarrassed at the enormity of her rudeness and the trouble it had caused, and steeled herself for her sister's justifiable annoyance.

"It was a dumb place for a private conversation." Skye gave Batty a sideways glance. "What? You thought I'd be furious, right? But I should have known better. Back when that was your room—when you were still little—Jane and I would sit at the top of the steps listening while Rosalind told you stories. I was always glad when you asked for stories about Mom."

Batty stared, dumbfounded. "I didn't know."

"How could you?" answered Skye. "Let's keep walking. I have someplace I want to show you."

Duchess and Cilantro tried to follow the usual paths, but Skye took them a different way, leading to the bridge over the creek, the one Batty should have used the day she got lost and hurt her ankle. It took a while to get across the bridge, for midway the dogs spotted a beaver dam in the water—a great piling up of branches and sticks—and even one brave brown beaver who stared defiantly at the barking invaders until Skye and Batty were able to drag them away.

Now Skye was taking them to a part of the woods Batty had never seen, not even in her trips across the creek with Rosalind. As they headed gradually uphill, they came across a double row of hugely overgrown lilac bushes, white, pink, and a dozen shades of purple. Even the dogs slowed down to enjoy this mysterious bit of civilization in the midst of wildness—this tunnel of intoxication that had to have been deliberately planted long ago. A little further on still, they abruptly came to a clearing with the bare remains of an ancient stone foundation. This had once been a house—there was the fireplace, and there, a gap where the door had been.

"This is my favorite place," said Skye.

Batty knew the privilege that was being bestowed. Skye had long kept her favorite place in Quigley Woods a secret, even from Jane, maybe even from Jeffrey.

"It's a really good one," she said.

"Cecilia Lee and I used to play *Star Wars* here. I was always Han Solo and she was Luke, and when she had to bring her little sister along, we made her be C-3PO," she said. "You don't remember Cecilia. She moved away in the middle of fourth grade."

"So you were crossing the creek by yourself when you were *nine*?"

"I started at seven, actually, but back then I'd bring Hound, too, when I could drag him away from you, so I wasn't exactly by myself." Skye sat down while Duchess sniffed among the stones. "But I freely admit that it was dangerous to come over here when I was that young, and I probably shouldn't have told you. Promise you won't tell Ben or Lydia. Swear."

"I swear. Penderwick Family Honor. But, Skye . . ."

"Hmm?"

"Didn't Rosalind know that you were coming over here?"

"She was busy helping Dad with you by then. Nick caught me once, though."

"Nick!" So it was a habit of his, catching Penderwicks.

"He told me that I should never come back because there was quicksand, but I researched how to

316

survive quicksand. You're supposed to do this"—Skye spread her arms wide—"and shout for help. It sounded so interesting, I was always a bit disappointed not to fall into any."

"Nick told me that he made up the quicksand."

"He did? Good old Nick." Skye reeled in Duchess, who thought she'd smelled a fox and was itching to go say hello. "So, Batty, I've got some apologies, too."

"You don't have to." Batty curled up a little inside.

"Yes, I do. Like about making Jeffrey go away. Dad told me about you trying to get to Boston."

"Yes."

"That was pretty brave."

"And stupid."

"And stupid," agreed Skye. "Batty, I know that's hard on you, not seeing him—it must be, or you wouldn't have tried so hard. Why did you—I mean, what do you talk about when you're with him, anyway? Just music?"

Batty tried to think. She could talk to Jeffrey about everything and anything, but their conversations always came back to music. "Mostly."

"When he talks about music to me, my brain turns to mush." Skye leaned down to scratch Duchess's ears. "Too bad you're not my age. He could have his dopey crush on you and leave me alone."

"Well, I'm not your age." Batty wasn't ready for any dopey crushes.

"That's true. Here's the other apology." Skye took

317

a deep breath. "I'm also sorry I've never been a very good sister to you. Or even nice to you, I guess."

"Don't apologize about that! Please."

"Why not? Good grief, don't cry."

"You weren't nice to me because you didn't like me. You were *honest*."

"Honest. Yes, I'm always that, even when I shouldn't be." Skye went back to Duchess's ears. "I've been trying to remember how it felt, you know, losing Mom. I think—I *thought*—I was her favorite. I thought that I was more *hers* than Rosy and Jane were because I looked so much like her, I guess, and they looked like Dad. And then you were born, and Mom died. . . . I don't know, maybe if you'd had blond hair and blue eyes, I would have felt closer to you. But Rosalind fell so in love with you, and Jane always had her crazy imagination to keep her company, and even Hound started spending every minute with you. You know, I used to think I was *his* favorite, too, before you came along. Sounds like I was a conceited child, doesn't it, seeing myself as everybody's favorite. Compared to me, Lydia's humble, right?"

Batty was too lost in her thoughts to answer. That photo in her father's box of pictures—the one in which a blissfully happy Skye was holding the puppy who became Hound—no wonder Batty hadn't wanted it upstairs with the other Hound photos. Because it had made her jealous of Skye. Skye, who had known Hound from the beginning of his life, and who had been Hound's favorite until she could no longer *drag him away* from her new baby sister.

"I took Hound from you, too," she said to Skye. "I can't believe you don't hate me."

"You didn't take Hound from me, Batty. You were a tiny baby."

"I took Mom from you, and then I took Hound from you, and then I couldn't even take care of him."

"What are you talking about?"

"You know what I'm talking about—you know, you know. I didn't take good enough care of Hound and he died!"

"Wow." Skye stood up, walked Duchess around in a circle, then came back to Batty. "Here's what I know. Not even I, Skye Magee Penderwick, can come up with one reason to blame you for Hound's death. And if *I* can't, no one can."

"But I should have—"

"You should have what? Slept next to him every night on the floor when he got too weak to climb onto your bed? Coaxed him to eat by letting him lick food off your fingers, a tiny bit at a time? Held him, talked to him for hours? You did all that. The rest of us helped, but you did most of it. Don't you remember? Holy bananas, use some logic. And close your mouth. You look goofy."

Batty closed her mouth, which had fallen open in shock.

"That's better," said Skye. "Now let's go back.

Rosalind said I could make your cake as part of my expiation of guilt."

Skye loathed baking and was terrible at it, but Batty's world had been turned upside down too many times—she no longer knew what to believe. "Really?"

"No, not really, you nutburger. I'm not going to wreck your cake for you."

The cake was delicious. All the food was delicious. Batty's birthday presents were lovely. Tommy did come—and everyone liked watching how he and Rosalind kept careful track of each other while pretending not to. But it was impossible that the party could be anything other than sad, because Nick was packed and ready to leave as soon as it was over. Batty tried to be cheerful. Everyone did. Mr. Geiger and Jane made the best job of it, throwing dumb jokes back and forth. Tommy helped by laughing at the dumb jokes and putting his arm around his mother each time she started to cry. Only Ben couldn't manage any cheer at all, weeping openly off and on during dinner and birthday cake.

Toward the end of the party, when Lydia was toppling over with sleepiness, Batty watched as Nick slowly made his way from one Penderwick to the next, getting and giving hugs and letting those who needed to cry do so on his shoulder. He stayed for a long time with Ben, crouched next to him, talking softly. Jane would be next, Batty knew, and then Batty herself, except that she didn't want to say good-bye to him. Maybe she would just sneak away into the evening shadows. Nick wouldn't notice. There were, after all, so many Penderwicks.

She should have known better.

"Running away again?" he asked, finding her around the side of the house.

"No," she answered. "Yes."

"I'll be back before you know it, annoying you all over again."

"Yes," she said. "I mean, no, you don't annoy me, Nick."

"Sure I do. Now listen up. I have some orders for you before I go."

"Choose a sport."

"Yes, that." He nodded his approval. "But also, I want there to be a dog in this house before I come home next time. Long before."

She looked at him with dismay. "I'm not ready—you know that."

"But you're getting closer."

Batty thought about that, and about what Skye had told her that afternoon in Quigley Woods.

"Nick, Skye said it wasn't my fault that Hound died."

"Of course it wasn't your fault. Who ever said it was?" He shook his head in disbelief. "Okay, so you're getting closer to being ready for a new dog, Ben's been ready for a while, and Lydia could use the competition.

321

Battikins, you don't have to love a new dog as much as you loved Hound. You don't have to love it at all. Just let it live here."

"I don't know."

"Think about it. Promise me you'll think about it."

"I promise."

"And no more running away. Promise that, too."

Batty was crying too hard now to say anything, but Nick seemed satisfied. As he kissed her cheek, Batty squeezed her eyes shut, not able to watch him leave.

A few minutes later, Rosalind found Batty, sat down beside her, and waited patiently until she'd stopped crying.

"Did Nick say good-bye to you, Batty?" she asked then.

"He told me to stop running away."

"That was good advice. Will you listen?"

"Yes." Noticing that there were words written on Rosalind's arm—words that hadn't been there before—Batty pushed up her sister's sleeve to get a better look. "'Choose wisely.' Did Nick write that?"

"He said it was either that or 'Dear Tommy, I adore you and want you back.'"

"You do want Tommy back, don't you?"

"Yes. Yes, I do, but since I don't know what he wants, I decided not to have my adoration brazenly advertised."

"Um, Rosy—" Batty tried making "be quiet" faces

at Rosalind, but they must not have been good ones, because Rosalind didn't get even a little quieter.

"On the one hand, I don't want to make assumptions or put pressure on him, and on the other"—Rosalind held up her left hand and stared at it, still missing Batty's attempts to silence her—"I don't want to discourage him by being too cool and distant."

Giving up on subtlety, Batty waved at the person walking toward them. "Hi, Tommy."

Never in Batty's life had she seen Rosalind blush so quickly and thoroughly. Nor had she ever seen that particular expression on her oldest sister's face—combined pride, embarrassment, and out-and-out love.

"Hey, Batty," answered Tommy, and he, too, had a new expression on his face—equal parts hope and caution. "Rosy, I need to go home to see Nick off and be with my parents for a while, but maybe later you and I could talk?"

"Maybe," said Rosalind, desperately trying to control her blush.

"She doesn't mean maybe," cried Batty as Tommy's expression turned into disappointment.

"What does she mean, then?" he asked.

"Choose wisely," Batty whispered to Rosalind.

"I mean, Tommy," said Rosalind slowly, "that I would like to talk with you later."

His irresistible Geiger grin broke out. "I'll come back over when I'm sure my mom's okay. And no changing your mind, Rosalind Penderwick, or I'll hunt you down and talk to you anyway."

"Tough guy." Rosalind's face now mirrored his, and glowed with happiness. "Leave us."

As Tommy sauntered away, Rosalind watched him, enrapt, and Batty watched them both, wondering at these strange rites of teenage-dom. Keiko might understand them better, and she would certainly be fascinated, but this was one romantic scene Batty would keep to herself. It was too private to share, even with Keiko.

"Do you think I was cool and distant with him?" Rosalind asked Batty when he was out of sight.

Hardly, thought Batty. "Nope. You were just right."

"Thank goodness." Rosalind dug into her pocket and brought out a little box that she handed to Batty. "Here's something for you."

"Another present?" Rosalind had already given her one gift, a pretty top to go with a skirt Jane had made for her.

"This is special. Open it."

It was a necklace, a thin chain with a tiny squiggle of gold hanging from it.

"A note on a chain!" said Batty.

"A note of music," agreed Rosalind. "Just right, don't you think?"

Batty dove into her oldest sister's arms.

CHAPTER TWENTY-THREE
One More Gift

A FEW HOURS LATER, Batty was back in her room, lying on the floor with Funty and Gibson—she was weary of being in bed after all those days spent there—and thinking. She had some decisions to make. Not yet, though, not yet. She needed to try just one more time.

"Stand up, Batty," she said, doing so, "and open yourself to the music."

Two deep breaths, and then just like every other time she'd tried in the last few days, all she got was that gruesome croak.

"Okay, I get it." She went back to lying on the floor.

Her voice, her orchid in a daisy field, was gone and seemed to have no intention of coming back. Batty had briefly considered the notion that it had been her imagination—part of the strange dreams she'd suffered through—and even asked Keiko if she'd gone cuckoo and made up Mrs. Grunfeld and her enthusiasm over Batty's voice. Keiko had told her not to be a dope. So that was a relief.

But still, she couldn't sing. She would have to get used to that, somehow.

It helped that she'd kept her voice secret from her family. They need never know what she'd been given for a brief time, what she'd lost. And Jeffrey! Thank goodness Nick had stopped her from going to Boston. Her voice had already been missing then, but because the missing hadn't yet seemed final the way it did now, she might have gone on and on about Mrs. Grunfeld and singing and touring Europe with Jeffrey and his father. And now she'd be stuck telling Jeffrey that it was over, and he'd be disappointed for her. Batty thought she could learn to bear her own disappointment but not anyone else's.

There was a knock on her door—that is, three quick knocks and a slap.

"Come in, Ben," she said.

Ben opened the door but didn't come in. "Can I have another piece of your cake? Dad said I should ask you."

"Yes, but leave some for me."

"Okay." He closed the door again.

In the end, what had she lost? Nothing real—just

a brief fantasy. She would rededicate herself to the piano, and maybe she would indeed someday take up a second instrument, just like she'd told Iantha. Not the clarinet, though. The cello, maybe. Or the double bass! What a good idea. Double basses were often included in jazz combos—so she could still tour with Jeffrey and his dad. It would be much better than singing, because the bass is always at the back of the stage, and the player is practically hidden behind it anyway. Much better for a shy girl than singing at the microphone, front and center.

Her thoughts were interrupted by another knock, or rather an erratic pounding, by what sounded like suspiciously small fists. Batty sprang up and rushed to open the door before Lydia had time to do heaven knows what out there in the hall. But she was safely ensconced in her mother's arms, scrubbed and ready for bed.

"We want to make sure you had a good birthday," said Iantha.

"Yes, I did, Mom." Batty wrapped her arms around both of them, forming a kind of Lydia sandwich. "Thank you again for my presents."

Iantha had gone a bit overboard, getting Batty a pile of books, including several more by Frank Cottrell Boyce, an adorable plaid jacket with a hood and extra-big pockets, *and* a gift certificate to the store in Wooton that sold sheet music.

"I am stuck," said Lydia.

Batty unwrapped herself. "What you are is goofy."

"Sing, Batty?"

"Not tonight, Lydia."

Then they were gone, too, and Batty could lie down again. She wondered how long it would take Lydia to forget Batty's former and glorious singing voice. *Not too long, please.* Though she wasn't optimistic—look at how Lydia was still clinging to poor dead Frank in his box.

She wondered when to tell Jeffrey about her double bass idea. Not that she was likely to have the chance to talk to him about anything for a long time. She was almost glad of that, though. No, she *was* glad she wouldn't see him for a long time. It would give her a chance to let the memory of singing drift so far away that she didn't miss it anymore. The next time she saw Jeffrey—which would be when Skye had softened, or maybe when the moon turned to cheese— Batty would be happy and complete, with no regrets and perhaps even some knowledge of the double bass.

This helped with one of her decisions: Yes, she should keep up the dog-walking business. Double basses were sure to be expensive.

Now there was a tap on her door, but before Batty could get up, Jane had opened it and stuck in her head.

"Thought you'd want to know that Rosalind and Tommy just left for a walk, and they were holding hands. Isn't that great?"

"Yes! Does Ben know?"

"I'll tell him. And may I give Artie a piece of your cake?"

"Just leave me one more piece, okay?"

As for her other decision—that would really be Mrs. Grunfeld's to make. Batty hoped to continue going into the music room every Tuesday at recess, if only to talk about music, now that she couldn't sing.

There was another knock. Surely, Batty thought, she was running out of family members. This person was politely waiting for her to answer, so she got up and opened the door. It was her dad.

"Why, it's one of my many daughters," he said. "But which one?"

"The best one," Batty answered, hugging him. How lucky she was to have such a father.

"Good girl. Also, you should know that Rosalind and Tommy just left for a walk, holding hands."

"Jane already told me."

"Did she. Hmmm. I wonder if she's writing about it yet."

"Probably. Dad, did you want another piece of my cake?"

"No, thanks. Just wanted to tell you happy birthday again and I love you and want for you everything that's wonderful in the world."

"Thank you."

"And there are no more big, scary secrets, right?"

"No," she said. Just a little, not-scary secret about

a marvelous voice that had been hers for too short a time.

"And you're not interested in boys yet, right?"

"No, Daddy. I promise."

"Good." He left and shut the door.

Should she lie down again? There was no one left to visit her, not with Rosalind out on a walk with Tommy. Except Skye, but Skye never visited. Even with the beginnings of their new understanding, that wasn't about to change. They still had too little to talk about.

She started back down to the floor, but—good grief—someone was knocking, and then speaking without waiting for the door to be opened.

"It's me, Skye, and I know Rosalind already gave you an extra gift, but I've got one, too, and mine's much better than hers."

"But I really liked your first gift," said Batty through the door. Skye's gift was one of the best of the day—a donation in Batty's name to an animal shelter.

"This one's different. Kind of annoying, and you can't keep him forever, and he's on strict orders to leave *me* alone, but I figured it was what you wanted the most. Have fun. Talk about music."

The door opened, Jeffrey came in, and the door shut again behind him.

"Hi," he said. "Happy birthday."

Batty was rooted in place, unprepared, trapped. This was a shock, not a gift.

"Skye gave me the last piece of your cake." Jeffrey was holding the plate with the cake, the last piece, as yet untouched. "Hope that's okay."

"I guess so."

"Wow, you're sure not glad to see me. You probably haven't forgiven me for running out on our breakfast. Not that I blame you. That was a lousy thing to do."

"No, I do forgive you."

He took a bite of the cake. "But?"

Batty glanced around the room, looking for a source of strength. There—on top of her record player—the Beethoven symphonies Jeffrey had sent her.

"No buts," she said. "Thank you for the presents. I tried to get to Boston to tell you in person, but that didn't exactly work out."

"Yeah, I heard about that. Gutsy move. Also insane."

"I know."

He sat on the edge of the bed, said hello to Funty and Gibson, and ate more cake. "Let me make it up to you. That special topic you told me about on Skye's birthday? Can we talk about it now?"

"No." She winced. Her Grand Eleventh Birthday Concert was dead and buried.

"Too late?"

"Yes, too late." And to Batty's fury, here came her tears again. Those awful tears, welling up in her eyes, sliding down her face, embarrassing her—hadn't she run out by now?

"Tell me what's wrong."

"I can't."

"Yes, you can."

"No, no, no." How *dare* he make demands after leaving her on her own for so long. "I didn't invite you here and I can't tell you. And that's my piece of cake you're eating!"

"I only ate a few bites. I'll leave the rest for you." Carefully he set the plate down on her desk. "Batty, you're supposed to tell me what I want to know. I'm your *mentore*, remember?"

"I can fire you. There, you're fired, and not my *mentore* anymore. Go away."

"No. I'm tired of Penderwicks telling me to go away when I've just gotten here. Batty, please, it's your old friend Jeffrey."

"If you won't go away, I will." But she couldn't go out into the hall, not while crying like a fool. She went instead into her closet, sat on a box of games, and listened through her sobs as Jeffrey moved around the room. It sounded like he was looking for something.

"Batty, where's the photograph of Hound I sent you? Did it get hurt during shipping?"

"No, it's fine." She owed him that.

"Where is it?"

"In here."

"In the closet? Why?"

"None of your business, Jeffrey. Please go away."

"No." The closet door opened, and there he was, staring down at her.

She stared back up at him, his familiar face blurry through her tears. Already she could feel her anger slipping away. She never had been able to stay upset with Jeffrey for more than a few moments. Even that time years ago when he'd accidentally mixed Funty up with the dirty laundry and Batty thought for sure that the blue elephant would come to pieces in the washing machine. But Jeffrey had been just as upset as she was and, in the end, Funty had come out of the wash not only intact but also cheerful and much cleaner.

"Jeffrey, Skye said it wasn't my fault that Hound died."

"Of course it wasn't."

"That's what Nick said, too."

"Where did you get the idea that it was your fault? Hound was an old dog with heart disease who'd lived a good life."

"But—"

"Listen to me, Batty. Dogs die. People die. Guinea pigs die! We do the best we can while they're alive, and then they die anyway. Right? Tell me that I'm right."

"You're right," she whispered.

"Thank you." He smiled. "Ready for some Beethoven?"

"Yes, I think so."

He went over to her record player, opened the box of symphonies, and put one on the turntable.

Two quick, crisp chords to start, then the quiet strings introducing the theme, one of Beethoven's most beautiful and stirring.

The *Eroica*, Jeffrey's favorite.

And now he was out there in her room, conducting. Batty leaned forward to better watch. She'd seen him do this for years—he called it play, swore he knew nothing of what he was doing—but to her it seemed that he was indeed bringing alive that magnificent music, thrilling to it, reveling in it, lost in it. And now Batty was lost in it, too, swept away by this outpouring of genius, coming to her from across the centuries, still fresh and alive. She listened and watched, and as she did, the theme returned, again and again, each time grander and more powerful, finally melting Batty's one last shred of pain, washing it away on an exhilarating, superb flood of music.

The first movement came to an end, and Jeffrey lowered his imaginary baton and bowed his head.

"Jeffrey," said Batty. "I'm ready now."

"To finish your cake?" He stopped the record before the second movement could begin.

"I didn't really care about the cake." She came back into the room.

"Then to talk?"

"No." She planted her feet and took two deep breaths. "To sing."

• • •

And thus Batty ended up with a Grand Eleventh Birthday Concert after all. Jeffrey let her sing only one song, "I'm Always Chasing Rainbows," before hustling her downstairs to the living room, where she sang it again for the entire family. Even Lydia, who had been put to bed, was brought out for this—Jeffrey insisted on it. There had been no plan, no rehearsal, and Batty wore no special outfit. But the astonished pride on everyone's face was just what she'd longed for. There were lots of tears, too, especially from her parents and Rosalind.

No tears from Batty, though. She was done with crying for now, and determined to keep it that way for a very long time.

CODA
The Following Spring

İT WAS A SATURDAY AFTERNOON in late March when the Penderwicks waited for Lieutenant Geiger's second return from war. Jane had put up freshly painted Welcome Home signs, helped again by Artie plus a few new boys, one of whom, to Mr. Penderwick's great annoyance, was yet another Donovan. The two older sisters had sent messages to be given to Nick when he arrived. Rosalind from her college in Rhode Island, where she was studying fiercely and without distraction, her heart safely stowed in Delaware with Tommy, faithful and true. And Skye from her college in California, also studying fiercely but with a heart still very much her own. She and Jeffrey, who was now in college in Boston, continued to be friends, despite many battles since the previous spring. Especially the big one at his high school graduation party, which no one ever spoke of, the memory of it being too awful for those who loved them both.

Batty and Ben waited in their living room. Ben was at the window, watching for the familiar blue truck. Batty was at her piano, accompanying herself on songs that Ms. Hinkel—chosen jointly by Jeffrey and Mrs. Grunfeld to be Batty's singing teacher— had assigned for their next lesson together, a lesson Batty would proudly help her parents pay for. Lydia ran in and out, hunting for anyone who would watch a demonstration of her latest passion, tap dancing— without taps, thank goodness. The rest of the family held vigil in their own ways, Jane upstairs, nervously reading from several books at once, a few pages here, a few pages there, and the parents in their study, talking softly together.

"Anything?" asked Batty, pausing in her music.

"Nope," answered Ben. "Not yet."

There had been much communication between Gardam Street and the remote mountains where Nick fought overseas: notes, pictures, boxes of food going out to him, reassuring news coming back when he could take time out from battles. At the coldest part of winter, his news had suddenly turned bad—a wound in his shoulder, much bleeding, a journey in a helicopter to the military hospital—but Nick had survived, healed, and gone back into service. Since then they'd longed for him to come home more than ever.

"Anything?" Batty asked again.

"Nope. Wait—I think—Batty, it's him! He's here! Mr. and Mrs. Geiger are coming outside!"

Scrambling off the piano bench, Batty shouted for Jane and their parents, then whistled, softly but with a certainty of being heard and obeyed. A big fluff of brown, with a plumed tail at back and at front a blunt nose and large, goofy eyes, rose up from his place beside the couch.

"Good boy, Feldspar," she said.

Feldspar sniffed at a second dog, emerging from behind the couch, this one sleek and gray, impossible to imagine as Feldspar's mother were it not for the eyes, just as silly on her as they were on him.

"Good girl, Sonata," said Batty. "You're finally going to meet Nick."

Sonata looked worshipfully at Batty, her master, her everything, but with doubts about meeting Nick. She'd been half wild when the Penderwicks brought her home from the animal shelter, unwilling to separate her from Feldspar, her runt and the last of her litter. Though no longer wild, she still flinched from new situations.

"You'll be fine." Batty laid her hand gently on Sonata's head, soothing her. "I'm with you."

They went out into the hallway, where the others were gathering, excited and flustered. Mr. Penderwick had forgotten his shoes, and Lydia her crown, though that had been happening more and more lately, as she was at long last moving out of her princess phase.

"We're all here?" asked Jane. "Father, mother, three sisters, one brother, two dogs?"

"*Gato,*" said Lydia.

"No, Asimov, you can't come." Iantha shut away the disgruntled cat, who'd fallen in love with Sonata and believed he should be able to go wherever she went.

Ben was jumping up and down like a yo-yo. "Hurry, hurry, hurry, hurry, hurry!"

"A little more calm, please," said Mr. Penderwick.

"We're all set now," said Iantha. "Ready?"

Batty grabbed two dog collars.

"Go!" exploded Ben.

Jane threw open the front door and out poured the Penderwicks, racing across Gardam Street to welcome home their hero.

When Jeanne Birdsall was young, she promised herself she'd be a writer someday—so that she could write books for children to discover and enjoy, just as she did at her local library. She is also the author of *The Penderwicks*, which won the National Book Award for Young People's Literature, *The Penderwicks on Gardam Street*, and *The Penderwicks at Point Mouette*.

Jeanne lives in Northampton, Massachusetts, with her husband and an assortment of animals, including a dog named Cagney. You can find out more about Jeanne, her books, and her animal friends at JeanneBirdsall.com.